HOLY DISORDERS

EDMUND CRISPIN

AVON
PUBLISHERS OF BARD, CAMELOT AND DISCUS BOOKS

All the characters and events portrayed in this story are fictitious.

AVON BOOKS
A division of
The Hearst Corporation
959 Eighth Avenue
New York, New York 10019

First Avon Printing, December, 1980

AVON TRADEMARK REG. U.S. PAT. OFF. AND IN
OTHER COUNTRIES, MARCA REGISTRADA, HECHO EN
U.S.A.

Printed in the U.S.A.

TO
MY PARENTS

NOTE

My sincere thanks are due to Mr. Philip Larkin for reading this book in manuscript and making a number of valuable suggestions.

E. C.

CONTENTS

Chapter One

INVITATION AND WARNING

"Continually at my bed's head
A hearse doth hang, which doth me tell
That I ere morning may be dead. . . ."
SOUTHWELL

As HIS TAXI BURROWED ITS WAY through the traffic outside Waterloo Station, like an over-zealous bee barging to the front of a dilatory swarm, Geoffrey Vintner re-read the letter and telegram which he had found on his breakfast table that morning.

He felt as unhappy as any man without pretension to the spirit of adventure might feel who has received a threatening letter accompanied by sufficient evidence to suggest that the threats contained in it will probably be carried out. Not for the first time that morning, he regretted that he had ever persuaded himself to set out on his uncomfortable errand, to leave his cottage in Surrey, his cats, his garden (whose disposition he changed almost daily in accordance with some new and generally impracticable fancy), and his estimable and long-suffering housekeeper, Mrs. Body. He was not, he considered (and the thought recurred with gloomy frequency as the series of adventures on which he was about to embark went its way), of a mould which engages very successfully in physical violence. Once one is over forty, one cannot, even in moments of high enthusiasm, throw oneself heartily into anonymous and mortal battles against unscrupulous men. And when, moreover, one is a finical bachelor, moderately well-off, bred in a secluded country

9

rectory, and with a mind undisturbed by sordid cares and overmastering passions, the thing begins to appear not only impossible but frankly ludicrous. It was no consolation to reflect that men like himself had fought with the courage and tenacity of bears all the way back to the Dunkirk beaches; they at least knew what they were up against.

Threats.

He groped in his coat pocket, pulled out a large, ancient revolver, and looked at it with that mixture of alarm and affection which dog-lovers bestow on a particularly ferocious animal. The driver regarded this proceeding bleakly in the driving-mirror as they entered upon the expanses of Waterloo Bridge. And a new thought entered Geoffrey Vintner's head as, observing this deprecatory glare, he hastily put the gun away again: people had been known to be abducted in taxis, which hovered about their houses until they emerged, and then conveyed them resistlessly away to some place like Limehouse, where they were dealt with by gangs of armed thugs. He gazed dubiously at the short, stocky figure which sat with rock-like immobility in front of him, dexterously skirting the roundabout at the north end of the bridge. Certainly there was only one train which he could have caught from Surrey that morning, in time to get his connection from Paddington, so his enemies, whoever they were, would have known when to meet him; on the other hand, he had had some considerable difficulty in finding a taxi at all, and without exception they had all seemed concerned more with eluding his attention than with trying to attract it. So that was probably all right.

He turned and looked with distaste at the traffic which pursued behind, with the erratic movements of topers following a leader from pub to pub. How people knew when they were being trailed he found himself unable to imagine. Moreover, he was not trained to the habit of observation; the outside world normally impressed itself on him as a vague and unmemorable succession of phantasms—a Red Indian could have walked through London by his side without his noticing anything untoward. He contemplated for a moment asking the driver to make a detour, in order to throw possible pursuers off the scent, but suspected that this would be unkindly received. And in any case, the whole thing was too preposterous; it would do no one any good to follow him publicly through the London crowds on a hot summer's midday.

In this, as it happened, he was wrong.

"Any visit which you make to Tolnbridge you will regret."

Nothing explicit about it, of course, but it had a businesslike air which was far from inspiring confidence. He noticed with that peculiarly galling sense of annoyance which comes from the shattering of some unimportant illusion that the paper and envelope were distinctive and expensive and the typewriter, to judge from its many typographical eccentricities, easily identifiable—provided one knew where to start looking for it. He abandoned himself to aggrievedness. Criminals should at least try to preserve the pretence of anonymity, and not flaunt unsolvable clues before their victims. The postmark, too—thanks to the conscientiousness of some employee of the G.P.O.—read quite legibly as Tolnbridge; which was what one would expect.

The telegram, loosely held in his left hand, fluttered to the floor. He picked it up, shook it fastidiously free of dirt, and read it through automatically, perhaps hoping to extract from the spidery, insubstantial capitals of the British telegraph system some shred of significance which had previously escaped him. That air of callous gaiety, he reflected bitterly, could have emanated from no one but the sender. It ran:

I AM AT TOLNBRIDGE STAYING AT THE CLERGY HOUSE PRIESTS PRIESTS PRIESTS THE PLACE IS BLACK WITH THEM COME AND PLAY THE CATHEDRAL SERVICES ALL THE ORGANISTS HAVE BEEN SHOT UP DISMAL BUSINESS THE MUSIC WASN'T AS BAD AS ALL THAT EITHER YOU'D BETTER COME AT ONCE BRING ME A BUTTERFLY NET I NEED ONE WIRE BACK COMING NOT COMING PREPARE FOR LONG STAY GERVASE FEN

Accompanying this had been a reply-paid form allowing for a reply of fifty words. It was with a sense of some

11

satisfaction that Geoffrey had filled it in: COMING VINTNER
—a satisfaction, however, tempered by the suspicion that
Fen would not even notice the sarcasm. Fen was like
that.

And now he doubted whether he would have sent
that reply at all had it not been for the telegraph-boy
hovering about outside the door and his own natural re-
luctance to take it to the post office later on. Most of our
decisions, he reflected, are forced on us by laziness. And,
of course, at that stage he had not yet opened his
letters. . . . There *were* compensations. The Tolnbridge
choir was a good one, and the organ, a four-manual Willis
one of the finest in the country. He remembered idly that
it had a horn stop which really sounded like a horn, a
lovely stopped diapason on the choir, a noble tuba,
a thirty-two-foot on the pedals which in its lower register sent a rhythmic pulse of vibration through the whole
building, unnerving the faithful. . . . But were these things
compensation enough?

In any case—his mental homily prolonged itself as the
taxi shot round Trafalgar Square—here he was, involved
against his will in some sordid conflict of law and disor-
der, and in some considerable personal danger. The
letter and the telegram in conjunction were proof enough
of that. What it was all about was another matter. The
telegram, suitably punctuated, suggested that some
enemy was engaged in a determined attempt to abolish,
by attrition, the church-music of Tolnbridge—the reason,
presumably, why his own proximate arrival was so much
resented. But this seemed unlikely, not to say fantastic.
The organists had been "shot up"—what on earth did
that mean? It suggested, ominously, machine-guns—but
then Fen was notoriously prone to exaggeration, and
cathedral towns in the West of England do not normally
harbour gangs. He sighed. Useless to speculate—he was
in it, with at least nine-tenths of his boats burnt and the
rest manifestly unseaworthy. The only thing to do was to
sit back and rely on fate and his own wits if anything happened—neither of which aids, he remembered without
satisfaction, had done him any very yeoman service in the
past. And what was all this about a butterfly-net . . . ?

The butterfly-net. He hadn't got it.

He glanced hastily at his watch, and banged on the glass as the taxi rounded Cambridge Circus preparatory to entering the Charing Cross Road.

"Regent Street," he said. The taxi performed a full circle and headed down Shaftesbury Avenue.

A following cab altered its course likewise.

The Regent Street emporium which Geoffrey Vintner eventually selected as being most likely to house a butterfly-net proved to be surprisingly empty, with assistants and customers sweltering in a mid-morning lethargy. It seemed to have been designed with the purpose of evading any overt admission of its function. There were pictures on the walls, and superfluous furnishings, and fat gilt cherubs; while vaguely symbolical figures, standing stiff as Pomeranian grenadiers, supported insouciantly in the small of their backs the ends of the banisters. Before going in, Geoffrey paused to buy a paper, reflecting that any intimations of gang warfare in Tolnbridge would certainly have reached the Press by now. But the Battle of Britain held the headlines, and after crashing into two people while engaged in a search among the smaller items, he postponed further investigation for the time being.

A gigantic placard showing the location of the various departments proved useless from the point of view of butterfly-nets, so he resorted to the enquiry counter. What Fen could want with such a thing as a butterfly-net it was impossible to imagine. Geoffrey had a momentary wild vision of the pair of them pursuing insects across the Devon moors, and looked again, even more doubtfully, at the telegram. But no; it could not by any stretch of the imagination be a mistake; and lepidoptery was as likely to be Fen's present obsession as anything else.

Butterfly-nets, he learned, were to be had from either the children's or the sports department; fortunately both were on the same floor. He examined the lift-girl with a professional air of suspicion as she closed the gates on him, and was rewarded with an exaggeratedly indignant stare (" 'aving an eyeful," she confided later to a friend). Thereupon he retired hastily into his paper, and as he was borne upward through the building, discovered and read the following:

"ATTACK ON MUSICIAN"

"The police have as yet no clue to the assailant of Dr. Dennis Brooks, Organist of Tolnbridge Cathedral, who was attacked and rendered unconscious while on his way home the evening before last."

Geoffrey cursed the papers for their lack of detail, Fen for his exaggeration, and himself for becoming involved in the business at all. This private ritual of commination concluded, he scratched his nose ruefully; *something* was going on, anyway. But what had happened to the deputy organist? Presumably he had been banged on the head as well.

The lift came to a shattering stop, and Geoffrey found himself precipitated into the midst of a vast mellay of sports equipment, tenanted only by one plump, pink young assistant, who stood gazing about him with the resignation and despair of Priam amid the ruins of Troy.

"Have you ever noticed," he said gloomily as Geoffrey approached, "the way no sports apparatus is ever a decent, symmetrical shape? You can't pile it up neatly like boxes or books—there are always little bits sticking out on all sides. Roller-skates are the worst." His tone deepened, indicating his especial abhorrence of these inconvenient objects. "And footballs roll off the shelf as soon as you put them up, and skis you are bound to fall over, and the moment you lean a cricket-bat against the wall it slides down again." He looked unhappily at Geoffrey. "Is there anything you want? Most people," he went on before Geoffrey could reply, "have given up sports for the war. I expect they're better off for it in the end. Muscular development only provides a foothold for fat." He sighed.

"What I really wanted was a butterfly-net," said Geoffrey absently; his mind still dwelt on the problem of the organists.

"A butter-fly net," repeated the young man sadly; he seemed to find this information particularly discouraging. "It's the same with them, you see," he said, pointing to a row of butterfly-nets propped against a wall. "If you

14

stand them on their heads, as it were, the net part sticks out and trips you up; and if you have them as they are now, they look top-heavy and disturb the eye." He went over and selected one.

"Isn't it rather long?" said Geoffrey, gazing without enthusiasm at the six feet of bamboo which confronted him.

"They have to be that," said the young man without any perceptible lightening of spirit, "or you'd never get near the butterflies at all. Not that you do very often, in any case," he added. "Most of it's just blind swiping, really. Would you be wanting a collector's box?"

"I don't think so."

"Ah, well. I don't blame you. They're inconvenient things, very heavy to carry about." He scrutinised the net again. "This will be seventeen-and-six. Ridiculous waste of money, really. I'll just take the price off."

The price was attached to the stem of the net with a piece of string that proved impervious to tugging.

"Won't it slip off?" said Geoffrey helpfully; and then, when quite obviously it wouldn't: "Well, it doesn't matter, anyway."

"It's no bother at all. I've got a pair of scissors." The pink young man felt helplessly in his pockets. "I must have left them in the office. I'm always doing that; and when I do remember, they tear holes in my pockets. Just a minute." He had disappeared before Geoffrey could stop him.

The man in the black slouch hat rose from his rather cramped position behind a counter laden with boxing-gloves near the stairhead, and made his way with considerable speed and stealth towards Geoffrey. He carried a blackjack and had the intent expression of one trying to trap a mosquito. The pink young assistant, however, did not stay away as long as he had hoped. Emerging from the office, he took in the situation without apparent surprise, and, acting with commendable presence of mind, put the butterfly-net over the assailant's head and pulled. The blackjack described an arc through the air and knocked over a pile of roller-skates with a horrifying crash. Geoffrey spun round just in time to see his would-be attacker overbalance backwards and collapse into the middle of a vast medley of sports equipment which stood in the middle of the floor. It expressed its unsymmetrical character by general dissolution. A number of footballs were precipitated to the top of the stairs, down which they careered with increasing momentum to the department below. The Enemy freed himself, cursing noisily, from the butterfly-net, got to his feet, and made for the stairs. The pink young man gave him a resounding crack on the back of his head with one end of a ski, and he fell down again. Geoffrey struggled with his revolver, which had become inextricably involved in the lining of his pocket.

Battle was at once engaged. The Enemy, who was showing remarkable powers of recovery, opened a frontal attack on Geoffrey. The pink young man threw a cricket-ball at him, but it missed and hit Geoffrey instead. Geoffrey fell over and upset a heap of ice-skates, over which the assailant in his turn fell. The pink young man tried to put the net over his head again, but missed his arm and overbalanced. The Enemy regained his feet and threw an iceskate at Geoffrey, which caught him a windy blow in the stomach as he was still endeavouring to get out his revolver. The pink young man, recovering his balance, smote the Enemy with a cricket-stump. The Enemy subsided, and the pink young man banged inexpertly at his head with a hockey-stick until he became silent. Geoffrey at last succeeded in getting out his revolver, to the accompaniment of an ominous tearing of cloth, and waved it wildly about him.

"Be careful with that," said the pink young man.

"What happened?"

"Malicious intent," said the other. He picked up the blackjack, tossed it in the air, and nodded sagely. "I'm afraid that butterfly-net's no good now," he added, with a relapse into his previous melancholy. "Torn to bits. You'd better take another." He went over and got one. "Seventeen-and-six, I think we said." Mechanically Geoffrey produced the money.

A roar of mingled rage and stupefaction from below indicated that the footballs had arrived at their destination. "Fielding!" a voice boomed up at them. "What the devil are you doing up there?"

"I think," said the young man pensively, "that it would be better if we left—*at once.*"

"But your job!" Geoffrey gazed at him helplessly.

"I've probably lost it, anyway, thanks to this. Something of this sort always seems to happen to me. The last place I was at one of the assistants went mad and took off all her clothes. I wonder if I've left anything?" He buffeted his pockets, as one who searches for matches. "I generally do. At least three pairs of gloves a year—in trains."

"Come on," said Geoffrey urgently. He was feeling unnaturally exhilarated, and obsessed by a primitive desire to escape from the scene of the disturbance. Footsteps clattered up the steps towards them. The lift-girl apocalyptically threw open the doors of the lift, announced, as one ushering in the day of judgement; "Sports, children's, books, ladies'——" shrieked out at the chaos confronting her, and closed the doors again, whence she and her passengers peered out like anxious rabbits awaiting the arrival of greenstuffs. The accidental touch of a button sent the lift shooting earthwards again; from it rapidly diminishing sounds of altercation could be heard.

Geoffrey and the pink young man ran for the stairs. On their way down, they met a shop-walker and two assistants, pounding grimly upwards.

"There's a lunatic up there trying to break up the stock," said the young man with a sudden blood-curdling intensity which, by contrast with his normal tones, sounded horrifyingly convincing. "Go and see what you can do—I'm off to fetch the police."

The shop-walker snatched Geoffrey's gun, which he was still brandishing, and leaped on upwards. Geoffrey engaged in feeble protests.

"Don't hang about," said the young man, tugging at his sleeve. They continued their precipitate downward rush to the street.

"Well, and what was all that about?" asked the young man, leaning back in his corner of the taxi and stretching out his legs.

Geoffrey deferred replying for a moment. He was engaged in a minute scrutiny of the driver, though obscurely conscious of not knowing what he expected this activity

17

to reveal. No chances must be taken, however; the encounter in the shop indicated that much. He transferred his suspicion to the young man, and prepared to make searching enquiries as to his trustworthiness. It suddenly struck him, however, that this might well appear ungracious, as it certainly would have done.

"I hardly know," he said lamely.

The young man appeared pleased. "Then we must go into the matter from the beginning," he announced. "He nearly got you, you know. Can't have that sort of thing." He proffered his determination to uphold the law a trifle inanely. "Where are you going?"

"Paddington," said Geoffrey, and added hastily: "That is to say—I mean—possibly." The conversation was not going well, and his brief feeling of exhilaration had vanished.

"I know what it is," said the young man. "You don't trust me. And quite right, too. A man in your position oughtn't to trust anyone. Still, I'm all right, you know; saved you getting a lump on your head the size of an Easter egg." He wiped his brow and loosened his collar. "My name's Fielding—Henry Fielding."

Geoffrey embarked without enthusiasm on a second-rate witticism. "Not the author of *Tom Jones,* I suppose?" He regretted it the moment it was out.

"*Tom Jones?* Never heard of it. A book, is it? Don't get much time for reading. And you?"

"I beg your pardon?"

"I mean, I introduced myself, so I thought you—"

"Oh, yes, of course. Geoffrey Vintner. And I must thank you for acting as promptly as you did; heaven knows what would have happened to me if you hadn't interfered."

"So do I."

"What do you mean—— Oh, I see. But it occurs to me now, you know, that we really ought to have stayed and seen the police. It's all very well dashing off like a couple of schoolboys, who've been robbing an orchard, but there are certain proprieties to be observed." Geoffrey became suddenly bored with this line of thought. "Anyway, I had to catch a train."

"And our friend," said Fielding, "was presumably trying to stop you. Which brings us back to the question of what it's all about." He wiped his brow again.

Geoffrey, however, was distracted, idly musing on a Passacaglia and Fugue commissioned from him for the New Year. It had not been going well in any case, and the interruption of his present mission seemed unlikely to prosper it. But not even prospective oblivion will prevent a composer from brooding despondently and maddeningly on his own works. Geoffrey embarked on a mental performance: Ta-ta; ta-ta-ta-*ti*-ta-*ti*. . . .

"I wonder," Fielding added, "if they've anticipated the failure of the first attack, and provided a second line of defence."

This unexpected confusion of military metaphors shook Geoffrey. The spectral caterwaulings were abruptly stilled. "I believe you said that to frighten me," he said. "Tell me what's going on. If I'm an enemy, I know already——"

"I didn't say——"

"And if I'm not, I may be able to help."

So in the end Geoffrey told him. As precise information it amounted to very little.

"I don't see that that helps much," Fielding objected when he had finished. He examined the telegram and letter. "And who is this Fen person, anyway?"

"Professor of English at Oxford. We were up together. I haven't seen much of him since, though I happened to hear he was going to be in Tolnbridge during the long vac. Why he should send for me——" Geoffrey made a gesture of humorous resignation, and upset the butterfly-net, which was poised precariously in a transverse position across the interior of the cab. With some acrimony they jerked it into place again.

"I can't think," said Geoffrey, after contemplating for a moment finishing his previous sentence and deciding against it, "why Fen insisted on my bringing that thing."

"Rather odd, surely? Is he a collector?"

"One never quite knows with Fen. In anyone else, though—well, yes, I suppose it would seem odd."

"He seems to know something about this Brooks business."

"Well, he's *there*, of course. And then," Geoffrey

added as a laborious afterthought, "he's a detective, in a way."

Fielding looked disconcerted; he had evidently been reserving this role for himself, and disliked the thought of competition. A little peevishly he asked:

"Not an official detective, surely?"

"No, no, amateur. But he's been very successful."

"Gervase Fen—I don't seem to have heard of him," said Fielding. Then after a moment's thought: "What a silly name. Is he in with the police?" His tone suggested Fen's complicity in some orgiastic and disgraceful organisation.

"I honestly don't know. It's only what I've heard."

"I wonder if you'd mind my coming with you to Tolnbridge? I'm sick of the store. And with the war on, it seems so remote from anything——"

"Couldn't you join up?"

"No, they won't have me. I volunteered last November, but they graded me *four*. I joined the A.R.P., of course, and I'm thinking of going in for this new L.D.V. racket, but blast it all——"

"You look healthy enough," said Geoffrey.

"So I am. Nothing wrong with me except shaky eyesight. They don't grade you four for that, do they?"

"No. Perhaps," Geoffrey suggested encouragingly, "you're suffering from some hidden, fatal disease you haven't known about."

Fielding ignored this. "I want to do something active about this war—something romantic." He mopped his brow again, looking the reverse of romantic. "I tried to join the Secret Service, but it was no good. You can't join the Secret Service in this country. Not just like that." And he slapped his hands together to indicate some platonic idea of facility.

Geoffrey considered. In view of what had happened it would almost certainly be very useful to have Fielding with him on his journey, and there was no reason to suspect him of ulterior motive.

". . . After all, war hasn't become so mechanised that solitary, individual daring no longer matters," Fielding was saying; he seemed transported to some Valhalla of Secret Service agents. "You'll laugh at me, of course"—

Geoffrey smiled a hasty and unconvincing negative—"but in the long run it is the people who dream of being men of action who *are* the men of action. Admittedly Don Quixote made a fool of himself with the windmills, but when all's said and done, there probably *were* giants about." He sighed gently as the taxi turned into the Marylebone Road.

"I should very much like to have you with me," said Geoffrey. "But look here—what about your job? One must have money."

"That'll be all right. I have some money of my own." Fielding assembled his features into a perfunctory expression of surprise. "Oh, I ought perhaps to have mentioned it. *Debrett, Who's Who*, and such publications, credit me with an earldom."

Geoffrey summoned up a cheerful laugh, but there was something in Fielding's assurance which forbade him to utter it.

"Only very minor, of course," the other hastened to explain. "And I've never done a thing to deserve it. I inherited it."

"Then what on earth," said Geoffrey, "were you doing in that shop?"

"Store," Fielding corrected him solemnly. "Well, I heard there was a shortage of people to serve in shops, owing to call-up and so on, so I thought that might be one way I could help. Only temporarily, of course," he added warily. "Just as a joke," he ended feebly.

Geoffrey suppressed his merriment with difficulty. Fielding suddenly chuckled.

"I suppose it *is* rather preposterous, when you come to think of it. By the way"—a sudden thought struck him—"are you Geoffrey Vintner, the composer?"

"Only very minor, of course."

They surveyed one another properly for the first time, and found the result pleasing. The taxi clattered into the murk of Paddington. A sudden noise disturbed them.

"Well, I'm damned," said Fielding. "The bloody net's fallen down again."

Chapter Two

DO NOT TRAVEL FOR
PLEASURE

*"A crowd is no company, and faces are but a gallery
of pictures, and talk but a tinkling cymbal where
there is no love."*

BACON

AFTER THE DIM, barn-like vastness of Waterloo, Paddington appeared like an infernal pit. Here there was not the
order, the strict division and segregation of mechanical
and human which prevailed at the larger station. Inextricably, engines and passengers seethed and milled together, the barriers provided for their separation seeming
mo more than the inconvenient erections of an obstacle-
race. The crowds, turgid, stormy, and densely-packed,
appeared more likely to clamber on to the backs of the
trains, like children piling on to a donkey at the sea-side
than merely to board them in the normal way. The loco-
motives panted and groaned like expiring hedgehogs prematurely overrun by hordes of predatory ants; any
attempt at departure, one felt, must infallibly crush and
dissipate these insects in their thousands—it would be impossible for them to disentangle themselves from the
buffers and connecting-rods in time.

Amongst the crowds, the heat banished comfort, but
stimulated the itch to uneasy and purposeless movement.
Certain main streams, between the bars, the platform, the
ticket-offices, the lavatories, and the main entrances, were
perhaps discernible; but they had only the conventional
boundaries of currents on a map—they overflowed their
banks amongst the merely impassive, who stood at the

angles of their confluence in attitudes of melancholy or despair. Observed from ground level, this mass of humanity exhibited, in its efforts to move hither and thither, surprising divergences from the horizontal; people pressed forward to their destinations leaning forward at a dangerous angle, or, peering round the bodies of those in front of them, presented the appearance of criminals half-decapitated. A great many troops, bearing ponderous white cylinders apparently filled with lead, elbowed their way apologetically about, or sat on kit-bags and allowed themselves to be buffeted from all angles. Railway officials controlled the scene with the uneasy authority of schoolmasters trying to extort courteous recognition from their pupils after term has ended.

"Good God," said Geoffrey as he struggled forward, carrying a suitcase with which he made periodic involuntary assaults on the knees of the passers-by, "are we even going to get *on* this train?"

Fielding, still inappropriately dressed in the morning clothes belonging to his recent occupation, merely grunted; the temperature seemed to overcome him. When they had progressed, clawing and pushing, another two yards, he said:

"What time is it supposed to go?"

"Not for three-quarters of an hour yet." The relevant part of the sentence was drowned in a sudden demoniac outburst of hooting and whistling. He repeated it at the top of his voice. "Three-quarters of an hour," he bellowed.

Fielding nodded, and then, surprisingly, vanished with a shouted explanation of which the only word audible was "clothes." A little bemused, Geoffrey laboured to the ticket-office. The tickets occupied him for some twenty minutes, but in any case the train seemed likely to depart late. He waved his bag in optimistic query at a porter, passing on some nameless, leisurely errand, and was ignored.

Then he went, reflecting a little sadly on the miseries which our indulgences cause us, to get a drink.

The refreshment-room was decorated with gilt and marble; their inappropriate splendours cast a singular gloom over the proceedings. By the forethought of those

24

responsible for getting people on to trains the clock had been put ten minutes fast, a device which led to frequent panics of departure among those who were under the impression that it showed the right time. They were immediately reassured by others, whose watches were slow. Upon discovery of the real hour, a second and more substantial panic occurred. Years of the Defence of the Realm Act had conditioned the British public to remain in bars until the latest possible moment.

Geoffrey deposited his bag by a pillar (someone immediately fell over it), and elbowed his way to the bar, which he clutched with the determination of a shipwrecked sailor who has reached a friendly shore. The sirens lurking behind it, with comparative freedom of movement, were engaged in friendly discourse with regular customers. A barrage of imperative glances and despairing cries for attention failed, for the most part, to move them. Some brandished coins in the hope that this display of affluence and good faith would jerk these figures into motion. Geoffrey found himself next to a dwarfish commercial traveller, who was treating one of the barmaids to a long, rambling fantasy about the disadvantages of early marriage, as freely exemplified by himself and many friends and relations. By pushing him malignantly out of the way, Geoffrey managed eventually to get a drink.

Fielding reappeared as inexplicably as he had gone, dressed in a sports coat and flannels and carrying a suitcase. He explained rather breathlessly that he had been back to his flat, and demanded beer. The ritual of entreaty was again enacted. *"Travelling,"* said Fielding with deep feeling.

"I hope we don't have to get in with any babies," said Geoffrey gloomily. "If they don't shriek out and crawl all over me, they're invariably sick."

There were babies—one, at least—but the first-class compartment containing it was the only one with two seats vacant—one of them, on to which Geoffrey at once hurled a mass of impedimenta in token of ownership, an outside corner. He then applied himself to getting Fen's butterfly-net on to the rack, assisted by Fielding, and watched with interest by the other occupants of the compartment. It was just too long. Geoffrey regarded it with hatred: it was growing, in his eyes, into a monstrous symbol of the inconvenience, shame and absurdity of his preposterous errand.

"Try standing it up against the window," said the man sitting in the corner opposite Geoffrey's. His plumpness and pinkness outdid Fielding's. Geoffrey felt, regarding him, like a man who while brandishing an Amati is suddenly confronted with a Strad.

They put this scheme into practice; whenever anyone moved his feet the net fell down again.

"What a thing to bring on a train," said the woman with the baby, *sotto voce*.

It was eventually decided to lay the net transversely across the carriage, from one rack to the other. The whole compartment rose—not with any enthusiasm, since it was so hot—to do justice to his idea. A woman seated in one of the other corners, with a face white and pock-marked like a plucked chicken's breast, complainingly shifted her luggage to make room. Then she sat down again and insulated herself unnecessarily against the surrounding humanity with a rug, which made Geoffrey hot even to look at. With a great deal of obscure mutual encouragement and admonition, such as "Up she goes" and "Steady, now," Geoffrey, Fielding, the fat man and a young clergyman who occupied the remaining corner hoisted the net into position. The baby, hitherto quiescent, awoke and embarked upon a running commentary of snorts and shrieks; it grunted like the pig-baby in *Alice*, until they expected it to be metamorphosed before their eyes. The mother jogged it ruthlessly up and down, and glared malignantly at the progenitors of the disturbance. People searching for seats peered into the compartment and attempted to assess the number of people engaged in this hullabaloo. One went so far as to open the door and ask if there was any room, but he was ignored, and soon went away again.

"Disgraceful!" said the woman with the baby. She bumped it up and down even more furiously than before, and cooed at it, adding to its noises with her own.

The net was by now secured at either end, and more or

26

less conveniently placed, except that anyone rising incautiously or coming into the compartment was liable to bang his head on it. Geoffrey profusely thanked his assistants, who sat down again looking hot but pleased. He turned back to transfer the remainder of his belongings from the seat on to the rack. They were now topped by a letter not his own, but plainly addressed to him. The paper and typing looked uncomfortably familiar. He opened it and read:

"There's still time to get off the train. We have our setbacks, but we can't go on failing indefinitely."

Ignoring Fielding's curious glance, he put it thoughtfully in his pocket and heaved the remainder of his things out of the way. In the confusion of a moment before, anyone in the compartment could have dropped that note, and for that matter—since the window was wide open—anyone could have flicked it in from outside. He tried to remember the dispositions of the various persons in the compartment, and failed. He sat down feeling somewhat alarmed.

"Another?" said Fielding; he raised his right eyebrow in elaborate query.

Geoffrey nodded dumbly and handed him the note. He whistled with noisy astonishment as he read it. "But who——?"

Geoffrey shook his head, still refusing to utter a sound. He hoped to convey by this means his suspicion of one of the occupants of the compartment. Any open discussion of the matter might, he obscurely felt, convey information of value to the enemy. The others were eyeing unenthusiastically this gnomic interchange.

But Fielding was for the moment oblivious of such innuendoes.

"Quick work," he said. "They must have had a second line of defence ready in case the business in the store failed. Simply a matter of phoning someone here while we were on our way. They're certainly taking no chances."

27

"I wish you'd remember," said Geoffrey a trifle peevishly, "that *I'm* the object of all this. It's no pleasure to *me* to have you sitting there gloating over the excellence of their arrangements."

No notice was taken of this. "And that means," Fielding continued impassively, "that the typewriter they used is somewhere in this neighbourhood—damn it, no it doesn't, though. The wording of that second note is so vague it could easily have been got ready beforehand." The failure of his calculation threw him into a profound despondency; he stared dejectedly at his feet.

Geoffrey meanwhile was carrying out an inventory of the other persons in the compartment. The man opposite, who had been so helpful over Fen's butterfly-net, had a well-to-do professional air. Geoffrey was inclined to put him down as a doctor, or a prosperous broker. His face was amiable, with that underlying shyness and melancholy which seems always to be beneath the surface in fat men; he had sparse straight hair, pale grey eyes with heavy lids like thick shutters of flesh, and very long lashes, like a girl's. The material of his suit was expensive, and it was competently tailored. He held a thick black book, one of the four volumes, Geoffrey observed with surprise, of Pareto's monumental *The Mind and Society*. Did doctors or brokers read such things on railway journeys? Covertly, he regarded his *vis-à-vis* with renewed interest.

Next door was the woman with the baby. Repeated jogging had now shaken the infant into a state of bemused incomprehension, and it emitted only faint and isolated shrieks. By compensation, it had begun to dribble. Its mother, a small woman vaguely and unanalysably slatternly in appearance, periodically wiped a grubby handkerchief with great force and determination across its face, so that its head almost fell off backwards; while not occupied in this way, she gazed at her companions with great dislike. Probably, Geoffrey reflected, she could be omitted from the list of suspects. The same could not be said for the clergyman sitting in the corner on her right, however. It was true that he looked ready, young, and ineffectual, but these were too much the characteristics of the stage curate not to be at once suspicious. He

28

was glancing occasionally, with anxious enquiry, at the woman with the rug. She, meanwhile, was engaged in that unnerving examination of other persons in the compartment which most people seem to regard as necessary at the beginning of a long railway journey. Eventually, feeling apparently that this had now been brought to the point where embarrassment was likely to become active discomfort, she said to the clergyman, looking sternly at a small wrist-watch:

"What time do we get into Tolnbridge?"

This query aroused some interest in other quarters. Both Geoffrey and Fielding started slightly, with well-drilled uniformity, and shot swift glances at the speaker, while in the Pareto-addict opposite Geoffrey some stirrings of attention were also discernible. All things considered, it was not very surprising that someone else in the compartment should be going to Tolnbridge, even though compared with Taunton and Exeter it was an unimportant stop; but Geoffrey at all events was too alarmed and uneasy to make such a simple deduction.

The clergyman seemed at a loss for an answer. He looked helplessly about him and said:

"I'm afraid I'm not sure, Mrs. Garbin. I could perhaps find out——?" He half-rose from his seat. The man opposite Geoffrey leaned forward.

"Five-forty-three," he said with decision. "But I'm afraid we're likely to lose time on the way." He took a gold watch from his waistcoat-pocket. "We're ten minutes late in starting already."

The woman with the rug nodded briskly. "In wartime, we must resign ourselves to that sort of thing," she said, her tone loaded with stoic resignation. "You are getting off there yourself?" she asked after a moment.

The fat man bowed his head. The reluctant and self-conscious democracy of the railway compartment was set into creaking motion. "Have you far to go?" he enquired of Geoffrey.

Geoffrey started. "I am going to Tolnbridge, too," he replied a trifle stiffly. "The trains are almost always late nowadays," he added, feeling his previous remark to be by itself an insufficient contribution to the general entertainment.

"Inevitably," said the clergyman, contributing his mite. "We are fortunate in being able to travel at all." He turned to the woman with the baby. "Have you a long journey, madam? It must be very tiring travelling with a child."

"I'm going further west than the rest of you," said the mother. "Much further west," she added. Her tone expressed a determination to remain in her seat as far west as possible, even if the train should be driven over Land's End and into the sea.

"Such a good boy," said the clergyman, gazing at the child with distaste. It spat ferociously at him.

"Now, Sally, you mustn't do that to the gentleman," said the mother. She glowered at him with unconcealed malevolence. He smiled unhappily. The fat man returned to his book. Fielding sat morose and silent, scanning an evening paper.

It was at this moment, amidst a shrieking of whistles which advertise immediate departure, that the irruption occurred. A man appeared in the corridor outside, carrying a heavy portmanteau, and peered through the window, bobbing up and down like a marionette in order to see what lay within. He then thrust the door aside and stepped aggressively over the threshold. He wore a shiny black suit with a bedraggled carnation in the buttonhole, bright brown shoes, a pearl tie-pin, a dirty grey trilby hat, and a lemon-colored handkerchief in his breast-pocket; his hands were nicotine-stained and his nails filthy; his complexion was sanguine, almost apoplectic, and he wiped his nose on the back of his hand as he trampled in over the clergyman's feet, hauling his case like a reluctant dog after him. It swung forward and struck the woman with the rug a resounding blow on the knee.

"No room!" she said as if at a signal. A confused murmur of admonition and discouragement went up in support of this remark. The man stared aggrievedly about him.

"Wadjer mean, no room?" he said loudly, "Djer think I'm gointa stand aht in the bloody corridor the 'ole journey? Because if yer do, yer bloody well wrong, see?" He warmed to his theme. "Just because yer travelling bloody first-class, yer needn't think yer got a right to occupy the 'ole train, see? People like me aren't goin' ter stand the 'ole way just so you plutocrats can stretch yer legs in comfort, see?" He became indignant. "I paid for a seat same as you 'ave, 'aven't I? *'Ere*"—he shot out a finger towards the fat man, who jumped visibly with fright. "You put that there arm up, an' we'll all 'ave a chance ter sit down, see?" The fat man hastily put the arm up, and the intruder, with expressions of noisy satisfaction, inserted himself into the gap thus created between the fat man and the mother and child.

"You mind your language when there are ladies present!" said the mother indignantly. The baby began to bellow again. "There—see what you've done to the child!"

The intruder ignored her. He produced a *Mirror* and *Herald,* and, after slapping the former down on his knee, opened the latter at full spread, so that his elbows waved within an inch of the noses of those on either side. The woman with the rug, after her first sortie, had recognised defeat in the monotonous stream of blasphemy and become silent. Geoffrey, Fielding and the clergyman, afflicted by a *bourgeois* terror of offending this unruly manifestation of the lower classes, sat impotent and disapproving. Only the mother, who maintained her intransigence with scornful glances, and the fat man, whose position was more desperate, still showed resistence.

"I suppose," said the fat man, abandoning his Pareto, "that you've got a first-class ticket?"

A deathly silence followed this question. The intruder jerked himself slowly up from his paper, like a pugilist who has been unfairly smitten in the belly and is gathering forces ponderously together for retaliation. The others looked on aghast. Even the fat man quailed, unnerved by the ominous delay in answering his query.

"What's it got ter do with *you?*" asked the intruder at last, slapping his *Herald* shut. A dramatic hush ensued. "Not the bloody ticket-collector, are yer?" The fat man remained dumb. "Just 'cos I ain't as rich and idle as you, ain't I got a right ter sit in comfort, eh?"

"Comfort!" said the woman with the baby meaningly.

The intruder ignored her, continuing to apostrophise the fat man. "Snob, aren't yer? Too 'igh-and-mighty to 'ave the likes o' me in the same compartment with yer, are yer? Let me tell you"—he tapped the fat man abruptly on the waistcoat—"one o' ther things we're fightin' this war for is ter get rid o' the likes o' *you* an' give the likes er *me* a chance to spread ourselves a bit."

He spread himself, illustratively, kicking Fielding on the shin in the process. The baby wailed like a banshee. "*Caliban*," said the mother.

"Nonsense!" the fat man protested feebly. "That's got nothing to do with whether you've got a first-class ticket or not."

The intruder twisted himself bodily round and thrust his face into that of the fat man. "Oh, it ain't, ain't it?" He began to speak very rapidly. "When we get socialism, see, which is what we're fighting for, see, you and your like'll 'ave show some respect to me, see, instead of treating me like a lot of dirt, see?" Finding this line of thought exhausted, he transferred his attention to the fat man's book, removing it, despite faint protests, from his hands. He then inspected it slowly and with care, as a surgeon might some peculiarly loathsome cancer after removal.

"What's this?" he said. "Vilfreedo Pareeto," he announced to the compartment at large. "*Ther Mind and Society*," he read. " 'Oo's that—some bloody Wop, is it? 'Ere, you," he addressed Geoffrey. "You ever 'eard of 'im —Vilfreedo Pareeto?"

The fat man looked at Geoffrey appealingly. Treacherously and mendaciously, Geoffrey shook his head. Worlds would not have induced him to admit acquaintance with that sociologist.

The intruder nodded triumphantly, and turned to Fielding. "What abaht you?" he said, waving the volume. "You ever 'eard of this?" As treacherously, but with more truth, Fielding denied it. The fat man turned pale. So solemn were the proceedings, he might have been awaiting sentence from the Inquisition, the only two witnesses for the defence having been suborned against him.

The intruder breathed heavily with satisfaction. Portentously he turned the pages of the book. "Listen ter this," he commanded. " 'The principal nu-cle-us in a deriv-a-tive (a non-log-ico-ex-per-i-ment-al the-ory) is a res-i-due, or a number of res-i-dues, and around it other sec-ond-ar-y res-i-dues cluster.' Does that make sense, I arst yer? Does that make sense?" He glared at Geoffrey, who feebly shook his head. "Sec-ond-ar-y res-i-dues," repeated the intruder with scorn. "Lot o' nonsense, if yer arst me. 'Ere"—he turned back to the fat man again, hurling the book on to his knee, "you oughter 'ave something better ter do with yer time than read 'ighbrow books by Wops. And if yer 'aven't, see, you just mind yer own business, see, and don't go poking yer nose into other people's affairs, see?"

He turned back aggressively to the other occupants of the compartment. "Anybody got any objection ter my sitting 'ere, first-class or no?"

So successful had been the process of intimidation that no one uttered a sound.

Presently the train started.

All afternoon the train rattled and jolted through the English countryside, towards the red clay of Devon and the slow, immense surge of the Atlantic against the Cornish shore. Geoffrey dozed, gazed automatically out of the window, thought about his fugue or meditated with growing dismay on the events of the day. The possibility— almost, he decided, the certainty—that he had an enemy within a foot or two of him made Fielding's company very welcome. Of the why and wherefore of the whole business he thought but briefly; strictly there was nothing to think about. The occurrences which had followed his arriving down to breakfast that morning, in a perfectly normal and peaceable manner, seemed a nightmare phantasmagoria devoid of reason. Almost, he began to wonder if they had taken place at all. The human mind properly assimilates only those things it has become accustomed to; anything out-of-the-way affects it only in a purely superficial and objective sense. Geoffrey contemplated the attack on himself without a shred of real belief.

Fielding and the woman with the rug slept, shaking and jolting like inanimate beings as the train clattered over points. The young clergyman gazed vacantly into the corridor, and the mother rocked her baby, which had fallen into a fitful slumber, beset in all probability with nightmares. The intruder also had gone to sleep, and was snoring, his chin resting painfully on his tie-pin. The fat man eyed Geoffrey warily, and put down the *Daily Mirror*, which had been forced on him in a spirit of scornful condescension by the intruder, and which he had been reading unhappily ever since the train left Paddington. He grinned conspiratorially.

"Devil of a journey," he said.

Geoffrey grinned back. "I'm afraid you're worse off then I am. But it's bad enough in any case."

The fat man appeared to be considering deeply. When he again spoke, it was with some hesitation. "You, sir, are obviously an educated man—I wonder if you can help me out of a difficulty?"

Geoffrey looked at him in surprise. "If I can."

"An intellectual difficulty merely," said the fat man hastily. He seemed to think Geoffrey would imagine he was trying to borrow money. "However, I ought to introduce myself first. My name is Peace—Justinian Peace."

"Delighted to know you," said Geoffrey, and murmured his own name.

"Ah, the composer," said Peace amiably. "This is a great pleasure. Well now, Mr. Vintner,—my whole problem can be summed up in three words: I have *doubts*."

"Good heavens," said Geoffrey. "Not like Mr. Prendergast?"

"I beg your pardon?"

"In *Decline and Fall*."

"I'm afraid I've never read Gibbon," said the other. The admission appeared to irritate him in some obscure way. "The fact is that by profession I'm a psycho-analyst —quite a successful one, I suppose; successful certainly as far as money goes. The amount of money," he said confidentially, "which some people will pay for information which they could get from three hours' intelligent reading in any public library . . . However"—he became conscious that he was getting off the point—"there it is. I suppose in London I'm pretty well at the top of my profession. You may think we're all charlatans, of course—a lot of people do"—Geoffrey hurriedly shook his head—"but as far as I'm concerned, at least, I have tried to go about the business methodically and scientifi-

cally, and to do the best for my patients. Well, then——"
He paused and mopped his brow to emphasise the fact
that he was now coming to the crux of the matter; Geoffrey nodded encouragingly.

"As you know, the whole of modern psychology—and
psychoanalysis in particular—is based on the idea of the
unconscious; the conception that there is a section of the
mind in some sense separate from the conscious mind,
and which is responsible for our dreams, certain of our
impulses, and all the complex manifestations of the irrational in human life." His phraseology, Geoffrey
thought, was taking on the aspect of a popular text-book.
"From this concept all the conclusions of analytical
psychology are derived. Unfortunately, about a month
ago, it occurred to me to investigate the origins and ra-
tionale of this basic conception. A terrible thing happened, Mr. Vintner." He leaned forward and tapped
Geoffrey impressively on the knee. *I could not find one
shred of experimental or rational proof that the unconscious existed at all.*"

He sat back again; it was evident that he regarded this
statement as in some sense a personal triumph.

"The more I thought about it, the more convinced I
became that in fact it didn't exist. We know, after all,
nothing at all about the *conscious* mind, so why postulate,
quite arbitrarily, an *unconscious*, to explain anything we
can't understand? It's as if," he added with some vague
recollection of wartime cooking, "a man were to say he
was eating a mixture of butter and margarine when he
had never in his life tasted either."

Geoffrey regarded Peace with a jaundiced eye. "Interesting," he muttered. "Very interesting," he repeated beneath his breath, like a physician who has diagnosed
some obscure and offensive complaint. "One accepted it,
of course, as a thing no longer requiring any investigation,
like the movement of the earth round the sun. But I
don't quite see . . ."

"But you must see!" Peace interrupted excitedly. "It
strikes at the root of my profession, my occupation, my
income, my *life*." His voice rose to a squeak. "I can't go
on being a psycho-analyst when I don't believe in the un-

35

conscious any longer. It's as impossible as a vegetarian butcher."

Geoffrey sighed; his look conveyed that *he,* at least, could set no way out of the impasse. "Surely," he said, "the matter isn't as serious as all that."

Peace shook his head. "It is, I'm afraid," he said. "And when you come to think of it, isn't psycho-analysis *silly?* Anything can mean anything, you know. It's like that series of sums in which whatever number you start with the answer is always twenty-one."

"Well," said Geoffrey, "couldn't you start a system of psycho-analysis based only on the conscious mind?"

The other brightened; then his face fell again. "I suppose one *might,*" he said, "but I don't quite see how it's possible. Still, I'll think about it. Thank you for the suggestion." He became very despondent; Geoffrey hastened to change the subject.

"Have you ever been to Tolnbridge before?"

"Never," Peace replied; he seemed to regard this admission of deficiency as the very acme of his troubles. "It's very beautiful, I believe. Are you proposing to stay long?"

Geoffrey, for no very sound reason, became suddenly suspicious. "I'm not sure," he said.

"My brother-in-law," said Peace didactically, "is Precentor at the cathedral there, and I'm going to see my sister—the first time in several years. I confess I'm not looking forward to it. I don't get on with the clergy"—he lowered his voice, glancing furtively at its representative in the far corner. "I find they regard one as a sort of modern witch-doctor—quite rightly, I suppose," he concluded miserably, remembering his doubts.

Geoffrey's interest was aroused. "As it happens," he said, "I'm going to stay at the clergy-house myself, so we shall probably be seeing something of one another. I shall be playing the services, for a while at all events."

Peace nodded. "Ah, yes," he said, "That organist fellow was knocked out, of course. My sister told me over the phone this morning. Said she wasn't surprised, —fellow drinks like a fish, apparently. I suppose it would have been my brother-in-law who asked you to come down?"

"It *should* have been, by rights. Actually it was a friend of mine, Gervase Fen, who's staying at the clergy-house at the moment. Presumably he was authorised." Knowing Fen, Geoffrey was suddenly seized by a horrible doubt. But plainly the Enemy considered him to be authorised, or they wouldn't be wasting their time on him.

"Gervase Fen," said Peace meditatively. "I seem to know the name."

"A detective of sorts."

"I see—investigating the attack on this fellow Brooks, I suppose. And it was he who sent for you to act as deputy? Extraordinary the things the police take on themselves nowadays?"

"Not an official detective—amateur."

"Oh."

"So you're really just holidaying, then?"

"Not entirely. I have to see my brother-in-law about . . ." Peace suddenly checked himself. "A matter of business. Nothing important." Geoffrey did not fail to notice the alteration in his tone; and he seemed to think he had said too much in any case, for he leaned back and automatically took up the *Daily Mirror* again. Geoffrey felt he had been dismissed. There was one more question he wanted to ask, however.

"Did you by any chance happen to see me pick up a letter from my seat shortly after I came into the compartment?" he said.

Peace looked at him curiously for a moment. "Yes," he said slowly. "As it happens, I did. Nothing alarming, I hope."

"No, nothing alarming. You didn't notice how it got there, I suppose?"

The other paused for some moments before replying. "I'm afraid not," he said at last. "No, I'm afraid I didn't notice at all."

Geoffrey found himself being pursued with a butterfly-net across the Devon moors. The persons of his pursuers were vague, but they moved with great rapidity. He was not surprised to find Peace running beside him. "It is necessary," he said to Peace, "that we should run the unconscious to ground wherever it may be. We can hide there, and besides, I strongly suspect that Gervase Fen will be somewhere in that neighbourhood too." His companion made no reply,—he was too much occupied with the baby he was carrying. When they reached the cathedral, the pursuers were a good deal closer, and they ran at full speed to the altar, shouting: "Sanctuary! We demand sanctuary!" They were stopped beneath the rood-screen by a young clergyman. "We can't go on failing indefinitely," he said. "It is impossible for us to go on failing indefinitely." The pursuers were by now very near. Peace dropped the baby. It screamed, and then began to whistle shrilly, like a railway-engine. The noise grew in volume, like the swift approach of a tornado. . . .

The engine of the train passing in the opposite direction swept past the compartment, its whistle at full blast, as Geoffrey struggled back to consciousness. Without moving, he opened his eyes and looked about him. Peace slumbered in the opposite corner, the paper dropped from his hands; the intruder still snored; the mother was whispering softly to the baby, which moaned and struggled spasmodically. Fielding sat reading a book—he seemed curiously isolated and strange. Geoffrey felt that if he spoke to him he would turn without recognition in his face, a stranger merely. The clergyman and the woman with the rug were talking together in low tones, their words inaudible above the incessant, monotonous beating of the wheels. Geoffrey sat and stared, first at a disagreeable photograph of Salisbury Cathedral, and then at the "Instructions to Passengers in the Event of an Air Raid," which had been annotated by some passenger with overmuch time on his hands:

DRAW ALL BLINDS AS A PRECAUTION AGAINST—*nosey bastards*. DO NOT LEAVE THE CARRIAGE UNLESS REQUESTED BY A—*hot bit*.

He blinked sleepily about him, and tried to stop thinking about the heat.

The sirens wailed as the train began braking on the stretch into Taunton. All along the coast, the fierce merciless battle against the invading bombers began. The intruder awoke from his long sleep and gazed blearily out of the window. His hasty movements of departure came as a welcome diversion. He got to his feet, scowled round him, and reached up to the rack above Geoffrey's head, where his heavy portmanteau lay. It was, of course, not entirely surprising, in view of its weight, that he should have let it slip, and if it had fallen directly on to Geoffrey's head as he leaned forward to talk to Fielding, the consequences would have been serious. Fortunately, Fielding saw it coming, and pushed Geoffrey against the back of the seat with all his force. The portmanteau landed with a sickening thud on his knees.

A confused clamour arose. The agent of this disturbance did not, however, wait to make his apologies, but was out of the compartment and on to Taunton platform before the train had come to a stop. Geoffrey sat doubled up with agony, nursing his thighs; but happily the human thigh-bone is a solid object, and Peace showed himself a fairly expert doctor. As to a pursuit, that was out of the question. By the time order was restored, the train was in any case on the move again.

"He might have broken your neck!" said the woman with the baby indignantly.

"So he might," said Geoffrey painfully. Feeling very sick, he turned to Fielding. "Thanks—for the second time today."

Peace had unlocked the case, and was gazing with bewilderment at the medley of old iron it contained. "No wonder it was so heavy," he said. "But what on earth . . . ?" Abruptly he decided that this was not the time for investigation. "You'd better do some walking before stiffness sets in," he told Geoffrey. "You'll find it'll hurt, of course, but it's really the best thing."

Geoffrey crawled to his feet, banged his head against the butterfly net, and cursed noisily; this, he felt, was the last straw.

"I'll go and get a wash," he said. "One gets so filthy on these journeys." Actually he was afraid he was going to be sick.

"Better let me come with you," said Fielding, but Geoffrey brushed him impatiently aside; he was consumed by a hatred of all mankind. "I'll be all right," he mumbled.

39

He swayed down the corridor like a drunk on the deck of a storm-tossed ship. The lavatory, when he reached it, was occupied, but just as he was passing on to the next a young man came out, grinned apologetically, and stood aside to let him in. Geoffrey was contemplating his features gloomily in the mirror preparatory to turning round and locking the door when he realised that the young man had followed him in and was doing this for him.

The young man smiled. "Now we're shut in together," he said.

"Third time lucky," said Fielding cheerfully.

Geoffrey groaned, and again shook himself free of a nightmare. He was back in the compartment, whose occupants were regarding him with some concern; even the baby gaped enquiringly at him, as though demanding an explanation.

"What happened?" Geoffrey asked conventionally.

"I got the wind up when you didn't come back," said Fielding, "and set out to find you. Fortunately, it wasn't very difficult, and we were able to lug you back here. How do you feel?"

"Awful."

"You'll be all right," said Peace. "The blow must have upset you."

"I should damn well think it did," said Geoffrey indignantly. "Where are we?"

"Just coming into Tolnbridge now."

Geoffrey groaned again. "Past Exeter? He must have got off the train there."

"My dear fellow, are you all right? He got off the train at Taunton."

Geoffrey gazed confusedly about him. "No, no—the other. Oh, Lord!" His head was swimming too much to think clearly. He rubbed it ruefully, feeling it all over. "Where's the bruise?" he asked. "There must be a bruise."

Peace, who was collecting his things from the rack, looked round in surprise.

"Where he hit me," explained Geoffrey peevishly.

"My dear chap, nobody hit you," said Peace amicably. "You must be dreaming. You fainted, that's all. Fainted."

Chapter Three

GIBBERING CORSE

*"And then the furiously gibbering corse
Shakes, panglessly convulsed, and sightless stares."*

PATMORE

TOLNBRIDGE STANDS ON THE RIVER after which it is
named about four miles above the sandy, treacherous
estuary which flows into the English Channel. Up to Han-
overian times it was a port of some significance; but the
growth in the size of shipping, together with the progres-
sive silting-up of the river mouth, which is now penetrated
only by a fairly narrow channel, pretty rapidly took from
it that eminence, and it has fallen back into its pristine
status of a small and rather inconvenient market-town
for the farm products of that area of South Devon. There
is still a fishing industry and (before the war at least)
some holidaying, but the bulk of its prosperity has been
transferred to Tolnmouth, a little to the east of the estuary, which as a summer resort is second only to Torquay
on the Devon coast. Nor is Tolnbridge of much value
from the military or naval point of view; it had received
a certain amount of sporadic and spiteful attention from
the bombers, but the main part of the attack was concentrated further up the coast, and it suffered little damage.

The cathedral was built during the reign of Edward II,
when Tolnbridge was enjoying an unexampled prosperity
as the staple port for the wines of Bordeaux and Spain;

in style it comes, historically, somewhere about the time of the transition from Early English to Decorated, but few traces of the later method are to be found in it, and it is one of the last, as well as one of the finest, examples of that superb artistry which produced Salisbury Cathedral and many lovely parish churches. Comparatively, it is a small building; but it stands in the centre of the town in a position of such eminence that it appears larger than is really the case. The river rises to a natural plateau, about a quarter of a mile back, on which the older part of the town is built. Behind this again there is a long and steeply-sloping hill, at the very summit of which the cathedral stands—the hill itself devoid of buildings, except for the clergy-house at the south-western end. So, from the town, there is a magnificent vista up this long slope, planted with cypress, mountain-ash and larches, to the grey buttresses and slender, tapering spire which overhang the river. The effect would be overpowering were it not for the two smaller churches in the town below, whose spires, lifted in noble, unsuccessful emulation of their greater companion above, a little restore the balance and relieve the eye. Behind the cathedral, the hill slopes more gently down again to the newer part of the town, with the railway station and the paint factory, whose houses stream down on the northern side to join the old town and peter out to the south in a series of expensive and widely-spaced villas overlooking the estuary.

It is perhaps surprising that Tolnbridge did not share the fate of Crediton and succumb to the See of Exeter. But Exeter's diocese was large enough already, and Tolnbridge was suffered to remain a cathedral town. About seventy years after the erection of the cathedral, a tallow-maker of the town called Ephraim Pentyre, a miser and a notorious usurer, but a man who gave much money to the Church on the understanding that it should reserve him a front seat at the celestial entertainment, set out by the coast road on a pilgrimage to Canterbury (where he might, had he ever reached it, have encountered Chaucer's pilgrims in person). So niggardly was he, however, that he refused to take servants for his protection, with the consequence that beyond Weymouth he was set upon, murdered, and incontinentally robbed of his offering to the shrine of St. Thomas. This incompetence and stinginess earned him his canonisation, for his bones were returned to Tolnbridge and buried with much ceremony in the cathedral, where their miracles of healing attracted pilgrims from all over the country, Edward III himself visiting the shrine in order to be cured of scurvy (his own legendary abilities in that direction having apparently failed); with what success it is not known. This was the heyday of Tolnbridge's prosperity, none the less welcomed by the inhabitants because they remembered St. Ephraim with dislike, or because worse and blacker crimes than usury had been commonly laid to his account.

After that there was a slow but steady decline. Tolnbridge was too isolated to play any part in the great political and ecclesiastical disturbances which spasmodically racked the country up to the end of the eighteenth century, though upon occasion little symbolic wars were fought out on these issues among the townspeople, only too often with violence and atrocities. The transition from Mariolatry to Protestantism was made without fuss, the more so, as some said, because the old religion was allowed to persist and become vile in secret and abominable rituals. Some emphasis was given to these suggestions by a frenetic outburst of witch trials in the early seventeenth century, and by the equally frenetic outburst of witchcraft and devil-worship which provoked them, and in which several clergy of the diocese were disgracefully involved. It is doubtful, indeed, if there was ever such a concentrated, vehement and (by the standards of the day) well-justified persecution in the history of Europe; there were daily burnings on the cathedral hill, and, that curious feature of most witch trials, free confessions, given without torture, by some hundreds of women that they had had intercourse with the Devil and participated in the Black Mass. After a few years the commotion died down, as these things will, and left nothing behind but the blackened circle cut into the hillside and the iron post to which the women had been tied for burning. There were no further disturbances in Tolnbridge, of any kind; and by 1939 the town seemed to have settled down into a state of permanent inanition.

So at least Geoffrey maintained, in more forcible words, on his failing to get a taxi at the station. What he is actually recorded to have said is "What a damned hole!"

Now this was unjust, and Fielding, looking down past the cathedral at the roofs of the old town and the estuary beyond, felt it to be so. However, it was obviously not the time for argument. Geoffrey was smarting not only with physical pain (this had by now considerably abated), but also with a considerable mental irritation. There are limits beyond which human patience must not be tried; after a certain point, the crossword puzzle or cryptogram or riddle ceases to amuse and begins to infuriate. This point, in the present affair, Geoffrey had long since passed, and his last escape, far from leaving him pleased, maddened him with its pointlessness.

"What I cannot understand," he said for the tenth time, "is *why*, when they had me exactly where they wanted me, without a chance to resist or cry out, they didn't bang me on the head and shove me overboard."

Fielding regarded gloomily an aged porter who was prodding tentatively at a trunk in the hope, apparently, of provoking it to spontaneous movement. "Perhaps they were interrupted," was all he said.

"You can't be interrupted when you're locked in a lavatory."

"Perhaps they found you were the wrong person and sheered off."

"The wrong person!"

Fielding sighed. "No, it's not likely. Their organisation seems very good," he added with a sort of melancholy satisfaction. "Unless you imagined all that."

"Imagine it," said Geoffrey. "Of course I didn't."

"He wasn't just asking you the time?"

"The *time!* You don't follow people into lavatories and bolt the door simply in order to ask them the *time*."

Fielding sighed again; he breathed out lengthily and noisily. The discussion, he thought, could not profitably be continued. "Is it far?" he asked.

"Yes; *very* far," said Geoffrey, annoyed at being thus crudely unseated from his hobby-horse; he thought, too, that he perceived the animal being led away. But some-

44

thing else had occurred to Fielding, for he turned abruptly and said:

"Those letters."

Geoffrey looked at him in silence for a moment, and then searched his pockets. The letters were gone.

"Very thorough," said Fielding drily. "When they found you were coming here despite their warnings, they decided you shouldn't have any clue to the machine they were typed on."

"So that was it. Damn. But it still doesn't explain why I wasn't knocked out."

"When you're organising a thing like this, you can't give your agents a free hand to do whatever emergency dictates. Besides, this fellow may not even have known what was going on. I expect he was told simply to get the letters from you, and when you fainted there was no need to use violence." Fielding whistled gently. "They're fairly thorough."

The heat had grown somewhat less. Peace had made off, presumably towards the Precentor's house, in another direction. The woman with the rug and the young clergyman had long since disappeared. Looking at his watch, Geoffrey found that the train had got in only seven minutes late. He and Fielding started off down the station hill, Fielding carrying both bags, and Geoffrey the inescapable butterfly-net. On their right stood the cathedral, serenely beautiful. The great rose window in the south transept glowed momently at them with a rich, red beauty, and the gulls wheeled and screamed about the slender octagonal spire.

The medley of tobacconists and second-rate pubs huddled round the station soon gave place to a rather dreary street of small villas; and this in turn to the squalid, beautiful houses of the old town. A little beyond the beauty of these two worlds they turned off to the right, and shortly arrived at the wrought-iron gates of the clergy-house, which had been built in the eighteenth century to replace the old clergy-house adjoining the north transept; this being now used for storing lumber, holding choir-practices, and other miscellaneous and untidy purposes. The gates, suspended on either side from pillars of soft, lemon-coloured stone, opened upon a depressing vista of shrubs and lawns, bisected by an overgrown gravel drive which curved round to the front door, skirted the house, and led out beyond the extensive kitchen-gardens on to the cathedral hill itself. Geoffrey entered these regions with circumspection, peering intently at a withered laurel as though he expected it to contain springs, nets and lime for his discomfort.

In this realm of celibacy, the first thing they heard was a girl's voice. "Josephine!" it called; then with more force, and a tinge of irritation: "Come back!"

There was a sound of running footsteps, and a young girl, plainly the object of these cries, came panting round the side of the house. She could not have been more than fifteen, and she was long, thin, and trembling, with curls of bright gold, tangled and disordered. Her face was red, not only with effort, but also with perceptible anger. She stopped short on seeing the strangers, and after staring at them for a moment, darted off into the shrubbery at one side, whence the diminishing rustle of innumerable graceless plants marked her retreat.

They toiled towards the portico, a little shaken by this welcome, and suspecting, with some dismay, a domestic upheaval. They had not gone more than a few steps before the owner of the voice they had heard appeared also, in unenergetic pursuit. And this at least, Geoffrey thought, was not what one expected to find on cathedral precincts —a girl of about twenty-three, as dark as the other had been blonde, with blue, humorous eyes, a tip-tilted nose, red lips, and a slim, loose-limbed body. Her dress, though rich and sober enough, and her high heels gave, Geoffrey thought, a faint suggestion of the courtesan. Not that he objected to this. Having little experience of women, he classified them, *a priori* as it were, as either amateur prostitutes or domestic helps, and anyone not fitting snugly into one of these categories left him confused, suspicious and uncomprehending (this masculine failing is commoner than perhaps women imagine). Certainly in this case a touch of the *hetaira*, the Lais or Phryne, was present; but there was also a practicality, self-possession and intelligence which softened and diffused the impression.

Fundamentally, Geoffrey was afraid of women. His endeavours to categorise those he had met as either courtesan or domestic had led to dismal misunderstandings, since he had never known anyone remotely resembling either kind. He also laboured, as a result of reading books, under the delusion that every unmarried woman he met was hunting, with all the tricks and subterfuges of her deadly and mysterious sex, for a husband, and congratulated himself inwardly upon hair-raising escapes from several women who in point of fact had never even considered marrying him, and who had merely used him as a convenient temporary paramour and offered him the honourable courtesy of the sex, a good-night kiss at the end of an evening enjoyed at his expense. Beyond the age of thirty, he had gradually shunned acquaintance with these puzzling beings. Consequently, he approached this new example of the species with a trepidation accentuated by her obvious charm.

"Damn the child!" she said, and gave up the pursuit.

"Has she been naughty?" said Fielding simply. He asked the question with the ease and authority of one too essentially courteous to need the formal preliminaries of acquaintance.

The girl met him, with equal ease, on his own ground. "Do you think children should be spanked?" she said. "Girls of that age, that is? I know I was—but Josephine's such a proud, headstrong brat she takes it hard."

"I think you should avoid it if possible," said Fielding with unnecessary seriousness.

The girl laughed—a low, gurgling infectious chuckle. "I see—you think it was me. No, I haven't got to the stage of walloping children yet. Father did it—and I must say I hardly blame him. Would you believe it, Josephine tore up and burnt the whole of the manuscript of the book he was working on?" An almost imperceptible chill came into the atmosphere. There are acts of petulance and ill-temper, and there are acts of deliberate malice. Geoffrey changed the subject with painfully obvious intent.

"We ought to introduce ourselves," he said. "This is the Earl of—the Earl of—— What are you the Earl of?"

"It's not of the least importance," said Fielding. He had put down the bags and was despairingly towelling his face and neck with an immense white silk handkerchief. "Don't misunderstand me—if I thought that either of you would resent my being an earl, I should give you the full details immediately. But we might just as well say Henry Fielding, and be done with it."

"Not," the girl said, "the author of——?"

Geoffrey interrupted in some haste. "And I'm Geoffrey Vintner," he said. He made the assertion despondently, as though he scarcely expected anyone to credit it.

"How nice," said the girl with business-like conviction. "We often do your Communion Service here. I'm Frances Butler."

"Good. So now we all know each other," said Fielding. He paused and gazed expectantly at Geoffrey.

"Oh, yes," said Geoffrey. "We are looking for Fen— Gervase Fen."

"I thought you were," said the girl, gazing pointedly at the butterfly-net, which he still brandished like a banner in front of him, "because of *that.*"

Geoffrey regarded her gloomily for a moment. "Insects?" he ventured at last.

She nodded gravely.

"He's out at the moment, and I don't know when he'll be back again. I gather he's going to make some experiment to-night with *moths,* but we told him he couldn't do it here, because poor little Dutton, the Deputy Organist, is terrified of them at the best of times; and as it's got something to do with males flying hundreds of miles to get at a female in a darkened room, we thought that a clergy-house was as unsuitable place for such demonstrations. Besides, in the unlikely event of its succeeding, we couldn't possibly have the place full of moths. So I believe he's going to do it somewhere else."

Geoffrey sighed. "How characteristic!" he said. "He asks me to come down here, and then at the crucial moment disappears into the blue. I suppose he didn't mention my arrival?"

"Not a word."

"No." Geoffrey sighed; the burden of Atlas seemed to be upon him. "No, I might have expected that."

"Were you going to stay here?" asked the girl.

"Well, I imagined so. But I can't possibly push myself in if you're unprepared."

"I could manage one of you," said the girl dubiously,

48

"but not both, by any possible means. There just isn't a bed."

"I can find somewhere in the town to stay," said Fielding.

"You'd better go to the 'Whale and Coffin,'" said the girl.

"It sounds terrible."

"It *is* terrible, but there's nowhere any better. Look, Mr. Vintner, leave your bags in the porch. Someone will take them in later, I dare say. And would you like a wash?"

"What I really want," said Geoffrey, "is a drink. Several drinks."

"All right. We'll all go down to the 'Whale and Coffin.' It is after six, isn't it? Then we can talk about things."

"I don't want to drag you away . . ."

"Away from *what?* Don't be so silly. Come on, both of you. It's only three minutes from here."

Geoffrey had nearly arrived before he realised he was still carrying the butterfly-net. He cursed it inwardly, murmuring under his breath.

"Have a good, rousing swear," said the girl. "You'll feel better."

The "Whale and Coffin" turned out to be a large, low, rambling building of indefinite date situated in the middle of the old town. It was provided with innumerable bars, labelled variously: Bar, Saloon, Lounge Bar, Public Bar, Private Bar, and so on; these departments being ineffectually presided over by a small short-sighted, elderly man who hurried constantly from one to another, less with any hope of being useful, one felt, than because it had become a habit and he couldn't stop it. He peered astigmatically at Geoffrey as he ordered drinks.

"Stranger?" he said. "Not been here before?"

"No," said Geoffrey shortly. He refused to be kept from his beer by well-meaning chatter.

"I think you'll like it," said the other without particular confidence. "It's a good local brew and we get a nice crowd here." From his accent it was evident that he was not a Devon man. "Strange name for a pub, isn't it?"

"Very."

"You'd imagine there'd be some story connected with a name like that, wouldn't you?"

"Yes."

"There isn't, though. Someone just thought it up one day."

Geoffrey looked at him with contempt and moved shakily back to the others, carrying drinks. They had settled in a remote alcove. Frances Butler crossed her legs, smoothed out her skirt with automatic propriety, and said:

"You needn't have worried—Harry never talks to anyone for more than a minute at a time. I've watched him."

"Do you come here often?" asked Fielding.

"Oh, so-so. I don't haunt the place, if that's what you mean. But it's the nearest pub to the clergy-house."

"I thought," said Fielding vaguely, "you might have found a lot of silly prejudice about going to pubs at all—your father being Precentor, and so on."

"Can't help that," said Frances, and grinned. "I expect there is some, but they think I'm a tart as it is. Going to pubs doesn't affect matters much. And Daddy doesn't seem to mind—that's the chief thing. He brought me up terribly strictly till I was eighteen, but since then he's just given me a lot of money and let me do what I like. Poor old Meg—the housekeeper at the clergy-house—got ill, and one can't get servants for love or money nowadays, so I gave up living with Daddy and went to house-keep there. I don't think the men like it very much, though. Each of them's afraid the others will think he's got designs on me. You've no idea the way they keep clear of my room, and the rumpus they make when they're going to the bathroom."

She laughed, and drank pink gin with a theatrical air of wickedness. It occurred to Geoffrey that she probably got an innocent, childish enjoyment out of pretending to be wicked. He greatly doubted, at all events, if she actually was. But he realised that with his present knowledge of her an adequate assessment of her merits and demerits was out of the question. Certainly she was attractive—very attractive, he suddenly felt. And he sighed, recognising the enormity of his inexperience in love.

"Tired?" she asked.

"No. Just content." It was not, he reflected, entirely a lie, at that. "Do you know," he said, "that I've been attacked three times to-day?"

She laughed. "Attacked? What on earth do you mean?"

"One man tried to knock me on the head in a shop"— "Store," said Fielding automatically—"another tried to drop a suitcase full of iron on my head, and another locked me in a lavatory on the train. That is to say——" Geoffrey sturggled for a more suitable form of words. Put like that, it didn't sound nearly as serious as in fact it had been. "There were anonymous letters, too," he concluded lamely.

"But how awful," said the girl. "No—what a stupid thing to say. I mean"—she gestured helplessly—"well, why?"

"I don't know. That's just the point. But I think it's got something to do with the attack on Brooks here."

Frances put down her drink rather suddenly. The movement was a slight one, and in itself unimportant, but it brought a curious unease to the atmosphere. There was a long pause before she said:

"Do you mean that?" Her voice was suddenly very quiet.

"That's all I can think of. If it hadn't been for Fielding, I might now be dead—almost certainly should be, in fact."

When Frances took up her glass again, her hand was a fraction unsteady. But her voice was calm as she asked:

"Was Dr. Brooks a friend of yours?" The question seemed to have a greater urgency, a greater importance, than common sense would allow. Geoffrey shook his head.

"I only knew him slightly—a professional acquaintance." He hesitated. "You said 'was'——"

She laughed again, but there was no humor in it. "No, he's not dead, if that's what you mean. I——" She seemed abruptly to make up her mind about something; with intended deliberateness and ostentation the subject was changed. "And Daddy asked you to come down here and play the services in his place?"

Geoffrey acquiesced, repressing an almost irrepressible curiosity. "Well, no, not exactly. That is to say. I suppose he knew about it. Actually it was Fen who wired me to come." He became uncomfortable. "If I'm not wanted, it doesn't matter. I'm glad of the break, and I shall like to see Fen again. . . ." He stopped, conscious that the words were meaningless.

The girl's tone was lighter now. "Oh, I'm sure you're wanted—I don't know who else would have played, if you hadn't turned up."

"I was wondering—surely there's a deputy? In fact, you mentioned one."

"Little Dutton—yes. But *he's* in the middle of a nervous breakdown. The silly boy overworked himself, trying to get God knows what stupid musical degree. The doctor won't let him go near an organ at the moment."

Geoffrey nodded portentously. "That explains it," he said. In fact, he reflected, it explained very little. Frances had as good as refused to talk about the attack on Brooks —and, confound it, *he* ought to know the facts if anyone ought. He was summoning up courage to reopen the subject when the landlord hurried past, peering intently at a huge pocket-watch supplied with a magnifying-glass which raised the hands and the figures on the dial to grotesque dimensions. When he was almost out of the door he paused and came back to them.

"Didn't recognise you at first, Miss Butler," he said. He clipped his words with the nervousness of the very short-sighted. "How's Dr. Brooks getting on? Any improvement?"

"I haven't heard this evening." Frances spoke shortly. "Harry, you don't know if Professor Fen's in here this evening?"

"What, that tall, mad fellow?" There was something like awe in the landlord's voice. "He might be in one of the other bars. I'll look. But I don't think so."

"If you see him, you might tell him I'm here. And a friend of his, Mr. Vintner."

The landlord's reaction to this last piece of news was unexpected. He took a step back and began breathing very quickly. "Geoffrey Vintner!" he exclaimed.

"Really, Harry. What on earth's the matter with you? You look as if you'd seen a ghost."

The landlord hurriedly pulled himself together. "Sorry," he mumbled. "Didn't quite catch the name.

Thought you were referring to a friend of mine, who—who's dead." He stood wavering in front of them for a moment, and then made a little too rapidly for the door.

"Well, I'm damned!" said Frances in frank surprise.

"If it hadn't been for Fielding, I *should* have been dead, too," said Geoffrey aggrievedly. "Who is that man, anyway?"

"Harry James?" said Frances. "Don't know anything about him, really. He's had this pub for about five years —came from up north, I believe Staunch Presbyterian. Leading light in the local Conservative Club. In fact"—a thought seemed suddenly to strike her—"just the sort of respectable anonymity you'd expect from——" She checked herself, and added humorously: "From what?"

Geoffrey nodded gloomily. "Precisely. From what?"

"I suppose," said Fielding mournfully, "that beer you're drinking is all right?"

Geoffrey jumped visibly. It occurred to him that he was not, perhaps, feeling very well. "Don't be absurd," he said testily. "People don't go putting poison in people's beer. Or if they do," he added with rising indignation, "it's no use worrying about it until it happens, or we shall all go raving mad and have to be put away." He relapsed into sulks. "I shall keep an eye on Mr. James," he mumbled, and then, with sudden irritation: "And where the *hell* is Fen? Really, it's too bad of him not to be here when I arrive." He brooded on his wrongs, cherishing them individually.

"I don't quite understand," said Fielding cautiously, "about these"—he waved a hand, evoking a myriad phantom butterflies—"insects."

"You wouldn't understand," Geoffrey replied, "because you don't know Fen. My better self persuades me that he's a normal, sensible, extremely healthy-minded person, but there are times when I wonder if he isn't a bit cracked. Of course, everyone has these obsessions about some transient hobby or other, but Fen's personality is so"—he hesitated over words—"*large* and overwhelming, that when he gets bitten it seems like a cosmic upheaval. Everything's affected for miles around."

Frances chuckled. "It began," she said, "when he found a simply gigantic grasshopper on the clergy-house

53

lawn. I must say I've never seen anything quite so vast. He put it in a deep cardboard box and brought it in to dinner that night to show us. The bishop was dining." She gurgled, enchanted by the imminent and foreseeable climax. "When he took off the lid, poor Dutton nearly fainted. Then he poked at the wretched thing until we were all ready to scream. 'It's all right,' he said. 'It's biologically impossible for it to get out.' The first leap landed it in the Bishop's soup. I've never seen a man so pale. Finally it ended up in the hearth, where the dog ate it. 'Nature red in tooth and claw,' said the Bishop (we gave him a new plate of soup, but he wasn't happy about it). 'There,' said Fen, 'a perfect specimen, and it's gone. You can stop their noise,' he said, 'by pricking them with a pin.' We said we shouldn't be surprised."

Fielding rocked with silent laughter. Even Geoffrey giggled absurdly. "But I thought," he remarked, "that Fen was busy investigating this business about Brooks. He . . ."

The girl got up suddenly. In a moment, as it seemed, the laughter was gone. Just so might a child intent on play run out of her own front door into a garden never seen before, and better not seen. Just so might a man turn a casual remark to a friend in a darkened train, and see a dead mask. Frances took two short steps and turned. When she spoke, her voice was not as it had been.

"Sooner or later," she said, "you'll have to know. It may as well be now." She seemed struggling for utterance. "It was kept from the papers, but they would never have printed it in any case. It was—after a choir-practice. Dr. Brooks went back to the cathedral for something. They found him next morning, not unconscious, though there was a bruise on his head." She stopped, and for a moment covered her face with her hand. "Devilry. . . . You'll think I'm mad, but I'm not. Everything isn't well here. Things happen that can't be explained. You—you must——" She was violently agitated.

Fielding half rose. "Look here, Miss Butler——"

But she brushed him aside, and went on speaking more rapidly than before. "I'm all right. Thank God it isn't me. They took him to the hospital—in secrecy. He's had moments of sanity, but they haven't been many. He was locked in, and the key was lying outside—they found it on the grass. An empty cathedral isn't a good place to be in all night. Ever since they brought him away he's talked and babbled and raved—about the slab of a tomb that moved, and a hanging man."

Chapter Four

TEETH OF TRAPS

*"They were in one of many mouths of Hell
Not seen of seers in visions; only felt
As teeth of traps. . . ."*

OWEN

THE CLERGY-HOUSE DRAWING-ROOM was a large one, shabby but comfortable, well-lighted, and decorated, not with Pre-Raphaelite Madonnas, but with caricatures by Spy of ecclesiastical dignitaries long dead and awaiting transfiguration, together with one original Rowlandson etching tucked away in a corner. This represented two obese clerics, one throwing bread contemptuously to an equally contemptuous rabble, the other surreptitiously embracing a large and simpering wench, very *décolletée*; a cathedral which was recognisably Tolnbridge stood in the background. A few scattered books showed tastes not far removed from the worldly: fiction by Huxley, Isherwood, and Katherine Mansfield; plays by Bridie and Congreve; and, in another but still noble sphere, John Dickson Carr, Nicholas Blake, Margery Allingham and Gladys Mitchell. The cathedral clergy are great readers— they have little else to do.

Geoffrey and Frances had left Fielding at the "Whale and Coffin" to unpack and were sitting together, talking a little restrainedly. Now they were alone, Geoffrey felt even more attracted by her, and she quieted his bachelor's misgivings (which she may have suspected) by an almost timorous reserve. The evening sunlight lay green and gold on the broad lawn outside the french windows, glistening on the thickly-clustered yellow roses and the shaggy chrysanthemum blooms. A faint scent of verbena drifted in from a plant which clung to the grey wall outside.

It appeared that since Brooks' arrival at the hospital little more had been heard of him. The nature and cause of his insanity were still unknown, except perhaps by the doctors who attended him, and no friends had been allowed to see him. Of near relatives he had only a brother, with whom he had been on the worst possible terms. This brother had been summoned by telegram, but had not appeared, and indeed it seemed doubtful whether he would have been the slightest help to anyone if he had. This much Frances knew, and no more.

There was still no sign of Fen.

Geoffrey asked who would be at dinner that night.

"Well, Daddy's coming over," said Frances. "And then there'll be Canon Garbin and Canon Spitshuker, and little Dutton, of course—the sub-organist. Oh, and Sir John Dallow's dropping in for coffee—there's to be some sort of meeting afterwards. Have you heard of him? He's the big noise on witchcraft in this country."

Geoffrey shook his head. "Is Canon Garbin married?"

"Yes. Why?"

"There was a Mrs. Garbin in the compartment we travelled down in. With a young clergyman."

"Oh, that was probably July Savernake. Come to think of it, he did say he'd be back to-day. I expect he'll be at dinner too."

"What about him?"

"How do you mean?"

"Well, what sort of person is he?"

She hesitated. "Well . . . he's Vicar at Maverley, about twelve miles from here. Got the living almost as soon as he was ordained." Geoffrey sensed a deliberate reservation behind the recital of facts, and wondered what its cause might be. "He spends half the year buying expensive books and wine, and playing the *curé bon viveur*, and the other half having to economise, and playing the 'poore persoun.' A see-saw sort of existence." Frances laughed apologetically. "That doesn't tell you much, I'm afraid. But you'll be meeting him, anyway."

Fielding came in, and Frances left to supervise the final

preparations for dinner. "Hideous little room I've got," said Fielding mournfully as he fell into a chair, "but it will do. How are you feeling?"

"A bit nightmarish."

"It is rather like that. Do you know, I've been wondering if those attacks on you weren't bogus from beginning to end—designed to conceal the reason for something else. Probably the attack on Brooks. All those preposterous warnings! *That* would bring you into the limelight all right—which is just what they wanted. I suppose they didn't care whether you were killed or just injured. Whoever it is, and whatever they're after, it seems they can afford to waste lives like water."

Geoffrey lit a cigarette and sucked at it without pleasure. "It sounds plausible, but there might be some other explanation."

"There's only one way of testing it out," said Fielding emphatically, "and that is by keeping quiet about it. If we once let out that we've rumbled it, they'll abandon the whole business. But if they think it's taking people in, they'll probably try something else—try to kill you again, for example."

Geoffrey sat up in annoyance. "A nice thing," he exclaimed bitterly, "asking me to keep quiet about a beastly theory, so as to encourage somebody to murder me. It's undoubtedly someone *here* by the way. The postmark on that letter was Tolnbridge, and it must have been someone connected with the cathedral to know I'd been sent for. . . ."

He broke off. Footsteps were approaching outside, accompanied by two voices raised in argument, the one shrill and voluble, the other deep and laconic. A touch of acerbity and resentment was audible beneath the tropes of polite discussion.

". . . But me dear Spitshuker you apparently fail to realise that by taking the universalist view you are, in effect, denying the reality of man's freedom to choose between good and evil. If we are *all* to go to heaven *anyway,* then that choice has no validity. It's as if one were to say that a guest at a tea-party has freedom to choose between muffins and crumpets when only crumpets are provided."

"I hardly think, Garbin, that you have grasped the essential point in all this, if you will forgive my saying so. You would concede, of course, that the Divinity is a god of Love?"

"Of course, of course. But you haven't answered——"

"Well, then. That being so, His aim must be the perfection of every one of His Creation. You will agree that even in the case of the greatest saint, perfection is impossible of attainment in the three-score years and ten which we have at our disposal. I am inclined, therefore, to believe that there must be an intermediate state, a purgatory——"

The door swung open, and Canon Spitshuker came into the room, closely followed by Canon Garbin. Canon Spitshuker was a little, plump, excitable man, with swanwhite hair and a pink face. By contrast, Canon Garbin was tall, dark, morose and normally laconic; he walked soberly, with his large, bony hands plunged deep into his coat pockets, while the other danced and gestured about him like a poodle accompanying a St. Bernard. Their juxtaposition as Canons of the same cathedral was a luckless one, since Canon Spitshuker was by long conviction a Tractarian, while Canon Garbin was a Low Churchman; furious altercations were constantly in progress between them on points of doctrine and ritual, never resolved. Unlike parallel lines, it was inconceivable that their views should ever meet, even at infinity.

The unexpected presence of Geoffrey and Fielding cut short Canon Spitshuker's oration. He spluttered for a moment like a faulty petrol-engine, then recovered himself, dashed forward, and wrung Geoffrey by the hand.

"How do you do?" he said. "I'm Spitshuker, and this"
—he pointed at the other, who stood regarding the scene with a faint but unmistakable disgust—"is my colleague, Dr. Garbin."

Garbin slightly bowed, an uncertain and derisive smile appearing momentarily on his face. Geoffrey murmured introductions.

"Henry Fielding?" Canon Spitshuker clucked delightedly. "Not," he added, "the author of _To_——?"

"No," said Fielding rather tersely. Canon Spitshuker seemed a little abashed.

"And you"—he paused for a moment, apparently testing the propriety of the question—"are staying here?"

Geoffrey explained the situation, Canon Spitshuker nodding his head in vigorous and unnecessary affirmation all the time. Canon Garbin crept into the room and deposited his long limbs circumspectly in an armchair.

"You must remember, Spitshuker," he said. "Professor Fen mentioned Mr. Vintner's name at the time of the business about poor Brooks, and Butler asked him to get in touch with him." He paused lengthily; then added, just in time to anticipate Spitshuker's next outburst: "We are very glad to see you. Very glad indeed. We shall greatly appreciate your help."

"Greatly appreciate it," Spitshuker chanted antiphonally.

"I was afraid," said Geoffrey, "knowing Fen, that he'd brought me down unofficially, as it were."

"You heard about Brooks, I suppose?" asked Spitshuker. "Poor fellow, poor fellow. A terrible and mysterious business. Let's hope that nothing of the kind happens to you."

"It *has* happened," Geoffrey was about to retort; but he thought better of it and restrained himself. "You don't know where Fen is?"

"I haven't the least idea. Wasn't he here to welcome you? Very bad, very bad. But I haven't seen much of him since he arrived—don't come into this house very much at any time. The living arrangements are unusual here. No cloisters—the prebends' houses are all scattered about the town. There's a Deanery, of course, and a Bishop's Palace of a sort, but the Bishop isn't there a great deal. Very uncomfortable—don't blame him. This house," said Spitshuker cheerfully, "is used as a sort of general rubbish-heap for minor canons and the sub-organist and any incumbents of the diocese who want to put up for a night or two. Can't think why Fen isn't staying at the Deanery—why you aren't, for that matter. Disgraceful. Still, you'll be comfortable enough here, I dare say. Frances—Miss Butler, that is—is an excellent housekeeper. I'd ask you to stay with me, only my housekeeper is ill at the moment, and to bring in guests, however pleasant, would be a trial." He paused for breath, while

Geoffrey uttered sounds expressive simultaneously of deprecation, civility, gratitude, complete understanding, sympathy and sad surprise.

"I think you'll find the choir in very good order," Spitshuker was proceeding irrepressibly, "and the organ, I'm told, is an excellent one." His mind switched subjects with the rapidity of a signalman changing points. "The Precentor has a brother-in-law staying with him, I understand, and is to bring him round this evening. Poor Frances will have yet another to cater for at dinner, I fear." He giggled. "But she can conjure up a banquet out of nothing—a most competent person. The Precentor's brother-in-law is a psycho-analyst, I believe," he pursued without waiting to take breath. "Interesting—extraordinarily interesting. We shall have to see what we can do to challenge his secular interpretation of the workings of the human mind."

Garbin, who had ostentatiously taken up and opened a book during this monologue, now looked up. "Don't be foolish, Spitshuker," he boomed with dreadful emphasis. "Peace has come here on a social visit, not to be dragooned into amateurish debates on serious subjects. My wife, by the way, seems to have travelled down with him this afternoon from London."

"Mrs. Garbin is back, then?" said Spitshuker. "Savernake came down with her, I suppose?"

Garbin nodded gloomily. "That young man," he said, "spends a good deal too much time away from his parish. I'm aware that it's too much to expect any parish priest nowadays to do more than merely conduct the services, but Savernake carries the business of ignoring his parishioners' affairs to an extreme. Butler, I believe, has complained to the Bishop about it."

"You don't mean," piped Spitshuker excitedly, "that Butler is trying to get rid of Savernake? Transfer him to another diocese, that is? I knew he never liked him, but—well——"

"Personally, I am in entire agreement with the Precentor," Garbin stated dogmatically. "Though I think a disciplinary reproof would be sufficient."

"Reverting to the question of Brooks," Geoffrey put in,

"has anyone here been able to think of an explanation of what happened to him?"

"One can conceive several possibilities," said Garbin slowly, "but I think it better not to discuss them at present."

"I asked because whatever is going on here seems rather to concern me. There have been to-day, two attempts on my life."

A dead hush fell unexpectedly on the little group. For what seemed an age no one spoke. Then Canon Spitshuker gasped slightly and said:

"My dear fellow——"

Words failed him. The hush was renewed. Geoffrey said:

"I've heard, you see, what happened to Brooks. And it seems to me that this is no time for false reticence. Of course I know nothing about your affairs here, and in the ordinary way of things wouldn't want to know. But it's quite obvious that my visit here was the cause of those attacks, and we—or the police—will have to start probing sooner or later."

Garbin looked up. He drummed his fingers on the arm of his chair, and seemed to be very carefully weighing his words. "You—or they," he said at last, "will find investigation a pariculary difficult business. There is no calling which requires a stricter attention to reputation than the Church. Things do, of course, happen. When they do, they are kept very quiet—very quiet indeed. I don't refer to—serious misbehaviour. Merely small things, which are perhaps more damning in the eyes of the world." He paused, labouring under some obscure emotional strain. "You know that Brooks is mad—stark, gibbering mad. I hope and devoutly pray that none of us was responsible for that. I think"—he smiled wryly—"that even Spitshuker will agree there is a hell prepared for whoever did that.

"For some human being was responsible, Mr. Vintner. Someone gave Brooks, when he was unconscious, a large dose of some drug—the details I don't know—nearly enough to kill him and quite enough to turn his brain, to make of him an invalid and a maniac for what little remainder of life God may give him. Was it sheer devilry, do you think—or a mistake? Was the intention to kill him, and was he left for dead?

"Brooks knew something, Mr. Vintner. Something which concerned the Cathedral, and which he must not be allowed to say. In his delirium he has often called for the police, has struggled to speak coherently and has never succeeded. The police are always beside his bed. They take down every word he says."

Garbin rose abruptly from his chair, thrust his long, bony hands into his pockets, and crossed to the window. He turned and faced the other three before he spoke again.

"What was it he saw, when he walked alone about the Cathedral? What was it he found there, that no one else has found?"

Dinner was over. It had not, from the social point of view, been a successful meal. The events of the last two days weighed too heavily on the minds of those present to allow more than sporadic, half-hearted conversation, always carefully directed away from the obsessing thought. Even the normally jovial Peace, who had come over to dinner from the Precentor's house, where he was staying, seemed affected by the atmosphere, and after opening the proceedings chattily lapsed gradually into a silence from which he emerged only to give occasional startled replies when he was addressed. Frances kept things moving at a rate just clear of open embarrassment and discomfort.

The Precentor had not put in an appearance, so there were eight of them at the table—Frances, Garbin, Spitshuker, the young clergyman Savernake, whom they had seen in the train, Geoffrey, Fielding, Peace and the sub-organist, Dutton, an acutely self-conscious young man with a massive white face spotted with orange freckles, and a shock of pale ginger hair, through which he constantly ran his cubby fingers. There was, it appeared, to be some kind of unofficial meeting of cathedral officers after dinner (without the Dean, who would normally have presided, but who was temporarily away)—obviously to discuss the repercussions of the Brooks affair, though this was not made explicit. The Precentor,

Frances' father, whom Geoffrey was curious to meet, would appear for that, and so would the Chancellor, Sir John Dallow. Geoffrey recalled, suddenly, the affair of Josephine and the burning of the Precentor's manuscript, and wondered why the girl was not with them; a casual question, put to Frances, told him that she had gone back to her own home.

Geoffrey found himself next to Savernake, but the acquaintanceship made little progress. After a start of recognition when Geoffrey was introduced to him, the young clergyman became taciturn and nervous. Geoffrey, venturing a straightforward reference to the situation, said:

"The police have made a thorough search of the cathedral, I suppose?"

Savernake nodded. "Thorough—very thorough indeed." He spoke in that exaggerated drawl which so often passes incorrectly for the Oxford accent. "But, of course, it was useless. No one will find—what there is to be found, unless he stays alone there as Brooks did."

"And then——?" Geoffrey left the rest of the question unspoken. But Savernake only shrugged, cracked the joints of his long, thin fingers alarmingly, and smiled.

Garbin and Spitshuker engaged in a private controversy on some obscure theological point, which lasted until dinner was over. Peace, Frances (from whom Geoffrey was regrettably distant) and Fielding carried on a three-cornered argument about a recent London play. Dutton was mostly silent, throwing occasional desperate remarks into such conversation as met his ears. Decidedly, not an inspiriting meal.

Coffee was in the drawing-room. There rose to meet them as they came in, Garbin and Spitshuker still engaged in surreptitious altercation, a little old man of phenomenal thinness, with a sharp nose, small beady eyes which never for more than a moment held your own, and a crown of sparse and wispy white hair—Sir John Dallow, Chancellor of the Cathedral. In speech he alternately gabbled and drawled. His mannerisms were at once like and unlike Spitshuker's. There were the same incessant gestures, the same dancing and posturing. But whereas in Spitshuker these were signs of energy, in Dallow, they appeared more as neurotic excitement. Looking at the two men, Geoffrey could think of no better comparison between them than that Dallow was an angle, and Spitshuker a curve; and probably, he thought with amusement, that was due as much to the difference between their figures as to anything else.

Dallow rose with conscious affectation as they came in brushing with the backs of his fingers at an invisible speck of dust on his lapel. He wore no clerical garments of any kind—only a dandified lounge suit and a tie of slightly shocking red. He darted forward to meet Frances as she preceded the others into the room, seized her hand and held it in a lingering parody of the chivalrous man.

"My dear Frances," he gabbled, "you will, I'm sure, forgive my letting myself into the house and settling down in this unconventional way." He had a disconcerting trick of thrusting his face close to the face of the person to whom he was talking. "I realised that I was a little early, and I he-e-sitated"—he drawled out the word, and then went on with a rush—"to *disturb* you . . . at your meal." His small eyes looked quickly about the gathering "Garbin. Spitshuker. Dutton— and how are you now, my dear fellow? And . . . ?" He glanced at Peace, Geoffrey, and Fielding. Introductions were made. "So pleased," murmured Dallow. "So pleased." He conducted Frances with bird-like movements to a chair, and sat down beside her.

"Butler is not here yet?" he enquired generally. "I hope —indeed I hope—that he will be in time for the meeting. The matter is so urgent—so terribly urgent." With a sharp movement, he began feeling in his pockets, and finally produced a large key. "I have been to the hospital," he said, holding it up, "and the police asked me to return you—this." He laid it delicately on a table beside him.

There was a moment's silence. Then Frances said:
"Is it——?"

Dallow nodded and grimaced. "Exactly. The cathedral key—more properly I should say the key to the door in the north transept. That key which hangs normally"—he emphasised the word—"in the front porch of this clergyhouse, for the use of its occupants."

"My dear Dallow," piped Spitshuker in sudden excitement, "are you trying to tell us that that—*that*—is the key which Brooks——" His voice trailed away.

Dallow nodded. "Precisely that." He looked at Frances. "You knew it was missing?"

"I? I hadn't any idea. I never need to use it. Mr. Dutton, what about you?"

The sub-organist shifted. "I never go into the cathedral now. Doctor's orders. Perhaps one of the other two——?"

"But they've been away for three days now. *Nobody* had occasion to notice it was gone. What's more, anyone could have walked in and taken it."

"Precisely what I told the police," said Dallow. "The 'C.H.' engraved on it left no doubt of its provenance. They will probably have to ask questions about it. In the meantime, they're finished with it, and asked me to bring it back. No finger-prints, I gather."

"What I can't understand," said Garbin, "is why Brooks wasn't using his own key to get into the cathedral. He's had one ever since we were authorised to lock the cathedral at seven at nights."

Dallow leaned forward. "My *de*-e-ar Garbin. You miss the point. Brooks *did* use his own key. But whoever was in the Cathedral with him—used *this* one." He tapped it slowly. "Brooks' key was found on him. This other, as you know, was found lying on the grass outside the north transept."

Fielding looked up. "That's curious."

"Very curious, Mr. Fielding. Why, you would ask, did our intruder not return the key here when he had locked the door behind him?"

"Ah, but our intruder overlooked that. And you must remember that in all probability poor Brooks was left for dead."

"Still less reason for locking it," said Dutton, wedging himself painfully into the conversation. They stared at him with that unanimous surprise which naturally shy people seem always to attract to themselves. You would have imagined that a white mouse was liable to pop out of his mouth at any moment.

"But there was a reason, of course," Spitshuker squeaked excitedly. "That is—supposing our intruder wanted to keep his crime secret for as long as possible.

67

The police try all doors of the cathedral at least three times during the night. If one of them was found open, naturally they would investigate at once. I understand that the longer a body remains undiscovered, the less easy it is to fix with precision the time of death, and so to use the method of investigation by alibi." He seemed to feel that this statement showed too intimate a knowledge of criminology, for he added: "Or so I think I have been told."

"True—perfectly true, my *de*-e-ar Spitshuker," said Dallow in benign confirmation.

"But that still doesn't account for the fact that the key was thrown away, and not returned," Peace interposed.

"I think I can explain that," Frances replied grimly. "At ten o'clock sharp every night the door of this house is latched. After that time, only the four of us with latch-keys—Notewind and Filts, the two minor canons who live here, Dutton and myself—can get in. Your criminal would hardly risk breaking into the house simply to return a key."

"And that means"—Garbin's deep voice almost startled them—"that those four are thus far freed from suspicion." Frances shrugged indifferently. "If we haven't been talking nonsense—as we probably have—I suppose it does."

"It seems very important," said Geoffrey, "because from what I've heard so far it seems as if the thing may have happened at any time. What time did the choir-practice finish, by the way?"

"It has to be over by a quarter to nine," said Spitshuker, "because the boys must be back at their homes by nine. And if I remember, one of the Decani altos, who was the last to leave, said he got home about ten past. Brooks merely told him that he proposed practising for a while—which I suppose he may have done. But he was nowhere near the organ when they found him." Spitshuker turned to the Chancellor. "How was he, by the way?"

"He is dead."

It was a new voice that had spoken. Simultaneously they turned towards the door. The Precentor, Dr. Butler, stood there looking at them with the coldest eyes Geoffrey had ever seen in a human being. He had the frame and height of a giant, and hair the colour of dirty ice. His face, where the bones showed so prominently, was tanned a dark brown. He was about fifty, prematurely grey.

Frances jumped up. "Daddy . . ."

The Precentor advanced towards Geoffrey. "Mr. Vintner? It was kind of you to come." He turned back to the others. "Yes, Brooks is dead. About three hours ago he recovered his reason."

"Recovered!"

"Yes. He woke from a long and merciful sleep and asked quite coherently to see the police. Of course, the officer was by his side in a moment, but he seemed so exhausted that he could utter only a few unintelligible words before he went to sleep again. A short while after it was time for him to take some medicine—a solution of caffein, I believe. It was prepared in the dispensary by one of the nurses, and taken out, with other equipment, on a trolley. The foolish girl then left it in the entrance hall of the hospital while she was called away to another patient. The entrance-hall is unwatched, and open to all comers."

He paused, and again the cold eyes glanced round the gathering. His self-possession was almost intolerable.

"She returned," he went on, "and took the medicine in to him. It was criminal negligence, was it not, to leave the glass untended in that way? They roused him, and in front of two nurses and a police officer he drank the caffein solution together with a fatal quantity of atropine. Ten minutes later—rather over two hours ago—he died, in extreme and violent agony." Butler paused again, and again looked round. "And the irony of it is that they thought it was only a return of his delirium. For five minutes, before they saw something was seriously wrong, they held him down and allowed the poison to do its work."

There was dead silence. No one moved a muscle.

"And now, gentlemen," said the Precentor without emotion of any kind in his voice, "we will proceed with our meeting."

Chapter Five

CONJECTURES

"Here's a wild fellow."
SHAKESPEARE

GEOFFREY ORDERED ANOTHER PINT and began to see matters in a more rosy light. He even withdrew himself momentarily from morbid questioning and looked about him. The bar of the "Whale and Coffin" was crowded— crowded with people who knew nothing, he reflected, of what he and the others had heard in the clergy-house drawing-room hardly more than half an hour ago. They chattered with stoic resignation about the state of the war, the quality of the beer, and the minor inconveniences of being alive. They drank, if not with gusto, at least with the appearance of enjoyment—most of them men, though in one corner sat a plump, well-dressed, painted woman of middle-age sipping in a tolerant, lady-like manner at a glass of oily-looking stout, while in another a pale, anae- mic, characterless shop-girl drank silently in the company of an equally pale, anaemic, characterless young man. There was not riotous enjoyment, but there was at least peace.

The appearance of peace, thought Geoffrey. What is peace? An ice-cream cornet in the sun? Certainly there was no peace in Tolnbridge, no serenity. Beneath the placid, quotidian ritual of the cathedral town lurked un- known forces which were moving ponderously devastat- ingly to the surface. Beneath the familiar mask of any of these people hatred and murder might lie. The landlord Geoffrey had not seen after his first visit—a fact which caused him both annoyance and relief: annoyance because he had returned here determined to confront the man and demand an explanation of his behaviour earlier on, and relief because he had not looked forward to the encounter with any special confidence. The blessings of enforced procrastination! On his left, a soldier was engaged in an interminable narrative about some minor mishap of Army life.

". . . So there 'e was in the front o' the lorry, see, and the 'ill full of ruddy 'oles like a sieve, and 'im bumpin' up an' down like a ruddy marionette, see . . ."

The voice faded to trite memory. A tall, heavily-built man came in and elbowed his way to the bar. Evidently he was a person of some consequence, for conversation wavered on his arrival, and the drinkers regarded him with curiosity and interest. They appeared to be anticipating from him some oracular pronouncement. But he only ordered a bitter and a packet of Players, and the talk became general again.

". . . There 'e was, see, the ruddy 'ill pitted with 'oles, an' the grenades dencin' about in the back like peas in a saucepan . . ."

Civilised people, thought Geoffrey, react oddly to the news of violent death. No one had screamed, or drawn in his breath with an alarming hiss; very little had been said, even, the party having broken up almost immediately, to allow the Chapter to get on with their meeting. Frances, refusing an invitation to drink, had gone to her room with a book; Fielding, whose reactions to the proximity of the sea were conventional, had announced his intention of going down to the rocks to potter; Dutton had gone to bed; and Peace had vanished, no one knew whither. An obscure irritation haunted Geoffrey that none of these people had felt the need of alcohol as he had; he felt morally weak. It was true that he had resisted the temptation for ten minutes when he had made a cursory and uninspiring examination of the garden, but still, it had mastered him in the end—that and a pressing desire, he added to himself in hasty and unconvincing extenuation, to see the landlord of the "Whale and Coffin" again.

He, however, was plainly not here, or else was lurking in some other corner of his establishment.

The evening was warm, and not conducive to thought; the drinkers lunged out ineffectually at the flies which sailed past their noses. There were not, in any case, sufficient data to make an examination of events. Geoffrey thought first of his fugue and then, becoming bored with this, as is the way of artists with their own works, mentally pigeon-holed it, and thought of Frances instead. The beer slowly toppled him to the edge of a swamp of maudlin sentiment. Intellect stood aside and informed him of this fact. He ignored it, abandoning himself to the luxury, and helping it on its way by more beer. He categorised, by comparison, the charms of his liking, his true love, his sweeting—"Sweeting," charming word, said Intellect, vainly endeavouring to divert him into a discussion of the degeneration of language: pity it's gone out of use. Lips like—like what? Coral? Cherries? No, no; trite, conventional. That sort of thing, said Intellect, still trying to stem the tide, went out with Jacobean literature. *My mistress' eyes,* it quoted, *are nothing like the sun. Coral is far more red than her lips' red; If snow be white, why then her breasts are dun; If hairs be wires, black wires grow on her head. . . .* Emotion replied indignantly with *Shall I compare thee to a summer's day?* but being uncertain as to how the poem went on, was forced to fall back on peevish mumblings.

Intellect's victory, however, was only temporary. What, thought Geoffrey, if I were to ask her to marry me? Bachelorhood, complacent in a hitherto indefeasible citadel, was startled into attention and began to peer anxiously from behind its fortifications. Discomfort, it whispered persuasively: inconvenience. All your small luxuries, your careful arrangements for peace of mind, would go by the board if you got married. Women are contemptuous of such things, or if she should turn out not to be, why marry her at all? Why have a mirror to reflect your own fads, to flatter your face? Pointless and silly. You'd much better remain as you are. Your work, too—a wife would insist on being taken out just when you were struggling with a particularly good idea. And what would become of your Violin Concerto with a baby howling about the house?

You're an artist. Artists shouldn't get married. A little mild flirtation, perhaps, but nothing more.

Before the undoubted common sense of these remarks, all that Emotion could do was to mutter gloomily but doggedly: I love her. And at this a real panic broke out in the citadel. Windows were banged, the portcullis closed, the drawbridge lowered. . . .

"I wonder if you can give me a light?"

Geoffrey started back to consciousness of his surroundings. The tall man who had just come in was flourishing an unlighted cigarette questioningly before him.

"Ever since Norway," said the man, "matches have been getting scarcer and scarcer."

The fact was unquestionable, and seemed to provide little opportunity for comment. Geoffrey produced a lighter and jabbed viciously at it with his thumb. At the twelfth attempt the man smiled, a little sadly. "Tricky things," he said.

"I filled it this morning, and I think I overdid it." Geoffrey shook the lighter; quantities of fluid splashed on to the floor. "I'll give it one more try."

The resultant sheet of flame nearly took their faces off. And it was as the tall man was dubiously approaching it with his cigarette that the other thing happened.

There were leading off from the bar three doors which gave access to small private rooms where it was possible for a few people to drink in relative privacy. From behind one of these, unnerving sounds were suddenly heard—tremendous crashes, over-turning of furniture, curses, grunts, and the noise of rapid movement and heavy breathing; then renewed crashes. The bar listened and gaped in stupefaction. Then the man who had asked Geoffrey for a light strode with an air of authority to the door and flung it open. Geoffrey followed him. The others crowded behind.

At first nothing could be seen but a small room with the furniture somewhat disarranged. From an angle, however, sounds of intense activity could be heard, and someone swearing in several languages. Geoffrey and the tall man went in. The crowd behind them stood goggle-eyed with hushed expectancy.

The *bagarre*, when discovered, was not precisely what

74

had been expected. On his knees in a corner was a tall, lanky man. In one hand he held a large glass of whisky, in the other a walking-stick, with which he prodded at some small, mobile object hovering above the floor. This was shortly revealed to be a common house-fly, avoiding the attacks with ease and evident enjoyment. How long this scene might have continued it is impossible to say. But the fly, tiring of the amusement, presently took wing and prepared to depart. Its assailant, plainly maddened by this unexpected manoeuvre, aimed the contents of his glass at it, and missed. The fly flew at top speed towards his nose, made impact, went into reverse, and then with what even to the unimaginative was manifestly a shriek of delight, made off through the window.

The man climbed tranquilly to his feet, dusting his knees in a conventional manner. Dark hair, ineffectually plastered down with water, stuck out in spikes from the back of his head. His cheeks glowed like apples, giving evidence of an almost intolerable health and high spirits. Despite the warmth of the evening, he was muffled in an enormous raincoat, and had on an extraordinary hat.

"Good *God!*" said Geoffrey with deep feeling.

Gervase Fen, Professor of English Language and Literature in the University of Oxford, gazed placidly about him. "The trouble about flies," he said without preliminary, "is that they never *learn*. You'd think that if you were as small as that, and landed on an animate object of immense size which heaved and banged and shouted at you, you'd go away and shut yourself up in a cupboard for ever. But not flies. They just circle round and come back again. It's the same with windows. Generations of flies have batted themselves silly against windows without ever discovering that you can't get through them."

The inhabitants of the bar had returned with indifference to their former stations. The tall man who had asked Geoffrey for a light said to Fen:

"I've been looking for you everywhere, sir. No one seemed to know what had become of you."

Fen nodded vaguely. "Inspector Garratt, isn't it? More about Brooks?"

Geoffrey, suppressing his annoyance with difficulty, said: "And I'm Geoffrey Vintner."

75

"I know that," said Fen.

"Well aren't you going to welcome me?"

"Oh? Oh?" said Fen. "And what can I do for you?"

"You asked me down here to play the services."

"Oh, did I? Did I?" said Fen. "I thought I'd asked old Raikes, from St. Christopher's. Not that he'd have been any good," he added thoughtfully. "He's been bedridden for years."

Geoffrey sat down, speechless with fury. "To think I come all the way down here, getting myself attacked three times on the way——"

"What's that, sir?" asked the Inspector, turning to him sharply.

"*Attacked.*"

Fen groaned. "More complication. And I came down here for a peaceful holiday. Well, let's get some drinks and have it all out."

They had it all out. First the Inspector, who gave a bare outline of the facts about Brooks' murder, as Geoffrey had heard them, and then Geoffrey, who gave a much less bare—in fact, a somewhat embroidered—account of the attacks on himself. He felt this to be justified by the unsatisfactory, and essentially unconvincing, nature of these attacks. Even so, they didn't seem greatly to perturb Fen and the Inspector, which annoyed Geoffrey considerably.

"I shall help," said Fen in a determined manner when Geoffrey finally fell silent.

"Good," said the Inspector. "The Yard warned us we shouldn't be able to stop you." Fen glared. "I think they still remember that business at Caxton's Folly, before the war."

"Ah," put in Fen complacently. "Caxton's Folly. *That* was a case, if you like." A thought suddenly disturbed him. "The Yard?" he added abruptly. "You haven't handed over to them?"

The Inspector sighed. "We haven't made much progress on our own, sir. And the death of Brooks this afternoon has made things worse, not better. Oh, we've questioned everyone within reach, you can be sure of that—though not a second time, of course, since Brooks was killed. That remains to be done." He nodded gloomily, as a general surveying a peculiarly unsuitable terrain before battle. "But what's the use? We don't even know what sort of questions to ask. Brooks hadn't an enemy in the world,—our only pointer is this improbable something he seems to have seen. *So*—the Chief Constable got on to the Yard. I believe they were going to send down one of their best men—fellow called Appleby——"

"Appleby! Appleby!" howled Fen indignantly. "What do they want with Appleby when I'm here?" He calmed down slightly. "I admit," he said, "that he's very good—*very* good," he ended gloomily. "But I don't see——"

With an effort, Geoffrey leaned forward, hoping thereby to produce an appearance of emphasis. "My dear Gervase: surely in a matter as serious as murder, *anyone* who can help——"

"Don't preach at me," said Fen peevishly.

"Well, we have a free hand for a day or so," continued the Inspector, regardless of interruptions. "If we can't discover something by then, it'll *have* to be the Yard."

"Of course we can discover something," said Fen magnificently. He paused in some perplexity. "But what? The thing divides itself into three problems, doesn't it? First, the attacks on Geoffrey here; second, the attack on Brooks in the cathedral; and third, the murder of Brooks. We might do worse than to take them separately and see what we can make of each." He considered. "You, Geoffrey, were attacked by three different people—all pretty certainly hired thugs. I wonder what happened to the fellow in the store? Do you think there's any chance of his having got away?" He turned to the Inspector. "You haven't heard anything, I suppose?"

The Inspector shook his head. "No reason why the London people should think it had anything to do with us. But I can ring up and find out." He made a note on a grubby envelope.

"So much for that," said Fen. "Not much use trying to trace the other two men. What happened to the case that was dropped on you, Geoffery?"

"It was left in the train, I think. Yes, I'm sure it was."

"There might be prints," said the Inspector. "The man who tried to do you in was probably an old lag we've got on record somewhere. Not that I expect it'd do much

77

good if we did pick him up. He wouldn't know much about it. Still, I'll try and get hold of the case. *Routine,* you know. 'The police may not have the dash and brilliance of the amateur investigator, but it is only by their patient and methodical investigation of the smallest details that the criminal, *etcetera, etcetera, etcetera.*'" He fished out his envelope and made another note on it. "The 5.43 in here, wasn't it?"

"Then there were the two threatening letters," Fen went on. "Any idea as to why anyone should want to stop you coming here?"

"I think," said Geoffrey, brazenly plagiarising, "that the whole thing was probably a blind to conceal the real reason for the attack on Brooks—to concentrate our attention on the fact that it was *organists* who were being attacked——"

"Nonsense," Fen interposed rudely. "You don't go to all that elaborate trouble just to cover up." He was prone to slightly out-of-date Americanisms. "Why not the obvious explanation—that they didn't want anyone playing the organ for two or three days?"

"That's silly."

"No, it isn't," said Fen irritably. "Look here. It's pretty obvious that Brooks saw something in that cathedral which incriminated somebody. Suppose it was somehow connected with the organ. Brooks sees it, they know he's seen it, and they try to bump him off." (Here Geoffrey gave a feeble moan of protest.) "Well, and good. They imagine they've succeeded, and that they're safe. Then next morning they get a nasty shock when they find that Brooks is still alive, and quite capable of blowing the words." (Geofffrey moaned again.) "So they make a second attempt, and this time they succeed. But they realise everyone will know by now that there's something of importance hidden in the cathedral (if Brooks had been found dead, no one need have guessed), and they want to get it away. Difficulty the first: the cathedral is well guarded"—Fen glanced at the Inspector, who nodded—"And no unauthorised person can get in except when it's open for services. Difficulty the second: they want to get at the organ-loft, or thereabouts, and that, despite the demise of Brooks, will during services be occupied—by

78

one Geoffrey Vintner, quite publicly summoned for the purpose. Moral: put Mr. Vintner out of action, and keep the organ-loft clear."

"It sounds plausible," said the Inspector. "In fact, it's the only explanation I can think of." ("You didn't think of it," muttered Fen. "I did.") "But"—he shrugged helplessly—"what is this mysterious something?"

"Presumably you've had the place searched?"

"It's been searched all right," said the Inspector grimly. "No results, of course—but then, we'd no idea what we were looking for. We did look in the works of the organ"—("*Works*," said Geoffrey faintly)—"but . . . well, there was nothing that we could see."

"Tombs?" suggested Fen.

"We didn't open them, of course. But then neither, one imagines, did Brooks."

Geoffrey intervened. "You say no *unauthorised* person has been able to get in, except at service times, since Brooks was found. Presumably that wouldn't include the clergy?"

"The gentlemen in Holy Orders? No, sir. But you can be sure that whenever they had occasion to go in, we kept an unobtrusive eye on them."

"Since the cathedral is under suspicion," said Fen, "presumably its sutlers are under suspicion as well."

"Exactly, sir. And that makes it more difficult. It's very awkward, having to try and pry into a canon." The bizarre effect of his phraseology startled the Inspector, and he was silent for a moment. "Well, what now?"

"The second problem," said Fen, "is the attack on Brooks in the cathedral. Any leads?"

"Pretty well nothing. He was knocked out and given an injection of atropine—intravenally, in the left forearm."

Fen interrupted: "I thought atropine was a soporific."

"No, it's an irritant—aphrodisiac—no, not that; what's the word I want?"

"Was it a fatal dose?" Fen asked.

"A fifth of a grain. It should have been fatal, but the action of these drugs still isn't properly understood. A sixteenth of a grain's generally given as the maximum safe dose. They diagnosed it pretty soon—lack of perspiration and saliva, and so on—and treated him with tannic acid, morphine, ether, caffein—everything they had. He would have recovered." The Inspector's voice was for a moment oddly shaken; Geoffrey suddenly realised the heavy responsibility of the man, and saw that it had told on him.

"You didn't find the hypodermic, of course?"

"No."

"It could be quite small?"

"That would depend on the solution. Atropine sulphate's soluble in the proportions one to three in ninety per cent alcohol; one to five hundred in water. But even so, it could have been tiny."

Fen mused, fidgeting slightly and shuffling his feet; he finished his whisky and pressed a plainly inoperative bell to summon more. "An odd method of murder. Gunshot, of course, would be too noisy—but a knife . . . or strangulation, or——? Messy, all of them. A woman's crime, perhaps. Or a man with a womanish mind." He pressed the bell again; it fell off the wall with a clatter. He regarded it thoughtfully for a moment, and then turned to the Inspector. "Would atropine be difficult to get?"

"I suppose so. Don't really know."

"If you're an inspector," said Fen, "what do you inspect? Tickets?" He laughed uproariously. The others regarded him coldly. When he had finished, the Inspector said: "If you got it at a chemist's, it would have to go on the poison register, of course. As far as the local chemists are concerned, we've been into all that already, and there's nothing in the least suspicious. We can't investigate every poison-book in the country, and besides, I'm pretty sure we're not dealing with a complete lunatic—not in that sense, anyway," he added reflectively. "No, there's nothing to be got from that angle, I'm certain. The knock Brooks got on the head was the usual blunt instrument, one supposes—scientifically placed, to require the minimum of strength: the whole thing suggests medical knowledge. Incidentally, it suggests premeditation as well. People don't go about carrying loaded hypodermics the way they do guns."

Geoffrey proffered an idea at this point, without much confidence. "Perhaps Brooks already knew that something was going on, and *they* knew *he* knew, and decided to silence him once and for all after the choir-practice."

Fen nodded approval. "Very good," he said. "Means? Motive? Opportunity?"

"*Motive*," said the Inspector heavily. "Can we define a little?" As it was evident that both Geoffrey and Fen were ready to define a great deal, and the question had been only rhetorically intended, he hastened to add: "The only clue we have is Brooks' ravings—when he was found by the Verger opening the church in the morning   " He stopped abruptly. "By the way, you'd like to question the Verger, I suppose?"

"No," said Fen.

"Ah," the Inspector replied unhappily. "Well, then. He said a good deal then, and later, when we got him to the hospital, and we got most of it down. A lot of it obviously had nothing to do with the matter in hand—he had some fancies, I can tell you, about that shameless hussy Helen Dukes in the Post Office——"

"Post Office, Post Office," said Fen. "What are we listening to a lot of stuff about the Post Office for?"

"And then naturally there were worries about the cathedral music," the Inspector went on unperturbed, "uppermost in his mind. It seems there'd been a quarrel with the Cantoris Bass over a solo—but that hardly seems to be a motive."

Fen heaved his long, lanky body irritably about in his chair, and fidgeted more than ever. "When are we going to get to the point?" he grumbled.

"Finally, there's a few things he said about the Cathedral itself. They seemed to cost him a lot of pain and fright, but they don't amount to much. You remember that passage in *The Moonstone*, where What's-his-name fills in the blanks of the old doctor's ravings to make a piece of beautifully grammatical English? Never seemed plausible to me: delirium doesn't work like that. The one flaw, I always think, in an otherwise excellent novel, though as *detective* writing I consider it's greatly overrated, like Poe's stories——"

"Oh, get on," said Fen. "What did Brooks say, anyway?"

The Inspector paused; then he took another envelope

from his pocket. "Why, sir, this was the burden of it." He read aloud:

"Wires. Man hanging—rope. Slab of tomb moved."

There was a brief silence. Geoffrey remembered the circumstances in which he had first heard those words; they affected him hardly less now. "An empty cathedral isn't a good place to be in all night"—even for the unimaginative. He remembered some words read in a story long ago: "In his unenlightened days he had read of meetings in such places which even now would hardly bear thinking of." And even if, as it seemed, the encounter had been material, in such surroundings it might well have shaken a man of strong nerves. This Geoffrey said.

Fen nodded. He appeared unexpectedly gloomy, but those who knew him well would have recognised this as a sign that certain things were becoming clear to him. He said nothing, but collected their glasses, and after a further glance at the offending bell-push, departed to get another round of drinks. Returning, he banged the glasses down on the table, sat down heavily, and said: "Well?"

The Inspector shrugged. "Night thoughts . . ." he murmured dubiously.

Fen drew in his breath sharply. "It is always my fate," he said, "to be involved with literary policemen. . . ." He waved his glass in a perfunctory and graceless toast, took a large mouthful of whisky, choked slightly, and went on in tones of bitter complaint: "Why does no one ever take things *literally* . . . *wires*. Radio, electricity"—he glared at the defunct apparatus on the floor—*"bell-pushes*. Hanging man—rope: men can hang from rope otherwise than by the neck; they can climb up and down it with definite and possibly criminal purposes in view. Slab of tomb moved: active or passive? Moved of its own accord, or *had been* moved?" He paused. "It seems fairly plain as far as it goes. And what part of the cathedral is inaccessible except by climbing a rope—no staircase?"

The Inspector's eyes shone with sudden comprehension; he half rose. Fen nodded.

"Exactly. The Bishop's Gallery."

Geoffrey gazed uncomprehendingly. "The what?"

Fen turned to him. "Of course. You don't know the cathedral well. The organ-loft is high up over the Decani

82

choir-stalls, on the south side of the chancel. From it a narrow gallery runs west, towards the nave, as far as the big column where the south transept begins; it can't be entered from that end. There are only two ways into it: first, from the organ-loft, an entrance which has been bricked up since the eighteenth century; and second, by a spiral staircase which leads down to a small room and then to an outside door, also walled up. In the small room lies the body of John Thurston, Bishop from 1688 to 1705, and the last of the witch-hunters—hence the name of the gallery above it. So apart from hauling down a lot of brick and plaster there's no way in except over the edge of the gallery." He turned to the Inspector. "I suppose the brick and plaster *hadn't* been tampered with?"

The Inspector shook his head; an indefinable sense of uneasiness was growing within him. "That was one of the likeliest places. No, it hadn't been touched—and it's quite impossible to disguise the traces of a thing like that if anyone's looking for it. Not that it wouldn't be fairly easy to burrow through that brick partition from the organ loft: it's thin, and it looks as if it was pretty hastily put up in the first place. But as to this rope business. I admit no one could get up and down from that gallery *except* by a rope—there's that padlocked wall tomb of St. Ephraim underneath, and it doesn't project so there's no foothold anywhere, nor on the columns at either side—they're slippery as glass. But how are you going to get your rope attached in the first place, before you begin climbing up it?"

Fen snorted contemptuously, and gulped his whisky. "This is filthy stuff," he said; and then: "An expert lassoist with a light hemp rope could do it easily. There's a row of crockets or something, along the gallery rail."

"But when you've got down again," the Inspector persisted. "You have to leave the rope hanging there, where someone will notice it."

"No, you don't," said Fen. "Not if your rope's long enough to allow a double length of it to reach the ground. You make a special sort of knot," he said vaguely, "and you climb down one strand, and then when you reach the bottom you pull the other, and it all comes undone." He sat back in a pleased manner.

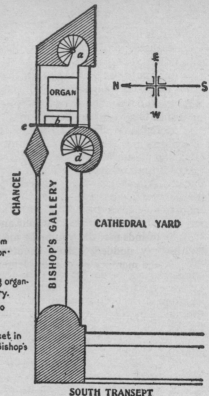

a. Spiral staircase leading from organ-loft to outside door.

b. Music cupboard.

c. Brick partition separating organ-loft from Bishop's Gallery.

d. Spiral staircase leading to Bishop's tomb.

The tomb of St. Ephraim is set in the wall directly below the Bishop's Gallery.

"Oh," said the Inspector suspiciously, "and what is this knot, may I ask?"

"It's called the Hook, Line and Sinker."

"Why is it called that?"

"Because," said Fen placidly, "the reader has to swallow it."[1]

"But what I want to know *is*," Geoffrey burst out, unable to contain himself any longer: "What are all these people *doing* shinning up and down ropes? We're no nearer to that than we were before."

"Wires," said Fen gnomically. He got up and began wandering about the room, apparently inspecting its decorations. "We must go over to the cathedral in a minute and visit, somehow or other, the Bishop's Gallery." He looked at the Inspector. "That can be arranged? It's annoying," he added balefully, "because I was going to make a particularly interesting experiment with moths this evening——" He interrupted himself and addressed Geoffrey. "That reminds me: did you bring me a butterfly net?"

Geoffrey nodded, hatred spontaneously arising within him at the memory of that implement. "It's at the clergy-house," he said. "Seventeen and six," he added. Fen ignored this.

"There's one more thing," said the Inspector, "and that's the murder of Brooks. Atropine again—through the mouth this time, of course. Criminal carelessness." His face darkened. "I think it's obvious that none of the hospital people was implicated, and that it was put in the medicine when it was left in the hall."

Fen looked up from his aimless circumambulations. "That's funny. It sounds like the merest chance. . . ."

"Nothing of the kind, sir. The nurse in charge of the dispensary is the scatter-brained kind, and she'd talked about Brooks—talked to every single person who came to enquire after him, I should think. Half Tolnbridge must have known he got that stuff every half-hour, regular as Fate. Just as she was wheeling it into the hall, a bell went

[1] This is outrageous, tantamount to accusing me of invention. The knot does of course exist, is known as the sheet bend, and is much used in climbing.—E. C.

—the bell of one of the private rooms she was in charge of—and she went off to answer it. She found the patient sound asleep and no one else in the room. By the time she got back, of course, the damage was done."

Fen groaned. "Oh, my ears and whiskers!" he said. "Adventurous, eh? No one was seen about?"

"Plenty of people were seen about. It was during visiting hours."

"It mightn't have been Brooks' medicine at all. But I suppose they didn't mind about a little thing like that."

(Another sentence came back to Geoffrey's mind: "They can afford to waste lives like water.")

Fen resumed his wanderings, the Inspector his logomachy. "All the people who might possible be connected with it—all the cathedral people, that is—I shall have to interview again this evening: Miss Butler, Dr. Butler, Dr. Garbin, Dr. Spitshuker, Mr. Dutton, Sir John Dallow, Mr. Savernake, now that he's back. . . ." He reeled off the list with the melancholy relish of a Satanist enumerating the circles of inferno. "But nothing will come of it," he said, suddenly abandoning all pretence and relapsing into a pathetic despair, "nothing at all."

"Come, come," said Geoffrey mechanically.

"I'd be obliged, sir," said the Inspector, pulling himself together slightly and addressing Fen, "if you'd take a look at the cathedral, and the Bishop's Gallery, while I'm seeing all these people. We shall have to get permission from the Precentor to get into the Gallery, but I hope there won't be any difficulty about that. I can give you a note to the men in charge, and they'll help you in every way you need." Fen nodded, and finished his drink. They all rose, the Inspector sighing, and Geoffrey feeling slightly hazy and adventurous with alcohol.

"Well," said the Inspector, "we're not quite as much in the dark as we were, though it's still mostly conjecture. Now we'll see what there really is in this infernal Gallery."

This, however, they were destined never to do.

Chapter Six

MURDER IN THE CATHEDRAL

*"To-night it doth inherit
The vasty hall of death."*
ARNOLD

THEY WALKED BACK from the "Whale and Coffin" to the clergy-house. Now it was ten to ten and a twilight haze was dusting the roofs of the town, a twilight mist softening the lines of the headland towards Tolnmouth and driving argent channels among the scattered white houses which hung on the low distant bank on the other side of the estuary. The melancholy crying of the gulls was almost silent. The sky, as if in a parting flourish before the onslaught of darkness, was the palest, most fragile blue. The curious, inexplicable stillness of evening was in the air—a stillness broken only by the cawing of a flock of rooks returning to their nests at the tops of a group of fir-trees. Dominating the town stood the cathedral, is spire raised proudly to heaven.

Geoffrey was limping badly; his bruise, he felt convinced, had grown to considerable dimensions by now, and a second, more formidable stiffness had set in. Moreover, matters were not improved by the speed at which Fen walked; he strode along at a great and unnecessary rate, talking incessantly about insects, cathedrals, crime, and Oxford University, and complaining impartially and slanderously (his normal manifestation of high spirits) about the conduct of the war, his personal comfort, the ingratitude of his contemporaries and the quality of certain proprietary brands of whisky. None the less, Geoffrey was happier than he had been all day. Fen had been found; something of the mystery had been cleared up; and he (Geoffrey) was in all probability the object of incidental and not special malice. He thought suddenly of a way in which the subject by inversion and the subject by diminution could be combined, and sang happily under his breath until even Fen, who was in the middle of some depressing tale about the habits of the common dung-beetle, was driven to comment on it. The Inspector walked for the most part in silence, plainly not listening to Fen, but inserting purposeless monosyllabic comments whenever a suitable opening occurred, like matches thrown upon the body of a stream.

They had not gone far before they met Fielding, on his way back from pottering, the bottoms of his trousers slightly stained with sea-water. He greeted them dejectedly, seeming still to be much afflicted by the heat, and was introduced to Fen and the Inspector.

("Not," said Fen before anyone could stop him, "the author of *Tom Jones?*")

As they walked on, Geoffrey put Fielding *au fait* with the situation, as far as he was able, and Fielding's dejection grew. Such mental inadequacy as *he* had displayed, his expression implied, boded ill for his hypothetical future as a secret agent. He was however slightly consoled on recognising that he had not known all the necessary facts.

"Things seem a bit clearer," he said to Geoffrey. His brow was puckered with anxiety. "What do you think one ought to do now?" Geoffrey sketchily indicated what plans were afoot, and he nodded.

"Very good," he said, apparently feeling that some comment was required of him. "But who's at the bottom of it all? That's what we've got to find out."

Geoffrey, who was only too ready to out-Watson Watson in this respect, made noises of dissent. "The best thing we can do," he stated dogmatically, "is to keep out of the way and not ask imbecile questions. There are two people in charge of this thing already. And God help the law," he added with feeling, "if people like us are ever landed with enforcing it."

"I think I'd be rather good at it," said Fielding staunchly. A pause. "Geoffrey?"

"Well?"

"Do you think either of these people could help me to get into the Secret Service?"

"Good heavens. Are you still nagging about that? You're unfitted, I tell you, unfitted——"

"I don't see why I'm any more unfitted than anyone else. You don't realise my position."

"I realise it perfectly well. You're a Romantic gone wrong—you're mad. . . . The Secret Service isn't all guns and beautiful spies and codes, you know," continued Geoffrey severely, who knew nothing at all about it. "It's just routine and office work and"—his imagination hastily came to the rescue—"hanging about in pubs listening to soldiers." ("Why?" said Fielding.) "You'll be saying there are spies here next—in Tolnbridge. . . ."

". . . And that's another thing," the Inspector was saying complainingly on Geoffrey's left. "There are *spies* here—enemy agents. Bits of information have been leaking out—nothing important, fortunately, but still, symptomatic. . . ."

Happily Fielding did not hear this. Geoffrey paused long enough to digest the monstrous intelligence and verify the seriousness of the Inspector before hastily diverting the conversation to other channels. Fen paid little attention. Mindful of his hobby, he had begun peering in shrubs and bushes in search of insects.

"How were the rocks?" said Geoffrey.

"Barbed wire," answered Fielding gloomily. "It gets caught in everything. I don't see that *that's* going to hold up an invasion very long, either." He paused in momentary perplexity. "Did you discover anything about the burning of the manuscript by that child?"

"Good Lord," said Geoffrey, startled. "No, I didn't. But I don't suppose that's got anything to do with it."

Fielding shook his head; from the gravity of his expression, it was clear that he regarded the incident as of the last importance. Also, it had been overlooked by the powers that were. He put it away in his mind with the naïve hopefulness of an investor who keeps worthless stock in the hope that it may one day make him immensely wealthy. "You saw the landlord?"

"No. He wasn't there."

Fielding looked at him with mild reproach. "You've been drinking all this time."

"*Certainly* I have been drinking," said Geoffrey with the imagined stateliness which alcohol induces.

". . . lays its eggs in a sort of milk-white bubble which refracts the head," Fen was saying. "Then about May the bubble bursts. . . ."

"By the way, sir," said the Inspector abruptly, "we never went into that matter about the tomb—you know, the slab of the tomb that had been moved."

"Oh, my fur and whiskers!" exclaimed Fen. "Nor we did. Did Brooks mean that old reprobate Thurston's tomb, do you suppose? But you said the brickwork hadn't been touched, and there isn't a slab, anyway. Slab. Slab." He flicked his fingers. "Got it! It must be that enormous wall-tomb of St. Ephraim, right under the Bishop's Gallery. That's the only one that hasn't been plastered in—it's got six big padlocks to hold it in position instead. I suppose the keys are somewhere or other." He pondered. "But I wonder why——? M'm. A try-out for a hiding-place, possibly. Perhaps Brooks saw one of the padlocks loose— unpleasantly like *Count Magnus*. We must try and locate those keys, Garratt, and have a look at the tomb."

"All I can say is this," said the Inspector aggressively, as though he were being accused of something, "nothing had been touched that I could see, and certainly none of the tombs that were plastered up." A thought struck him. "Perhaps he was raving after all," he added gloomily.

They rounded a bend in the road, by an evil-looking tobacconist's. Two soldiers sat on the running-board of an Army lorry, smoking and staring with sad absorption at the tarmac. Two shop-girls in short skirts passed by on the other side, giggling and casting *oeillades* after the manner of their kind. The soldiers made sounds jocosely expressive of lustful attention. The girls shrieked with nervous excitement and made off. The Inspector sighed. Fen made futile attempts to put a grasshopper into a match-box. In the distance Frances appeared, a model of beauty, walking towards them. Geoffrey, too, sighed: that

90

lithe perfection of grace could not be for him. Her hair shone a deeper, richer black in the evening light.

"Is the meeting over yet?" Geoffrey asked when she had joined them.

"Ages ago," she said lightly. "They've all gone—most of them, anyway." She did a tiny pirouette in the road.

"You seem happy," Geoffrey ventured.

"I'm excited."

"Why?"

"Oh, I don't know. I shouldn't be, I suppose, with all these awful things happening." She looked at him a little shyly. "It's nice seeing new people—*you* know. Why did you want to know if the meeting was over?"

"I must see your father about what I've got to play, and when, and where I'm going to see the choir, and try the organ, and——"

She laughed. Oh, business. Well, you won't catch Daddy at the clergy-house. I can tell you that. He went off up to the cathedral as soon as the meeting was over, half an hour ago at least."

Geoffrey intercepted a swift glance which passed between Fen and the Inspector. "Do you know what he intended doing, miss?" asked the Inspector.

The girl's face clouded. "He said—he said no one could get to know what happened to Brooks unless they did as he did, and stayed in the cathedral alone." She hesitated. "It seems silly."

"It will do no good, miss, if that's what you mean," the Inspector pontificated vaguely. "Nor, I suppose, will it do any harm. The clergy-house key arrived back safely, I take it?"

Frances nodded. "Sir John brought it just after dinner." She turned to Fen. "Are you going to be in to-night?"

"Yes," said Fen gloomily, as though this was the most offensive thing he had ever heard. "I was going to make a most interesting experiment with moths, but apparently that won't be possible now."

"You don't want supper or anything? Are you going back to the clergy-house now? I'm a bit anxious about Daddy—that was why I came to meet you."

"We're going to the clergy-house," said Fen, "to leave the Inspector, who's got some questions to ask about people's movements this afternoon. While he's doing that, Geoffrey and I are going up to the cathedral to have a rather particular look round—and incidentally, to see your father, as you say he's there."

"I shall be glad of that," said Frances a little shamefacedly. "I'm just a tiny bit frightened about his being there alone. After what's happened . . . Oh, I suppose I'm making too much of it." She smiled. "Anyway, he's wearing a four-leaf clover for luck, so it ought to be all right."

"He'll be safe enough, miss," said the Inspector automatically. "My men are still on guard there, you know. There's nothing much can happen to him, I fancy." He whistled a few notes, tunelessly and without spirit.

They turned in at the clergy-house gates, traversed the wilderness of unflowering shrubs, and entered by the front door. In the hall they found Canon Spitshuker, small, plump, and excitable as ever, struggling into a raincoat and carolling the Benedicite to himself. "Frances, my dear," he called out as they entered, "you will, I fear, find the house empty, the revellers gone. I alone remain —except, of course"—he fluttered his hands excitedly— "the good Dutton, who has retired to his room with a copy of *The Anatomy of Melancholy* and some tablets of luminal. Hardly the most inspiriting reading for a nervous subject, I should have said, but perhaps it has a quietening effect on some people. And how are the insects, Gervase? The Bishop, I think, will not readily forgive you that last *débâcle*." He paused, and his face clouded as he glanced at the Inspector. "Strange: I was almost forgetting . . . poor Brooks. . . . No doubt you will be wanting any assistance we can give you, Inspector, over this new . . . development."

The Inspector nodded. "If you please, sir. It's a matter of routine, you understand, more than anything else. Were you in a hurry to be getting home?"

"No, no. I can stop as long as you wish. No commitments, except for my hot milk and rum before bed." Spitshuker began struggling out of his raincoat again, ineffectually aided by Geoffrey; he emerged from it eventually with the suddenness of a cork from a bottle, and stood gasping slightly.

"I understand, then, sir," the Inspector pursued, "that

there's no one except yourself and Mr. Dutton left in the house?"

"Indeed, that is so. Mr. Peace—Butler's brother-in-law —was here talking to me until five minutes ago, but then he went off somewhere: you must have just missed him. We had a most interesting conversation—most interesting. It appears that he is afflicted by doubts, of a crucial nature, about the validity of his calling, but, as I endeavoured to explain to him, when one is dealing with doctrines about the mind which are, in comparison with those of Christianity, so hazy and unscientific——"

Frances came to the rescue. "Do you know if he was going up to the cathedral?"

"My dear young lady, he may have been. He said nothing about his destination. Perhaps he was intent on enjoying this delightful evening."

Fen, who had been pottering about the hall straightening pictures which he fancied were slightly askew, said: "I must meet Mr. Peace." He turned to Frances. "He's staying with your father?" Frances nodded.

"A friendly visit?" Fen went on.

Frances shrugged. "I think he's here on business. It seems odd, though. I've never met him before, and we've never visited him when we've been in Town." Fen made abstracted signs of affirmation: he straightened another picture. "Will you be wanting me?" said Frances to the Inspector. "If not, I must go and deal with things in the kitchen."

"Not for half an hour or so, miss."

"I'll be there or in my bedroom if you want me," she said; and departed.

"Come on, Geoffrey," said Fen, fidgeting about. "Let's get up to the cathedral before it's too dark to see anything." A thought struck him, and he turned to Spitshuker. "Do you happen to know if the Bishop's Gallery has ever been opened or—entered in any way, since it was first blocked up?"

Spitshuker glanced at him sharply, the sudden shrewdness of his gaze contrasting formidably with the slightly ineffectual mask he presented to the world. "The Bishop's Gallery?—my dear fellow. I think not—no, I think not. At least there is no record of it. It would be possible, I suppose, to climb up from the chancel by means of a rope—one cannot tell if that has been done. But there has been no *public*—as it were—opening of Bishop Thurston's tomb, and if it were ever mooted, much local superstition would be against it. The Bishop was, perhaps, not an ornament of the Church he served, and it is inevitable that there should be . . . tales. With a gallery thus isolated and containing only the corpse of a man, a trick of the light which made it seem as if someone were peering down . . ." He stopped.

Fen showed interest—an unusual spectacle. "You fancy you've seen something of the sort yourself?" he asked.

Spitshuker gestured. "As I said—a trick of the light. But we are not forbidden to believe in demons."

"Recently?"

"I think not."

Fen's interest rather noticeably waned. "So the Bishop looks down into the chancel, does he? He's never progressed further, one supposes?"

The Canon laughed, suddenly and harshly. "It is said that there are two—a man and a woman. But I shouldn't bother your head with fairy tales. Dallow will tell you the local beliefs, if you ask him: he is the expert on these things." He paused. "I doubt if your question was framed with a view to ghost-hunting."

Fen answered the implicit question. "It's necessary that we should get into that gallery," he said. "For that, we shall need the permission of the Dean and Chapter. Unfortunately we can't afford to wait. Do you think if we climb in over the parapet the Dean and Chapter will wink an eye?"

"My dear fellow, the Church is adept at winking eyes. Among the Jesuits it is known as casuistry. But how do you propose to accomplish this?"

"Geoffrey here will climb up a rope," said Fen firmly.

"Oh no, I won't."

"Somebody will, then. Of course, there's the problem of actually attaching the rope. I suppose there's no one in the town capable of throwing a lasso?"

Spitshuker looked dubious. "Harry James, the landlord of the 'Whale and Coffin,' did some cattle-farming in the Argentine once"—Geoffrey and Fielding flashed simultaneous ocular signals of triumphant finality at one another—"and perhaps you have to be expert with the lasso for that. On the other hand, perhaps not." He seemed dejected by his lack of precise information. "And besides, I fancy it is an aptitude one can quickly pick up—and equally quickly lose."

Mentally, Geoffrey admitted the justice of this; as a piece of evidence against the landlord of the "Whale and Coffin," it was equivocal, particularly since the notion of anyone's having climbed into the gallery at all was still pure theorising. But he was reluctant to abandon any scrap of information about that stocky, sinister, slightly ludicrous little figure who had known his name and who had been so astonished at his presence in Tolnbridge.

". . . We'll see," Fen was saying ominously, "what can be managed. It probably won't be possible to-night, in any case, but I want a chance to spy out the land. One other thing; the keys of St. Ephraim's tomb."

Spitshuker stared at him blankly. "The keys . . . ? Oh, ah, yes, to be sure: of the padlocks." He became faintly jocose. "You are not thinking, I hope, of instituting a general disinterment? The keys were in any case lost or destroyed—I forget which—some hundred and fifty years ago. St. Ephraim was originally buried in the chapel dedicated to him—the present tomb is a seventeenth-century erection, to which his remains (not much of them, one fancies) were then transferred. The padlocking is unusual, but not unknown—it's more normal, of course, with sarcophagi. The keys remained with the successive deans. . . . Yes; I believe I have it. The Deanery was burnt down late in the eighteenth century, and probably the keys were lost then. But there again, Dallow would be the man to ask."

"It would be easy enough to take impressions," said the Inspector.

"But my dear Inspector," squeaked Spitshuker, "why, I ask you: why? There is nothing of value behind that immense slab. A lead coffin with some dust and hair—that's all. There *were*, of course, rich offerings to the shrine, but all were seized by Henry VIII, and afterwards the cult died out, except locally."

"We have our own ideas about why, sir," said the In-

95

spector with traditional gruffness, "which, if you'll forgive me, I'll keep to myself for the moment." Rather insubstantial ideas, Geoffrey reflected, but forbore to comment on the fact.

Fen, who for the last minute had been rattling the umbrellas and sticks irritatingly about in the hall-stand, said: "Let's get off, for heaven's sake. What are we pottering about here for, I should like to know?" Before anyone could say anything more, he had vanished through the front door. Geoffrey and Fielding followed him. Out of the corner of his eye, Geoffrey saw Spitshuker and the Inspector go into the sitting-room.

They rounded the house and passed through the back garden amid a cloud of wordy and incoherent apologies from Fielding for encumbering them with his presence. The gate between the garden and the Cathedral grounds was locked, but Fen had borrowed Dutton's key. He was unusually preoccupied and solemn as they climbed the cathedral hill. The ground was dry and hard beneath their feet, the air preternaturally still; Geoffrey strained his eyes to catch a glimpse of the police who guarded the cathedral doors, but dusk was falling, and once one was actually on the hill, he realised, the trees and shrubs made it extremely difficult to see the cathedral at ground level; there were only brief occasional vistas, which a step further would annihilate. He thought he glimpsed a figure passing round to the north side of the building, but could not be sure.

They paused by the hollow where the witches had burned. It was overgrown, neglected. Weeds and brambles straggled over it. The iron post stood gaunt against the fading light. They found rings through which the ropes and chains had passed. The air of the place was almost unbearably desolate, but in imagination Geoffrey saw the hillside thronged, above and below, with men and women whose eyes glowed with lust and fright and appalling pleasure at the spectacle to be offered them. And a whisper ran through the crowd, swaying and bending their heads like the fingers of wind plucking at a field of corn, as the cart appeared, and they leaned forward to see better—the justices in their robes, the dean and chapter, the squires, and behind them the many-headed beast, the

rabble. A woman they had known—a next-door neighbour, perhaps—a familiar face now become a mask of
fear in whose presence they crossed fingers and muttered
the *Confiteor*. Who next? And in the breast of that
woman, what ecstasy of terror or vain repentance or affirmation? What crying to Apollyon and the God of
Flies . . . ? It needed little fancifulness to catch the echo
of such scenes, even now. And here, they had accumu-
lated—week after week, month after month, year after
year, until even the crowds were sick and satiated with
the screaming and the smell of burnt flesh and hair,
and only the necessary officers were present at the ending
of these wretches, and the people stayed in their houses,
wondering if it would not have been better to face the
malignant, tangible living rather than the piled sepulchres
of the malignant, intangible dead.

"This was the last part of the country," said Fen, "in
which the trial and burning of witches went on. Elsewhere
it had ceased fifty or sixty years earlier—and then hanging, not burning, had been the normal method of execution. The doings of Tolnbridge stank so throughout the
country that a Royal Commission was sent down to investigate. But when Bishop Thurston died the business
more or less ceased. One of the last celebrated witch-trials
in these islands was the Weir business in Edinburgh; that
was in 1670. Tolnbridge continued for forty years after
that, into the eighteenth century——the century of Johnson, and Pitt, and the French Revolution. Only a step to
our own times. A depressingly fragile barrier—and human
nature doesn't change much."

They moved on up the hill. "It's going to be too dark
to do anything elaborate," said Fen, "and the cathedral
isn't blacked out in the summer." He took a torch from
the pocket of his raincoat and flicked it on experimentally. "It's quite possible, of course, that we're wildly
astray in all our conjectures—though it seems the good
Precentor is with us, up to a point."

"What do you think he's doing?" Geoffrey asked.

"My dear good man, how do I know? Presumably what
he said he was going to do—waiting for the ghost and—
Hello!"

They had reached the top of the rise. Over them, immensely high it now seemed, towered the cathedral, sombre and powerful as a couched beast in the gathering gloom. They stood in the angle of the nave and the south transept, in a stretch of green turf. From where they were, three doors were visible; none of them was guarded.

Fielding gripped Geoffrey's arm. "Geoffrey!" he whispered. *"Where are the police?"*

And it was at that precise moment, in the sitting-room of the clergy-house, that Canon Spitshuker happened to remark to the Inspector:

". . . And so when I saw you'd taken your men off guard at the cathedral, I assumed . . ."

The Inspector was on his feet. "When you *what?"*

"Surely they all left in a motor-car about an hour ago now. Several of us saw them go."

The Inspector gazed at him incomprehendingly for a moment. The "Holy God!" he whispered, and ran for the telephone.

For a moment after Fielding's remark, the three stood stockstill, looking. Then the earth seemed to shake under them. In a moment more there came from within the building a dull, enormous crash. After that, silence.

Gervase Fen was the first to stir himself. He ran to the nearest door and tried the handle; it was locked. So also with the other two. They pelted round the cathedral to the other side, and there, to their surprise, almost ran—into Peace, who was hurrying anxiously in the opposite direction.

"What was that noise?" he shouted agitatedly. "What was that noise?"

"Don't ask imbecile questions," said Fen shortly, and proceeded to try the doors on the south side. Geoffrey discovered one which was open, and gave a crow of triumph.

"That's no good, you fool," shouted Fen. "It only leads to the organ-loft. You can't get into the cathedral that way. Useless here. Every damn door in the place is locked." They all rushed round again to the north side, vainly trying the west door on their way, and were there rewarded by the sight of the Inspector running like a madman up the hill, waving his arms and uttering unintelligible cries. Subsequently there appeared two constables, summoned by the Inspector over the telephone in blasphemous terms, and toiling up the slope on bicycles.

Fen glanced at his watch. "10.16," he said. "And it's about a minute since we heard that noise. Say 10.15."

"Can we break one of the doors down?" asked Fielding excitedly.

"You can try if you like," said Fen minatorily, "but it won't do the slightest good. We shall have to get a key —or else a rope, and Geoffry can climb down into the chancel from the organ loft." ("No," said Geoffrey.) "I rather suspect we shall find that the clergy-house key has gone again, but each of the Canons has one."

The Inspector and the constables arrived more or less simultaneously, all greatly out of breath. Fen, with a rapidity and concision which he could very well employ when he chose, explained things to the Inspector, who nodded.

"Some sort of blasted decoy," he said, breathing stertorously. "They're such fools, a little child could take them in. God look down and pity us. Where have they gone, I ask you: where have they gone?"

"Never mind all that," said Fen rudely. "What we've got to do is to get into the cathedral." A constable was dispatched with instructions to get a key; he careered off down the hill at a fine pace.

"I'm going up to the organ-loft," said Fen, "to find out what can be seen from there." They all followed him, toiling up a long spiral staircase. Then, abruptly and without warning, they were there.

The cathedral was sunk in intense gloom. A few last rays of light still struck through the clerestory windows, resting upon capitals stiff with foliage. Enormous shadows moved and flitted with terrifying quickness. Geoffrey could dimly see the big four-manual console of the organ, the structure overhead which bore the tall, painted pipes, and, on his left, a large music cupboard standing against the brick partition which separated the organ-loft from the Bishop's Gallery. He went with Fen and the Inspector to the high wooden fencing which overhung the chancel, and hoisting themselves up, they peered down. Fen's powerful electric torch cut into the darkness; motes of dust glittered and drifted in the beam; the light created a new world of shadows about them.

And so it was that Geoffrey, looking down, and a little to the left below the Bishop's Gallery, saw the great stone slab which lay poised and rocking, so gently and slowly, on the ground below; glimpsed the huge cavity—the tomb of St. Ephraim—which it had filled; and, as the light shifted, saw the black shoe of a man projecting from beneath that immense stone.

A stifled exclamation came from the Inspector: "There's someone under there. It's . . ."

He stopped. On the far side of the chancel rattled the wards of a lock, and a door was pushed open. The returning constable, finding no one about, was entering the cathedral. He stopped, startled by the torchlight, looked swiftly up at the organ-loft, and, hand on truncheon, advanced a few steps into the nave.

"Potter!" the Inspector shouted. "Stay by that door! We'll be round in a moment. Don't move from it, and don't let anyone out!" His voice awoke a thousand mocking echoes in the empty building. The constable saluted and returned to the door.

In three minutes they were standing about the stone slab, and the thing which lay under it. Every possible exit from the cathedral was guarded, and no one could get out. The united efforts of all the men had failed to shift the stone more than an inch or two.

"It's uncanny," Fielding whispered to Geoffrey. "No one here, and that damn slab bursting out of the wall as if . . ." He stopped suddenly, and they both glanced at the ugly black cavity in the wall. In the circumstances no further comment was needed.

The Inspector wiped his brow.

"We shall need a crane to get this thing off," he muttered.. "And there's no chance he's still alive: it must have smashed every bone in his body. I suppose there's no doubt——?"

Fen shook his head. "Not very much, I should think. . . . First Brooks, and now Dr. Butler, the Precentor. . . ."

Chapter Seven

MOTIVE

"Look always on the motive, not the deed."
YEATS

WHEN FIELDING had finally been persuaded to go home:
"Resurrection men," said the Inspector agitatedly.
"That's what's going on. Two tombs opened in less than
an hour." He banged angrily on the table. I went up that
rope into Bishop's Gallery myself—like a Model Home
Exhibition, it was. Dust and cobweb of centuries neatly
swept into corners. And nothing there. Nor in that smelly
tomb place down the staircase. The bird's flown. Whatever
it was, gone." He lit a cigarette with as much ferocity as if
it had personally offended him.

Fen, his long, lanky body stretched in one of the clergy-
house armchairs, drank some whisky and stared blankly in
front of him. "Well, that's what we should have expected,
isn't it?" he enquired. "It shows at least that we're on the
right track." His face hardened. "A strange business, Garratt,—very strange. Almost too strange to be real. Accident? No, no. Suicide? Ridiculous. Murder impossible, I
should have said—and what a method!" He swallowed
more whisky, and gently mused.

It was close on midnight. With tremendous efforts the
slab had finally been moved, and the pitiful, mangled remains of the Precentor taken away. Inch by inch, the doors
guarded every moment, the cathedral had been searched,
and without result; Geoffrey felt he would never forget

101

that grotesque, torch-lit hunting. And now the cathedral was to be watched all night—a further search to be made in the morning. For, unless there was someone still trapped there, what explanation could there be . . . ?

He started when Fen spoke to him. "You told the girl?"

Geoffrey swallowed. "Yes; she was in the kitchen here. She—didn't say anything. I didn't know what to say, either."

"And the mother?"

The Inspector shifted uneasily. "Canon Spitshuker has gone. It seemed the best thing." For a minute they were all silent. "To-morrow, of course, we shall have to see her ourselves—we shall have to see everyone."

Fen said:

"You talked about resurrection men. Was either of the coffins disturbed?"

"No, no, sir," the Inspector replied. "Not that we could see. A way of speaking merely." He sat down, and said suddenly and frankly: "I haven't the beginnings of an idea about it."

"I have glimmerings," said Fen. He poured himself out some more whisky. "But the whole thing bristles so with problems that one doesn't know where to begin. Take the most obvious point. All the doors were locked, and not a key in any of them, inside or out. No one except Peace about when we got there. No one in the cathedral when we searched (and, incidentally, no chance for anyone to get out anywhere while we waited for a key). All of which seems to dispose of anyone's shoving the slab on top of the poor man. And then, in heaven's name, what murderer is going to get a six-ton slab moved out, climb into a tomb, have the slab put back, and crouch there until his victim happens to come along? It's daft."

"What happened to the padlocks?" asked Geoffrey.

"Don't introduce irrelevancies," said Fen severely. ("We found them piled in a corner," the Inspector explained rapidly.)

"Are you paying attention," grumbled Fen, "or are you not? I don't *expect* anyone to attend to my lectures at Oxford, though heaven knows I try to make them interesting, and it isn't my fault if I have to talk about rubbish like——" He checked himself abruptly. "What was I saying?"

"Nothing in particular."

Fen glared malignantly about him. "Well, *you* say something, then. No," he added hastily, suddenly recollecting something, "don't for heaven's sake say anything. I want to know what happened to your police guard, Garratt."

The Inspector moaned dismally. "They got a typewritten message, signed by me (not that it isn't easy for anyone to copy my signature if they want to), telling them to get into the car and meet me at once at Luxford, which is a village about fifteen miles away. Off they went, the cretins, and they've only just got back."

"But who gave them the message?"

"Well—that's the odd part of it. It was Josephine Butler —Dr. Butler's other daughter."

Fen whistled noisily. "Well, well!" he said. "This is getting interesting. And who gave it her?"

"We don't know about that yet. But she told the sergeant in charge that she got it from a policeman."

"A policeman!" exclaimed Fen in stupefaction. "You're not wandering in your mind, I suppose, Garratt?" he added with oily kindness. "You didn't send the message yourself?"

"No, of course I didn't," said the Inspector irritably. "And that's what makes it so queer. Why get my men out of the way in order to commit an impossible murder?"

"I should have thought that was an easy one," Geoffrey put in. "It was to give whoever was responsible a chance to get away with whatever it was they'd got in the Bishop's Gallery."

"Lucid," said Fen.

Geoffrey ignored this. "It rather makes one suspect that the two things aren't connected at all. The Precentor may have met his death by accident—in fact, it seems the only possible thing——"

Fen snorted explosively. "Accident!" he said. "Nonsense. Even if he'd unlocked the tomb himself and found the slab was falling out on him, he'd have tried to save himself. And he would have fallen *backwards,* with his head away from the tomb. In fact he was flat on his face, with his head turned slightly inwards towards it." He reflected. "You didn't find the keys to the padlocks, I suppose?"

The Inspector made negative signals. "Not a sign. That rather puts the accident business out of court, too. *Court*. Lunacy court, that's what we shall want. And there's this Brooks business. We haven't even made a start on *that* yet."

"One thing at a time," said Fen tediously. "If at first you don't succeed, try, try, try again." A more useful reflection occurred to him. "While we're on the subject of keys, by the way: who got into the cathedral by means of which keys?"

"Oh, yes, you were right there," said the Inspector grudgingly. They waited until he should explain this gnomic pronouncement, Fen muttering "I'm always right" under his breath. "The clergy-house key *was* gone again, and what's more, this time it hasn't turned up; so presumably the criminal or criminals used that. As to Dr. Butler, he used his own key. It was found"—he hesitated, as at a distasteful memory—"among his clothes. So that, again, is that."

Fen nodded. "No leads anywhere, it seems. A weird business." He gestured impatiently. "I can't somehow get over the feeling that the whole thing's an accident—that it wasn't intended that way. . . ."

"One other thing occurred to me," said Geoffrey. "And that is that anyone who was in the cathedral might have got out by climbing up a rope into the organ-loft, hiding there when we first came in to look round, and then getting out when we left."

"Not possible, sir," said the Inspector, relieved at the opportunity of making some contribution, however negative, to the proceedings. "For one thing, we should certainly have seen if anyone had been there. For another, there's nothing in that loft or around it to attach a rope to. The organ seat's loose, and can't be fixed, or at any rate hadn't been—I had a look for that—and there's nothing else that would take the strain, or that isn't out of the question for some reason or other. I shall go over the ground again to-morrow, of course, but you can take my word for it there isn't a chance."

"It wouldn't be possible to get in from the Bishop's Gallery?"

"Not unless you flew. You can't see round that partition between them, let alone *climb*—it projects quite a way, you'll find."

"So there's absolutely no way from the organ-loft—or the stairway leading up to it—into the main part of the building?"

"None, sir; you can rest assured of that." Geoffrey sighed, and abandoned his idea to the limbo of wasted and well-meaning endeavour.

"And in that case . . ." said Fen and the Inspector simultaneously; they hooked little fingers. "Shakespeare," said the Inspector. "Herrick," said Fen. "And I wish," he added, "that someone would come into this room now who would tell us what this thing is that everyone's so anxious to do murder for."

There was a knock on the door. If the Archangel Gabriel had appeared to announce personally his intention of blowing the last trump in ten minutes' time, Geoffrey could not have been more surprised. What actually happened was that a pale, spectacled young man put his head round the door, and having apparently ascertained that no special perils lurked within, followed it into the room. He was dressed in a slightly greasy overall suit, and carried in one hand a length of wire and in the other an open pen-knife. A cigarette hung unregarded from a corner of his mouth. When he spoke, it was in a vague, abstracted murmur, slightly tinged with a cockney accent.

"Inspector Garratt?" he enquired generally. The Inspector rose.

"Name's Phipps," murmured the young man, scraping at the wire with his pen-knife. "C.I.D., radio. Told me at station I'd find you here. Front door open, nobody about, so just walked in." The telescoping of inessential words gave his conversation a curiously telegrammatic effect. "Mind if I speak you alone a moment?"

The Inspector made brief apologies and followed the young man into the hall. For some minutes Fen and Geoffrey sat in silence, broken only twice, once by Fen saying "Wires," and later by his pointing to the ceiling and remarking: "Privet-Hawk Moth, *Sphinx ligustri*."

In due time the Inspector returned, without the young man; plainly he was much moved. He sat down with caution, stared at the carpet, and said: "That's torn it!" Fen sang a little tune to himself; when he had finished he said cheerfully:

"If it's what it obviously is, no wonder you look glum."

The Inspector looked up. "See here, sir, I oughtn't to tell you this, nor you, Mr. Vintner; but I'm damned if I'll keep it to myself, all the same. You've probably guessed. They've located an enemy transmitting-set here, and they've been trying to narrow it down for the last two days. Pretty unobtrusively they've worked, too—our people never noticed them. There'd been nothing for forty-eight hours, and then suddenly this evening there was a short flash." He nodded grimly. "Just after my men at the cathedral went off on that fool's errand. So it's obvious now what there was in the Bishop's Gallery, isn't it—or, rather, in the tomb down the spiral staircase? And as pretty a hiding-place as you could want, too. But what a nerve—phew!" He mopped his brow.

Fen nodded gently. He was engaged in a remote and pleased contemplation of the moth on the ceiling.

"But there's another thing," the Inspector went on, "which makes it nastier. That set could only have been operated at nights, and that means someone connected with the cathedral must be an enemy agent—someone with access to a key. . . ." His voice trailed off; in a little while he said: "Brooks found out what was going on, and he had to be silenced. And so, I fancy, did Dr. Butler. You understand, sir, that this puts things on a different footing altogether. I shall have to ask the Yard to come down now, as fast as they can travel. I can't deal with this. I should have had a job dealing with the murders, but spying . . ." He shook his head. "It'll have to be the Yard."

Without shifting his gaze, Fen drank half a glass of whisky. "How annoying," he said mildly.

"Really, Gervase," said Geoffrey in exasperation. "Surely, when matters are as serious as this, purely personal considerations . . ."

"No!" Fen howled; he howled with such suddenness that he startled even the moth, which dashed itself frantically against the window-curtains. "I will *not* be lectured!

106

I know it's very grave, and all that, but I shall only fuddle myself if I try to get solemn about it. I'm not going to abandon the habits of a lifetime just because a lot of rattish transcendentalist Germans happen to be pottering about in my neighbourhood. Kant!" he hooted disgustedly. "There's a passage in the *Kritik der Reinen Vernunft* where——"

"Yes, yes," said the Inspector. "But the fact remains: it'll have to be the Yard."

"Don't keep saying that," replied Fen irritably. "Who will they send, anyway? I hope it's someone I know. If I get some results before they arrive," he added hopefully, "they might let me be in at the death."

The Inspector got up. "I'm going to write up my notes and go to bed," he said. "It's no use trying to interview anyone to-night. I'll be round here at 9:30 to-morrow morning, and I shall be very grateful for any ideas you may have. The Yard people may be there by then"—("It'll have to be the Yard," said Fen irritatingly)—"and we shall see," concluded the Inspector without much confidence, "what we shall see. He picked up his hat and moved to the door. "Good night, gentlemen. Not much sleep for me, I fear."

Fen waved a languid hand from the depths of his chair. "Good night, sweet Inspector," he called. "Good night, good night." He finished his whisky; furrows of earnest concentration appeared on his brow. "An odd climax, that wireless business—or anti-climax. Unsatisfactory, like the end of *Measure for Measure*. This is a complex business, Geoffrey. There are oddities . . ."

Geoffrey yawned. "Lord, but I'm tired. What a day! I can't believe it's only this morning I got your telegram and that letter. God grant I never go through a day like this again." He rubbed his thighs ruefully, and wandered to the door. "Two threatening letters, three attacks; and then on top of that I meet an earl serving in a shop and a landlord like something out of Graham Greene, and I overhear a murder."

Fen smiled sweetly. "I wonder if you're right," he said. "Good night, Geoffrey. *'Let no lamenting cries, nor doleful tears be heard all night within, not yet without, nor let false whispers, breeding hidden fears, break gentle sleep with misconceived doubt; let no deluding dreams, nor dreadful sights make sudden sad affrights. . . .'"*

Geoffrey left him trying to catch the moth in an empty matchbox.

Grotesque, thought Geoffrey as he lay in bed next morning, gazing with earnest fixity at the ceiling: a preposterous gallimaufry of hobgoblins and spies. The murders were very well in their way; at least it was demonstrable that they had occurred. But ghosts were inconceivable, enemy agents almost equally so. Daylight, he reflected, restores us to sanity, or at least to that blinkered and oblivious condition which we call sanity. Impossible murders, even, would find it difficult to withstand the penetrating virility of morning light. Plainly, something had been overlooked, or absurdly misinterpreted. The German transmitting set would prove to be the fumblings of a schoolboy of mechanical proclivities. When one came down to facts—well, what? When one came down to facts, Geoffrey was forced to admit, the notorious antisepsis of daylight seemed somehow lacking in effect. Nothing, essentially, had changed since the previous night; the events of yesterday, which, it was evident, the mind was only too willing to write off as perfervid delusions of its own, stood dismayingly impervious to such high-handed attempts at erasure; furthermore, they intruded distressingly upon the mind's naïf and virginal projects for its own placidity during the coming hours—a moral hangover, a blotted and scrawled-upon sheet of the copy-book defying removal. It poisoned all enjoyment. Geoffrey's mood became noticeably more atrabilious. He contemplated with nothing less than malevolence the ravaging incursions of Id upon the tranquil expanses of his personality.

No lust for the hunt, no anguished endeavour to discover the truth possessed him, he observed; and that, presumably, was why he was still in bed. The room had the pervasive melancholy aura of the almost permanently unoccupied; a few personal belongings, scattered about, battled bravely but ineffectually to make of it a habitation. Plainly the atmosphere would drive him out of it fairly shortly. But before that happened, something remained to be debated. Long experience had taught Geoffrey that

108

mental colloquy, however confidently embarked upon, generally ended in irrelevancy, divagation and chaos; he did not, however, quite realise that it is impossible for a man to think clearly and rationally about a woman when lying in bed. The subsequent proceedings of his mind were therefore confused and for the most part unworthy of attention. It did, however, emerge from them that although he might be in love with Frances it seemed in the highest degree doubtful if she was in love with him; that the thing to do was to find out about this; and that the time to do it was not the morning after her father had met with a violent death. Thus supplied with a course of action and an excuse for putting off embarking on it almost indefinitely, Geoffrey decided that there was no point in lying on his back any longer, and got up.

He careened down the corridor to the bathroom, sponge-bag and towel flowing gently behind him. A faint scuffling from within, as of rats disturbed at a meal, showed it to be occupied, conceivably by Fen. Goeffrey cautiously pushed open the door, and was confronted by the spectacle of Dutton, his face covered with soap, a cut-throat razor brandished suicidally in the region of his jugular vein, and making gestures of vague pudency; Geoffrey retreated. "Breakfast is three-quarters of an hour's time," a voice pursued him back to his room. "Good morning," it added as an afterthought.

Dutton having taken himself off, Geoffrey lay in a hot bath and reflected further on the events of the previous night. And as he reflected, an idea came into mind. It was an idea so simple, so plain, so obvious, that he was unable to imagine why it had not occurred to him before. And the more he considered it, the more likely it seemed, though certainly there were smaller problems which it left unsolved. Not quite a closed box, after all; in fact, not a closed box at all. . . .

He was almost amiable when Fen came in, wearing a violent purple-silk dressing-gown, and looking ruddier, lankier, and more irrepressible than ever.

"I'm going to shave while you're having your bath," he announced threateningly. "Otherwise I shall be late for breakfast." He lathered soap all over his face, flinging it freely about the room, and began making long, tearing passes at his cheeks and throat with a safety-razor. "Did you have a good night? That moth I caught is dead this morning."

"I'm not surprised. Why do you pretend to be interested in insects?"

"Pretend?" Fen examined his face without much enthusiasm in the mirror. "I don't pretend. Essentially I am a scientist, beguiled by chances into the messy, delusive business of literary criticism. You can see that from the clarity and precision of my mind." He beamed at this triumph of autology. "And I don't deny there's a romantic interest as well. Life in the insect world is all melodrama—*The Revenger's Tragedy* without any of the talk."

"And a pretty daft business *that* would be," said Geoffrey. He fished for some invisible object by the side of the bath. "Here's a toy boat." He put it on the water and pushed it to and fro.

"The Elizabethans"—Fen was evasive—"were not strong on plot. . . . The strength of their drama lay in the now lost art of rhetoric. They recognised the superiority of word over action as a means to enjoyable sensations. The Elizabethan groundling was a superior person, in point of culture, to the educated *bourgeois* of to-day." He paused, and dabbed styptic pencil on a cut. "Whose boat is that, I wonder?"

"Josephine Butler's, I expect: a relic of nonage." Geoffrey was engaged in squeezing water on to it from his sponge, in the hope of capsizing it. "Your grounding had no sense of humour, though. Otherwise he'd never have put up with Beatrice and Benedick." He surveyed the boat thoughtfully, and balanced a piece of soap on the deck; it fell off. "You heard about Josephine's burning her father's manuscript?"

"And being smacked? Yes. It doesn't seem to have much to do with anything. I should like to know what the manuscript was. Garbin would know—or Spitshuker. And it's odd she should have taken that message to the police at the cathedral. Again, it may not mean anything. There are too many peripheral elements in this thing. This centre's a nice convenient blank; the circumference swarms with cryptic sign-boards and notices."

"I think I have an idea."

"It's sure to be a wrong one." Fen blew powder on to his chin from a surgical-looking rubber bulb such as hairdressers use. He bundled his things indiscriminately into his sponge-bag.

"Don't you want to know what my idea is?"

"No," said Fen in parting, "I don't. And if you stay in that bath much longer you won't get any breakfast, I can tell you that. There's an idea for you to be going on with." He laughed irritatingly, and went out.

For Geoffrey, the choosing of a tie had developed into an elaborate ceremonial, involving reference to his suit and shirt, to the weather, and to an imperfect memory of what he had worn during the preceding ten or fourteen days. On this particular morning, having returned with some sense of anti-climax to the tie he had first selected, he gazed for rather longer than usual at his reflection in the dressing-table mirror. The impact of womanhood on one's life, he reflected, is to make one rather more attentive to one's imperfections than is normal. None the less, he *did* look at least ten years younger than his age; the slightly faun-like mischievousness of his face was, he supposed, not unattractive; light-blue eyes and close-cropped brown hair had, without doubt, their charms. . . From these complacent reflections he was interrupted by a subterranean booming which he supposed must mean breakfast. He bent his attention painfully upon the outside world again, and hurried downstairs.

Frances, he knew, would not be there; she had returned to spend the night with her mother, leaving a not inadequate old person of simple appearance to hold the fort in the meanwhile. Fen was already in the breakfast-room when Geoffrey arrived, gazing with every appearance of interest at a morning paper. Dutton shortly appeared, arranging freshly-cut flowers in a bowl with a curiously feminine competence and delicacy. They sat down to porridge, Dutton plainly feeling it incumbent on him, as the only resident present, to lead the conversation. After several false starts, he achieved the statement that it was a terrible thing. This as it happened was unfortunate, since conventional expressions were seldom a success with Fen. He regarded Dutton with interest.

"Is it? Is it?" he said, waving his spoon and scattering

111

milk about the table-cloth. "I knew very little about Dr. Butler. Not a communicative man, I should have said, or one easy to get on with."

Dutton looked cautiously at his plate; plainly he was considering the wisdom and propriety of discussing the dead man. "Uncommunicative, yes," he admitted eventually. "And liable for that reason to be—traduced." He offered this linguistic triumph with modest pride. Fen's interest grew. He said:

"He wasn't popular, then?"

Dutton scurried to cover his tracks. "I should hardly put it as strongly as that. About a man in his position there are always misunderstandings." A wave of blushes passed up his face and were engulfed in his ginger hair. It was very awkward. Fen, possessed of little patience at the best of times, abandoned finesse and said:

"For heaven's sake, don't hedge. What I want"—he pointed his spoon at the alarmed sub-organist—"is to hear what you know of the relations of all the people round here with the dead man." He became acrimonious. "You'll have to tell the police if they ask, so you may as well tell me. Cast off this skin of discretion," he added, waxing suddenly eloquent; and then, returning abruptly to a more homely plane: "Good heavens, man; don't you *like* gossiping about other people's affairs?"

It seemed that a powerful conflict was raging within Dutton's soul, between discretion and shyness on the one hand, and the desire to be friendly, and the centre of importance, on the other. Quite suddenly, the second party won, and he began to talk, and with hesitation at first, and then, as he found he was enjoying himself, with some zest and vigour. Fen and Geoffrey had little to do except. sit and listen.

"Dr. Butler," Dutton said, "made himself out to be, first and foremost, a scholar. As to what he was studying, I'm a bit vague, but I think it was something to do with theology. Garbin's a strong man in that line, too—I believe his book on the Albigensian heresy is *the* work on the subject—and he always maintained that the Precentor's scholarship was half bogus. They had quarrels—one in particular over some important incunabulum which Garbin was editing for the Press and which the Precentor

112

cribbed from for an article in a learned magazine: I think Garbin nearly gave up his prebend because of that. When Dr. Butler died they were both working on a book on the same subject more or less, and the rivalry was terrific." Dutton considered. "I don't know that that would be a motive for murder, though, particularly if Garbin's scholarship was as much superior as he pretended it was."

"We think we know the motive," said Fen, "but I want to get a general picture of all these people. Go on."

"The Precentor quarrelled with poor Brooks over the music, but then precentors and organists are always at loggerheads. I must say, though, that Dr. Butler was quite exceptionally high-handed about the music. But Brooks was a bit of a tactician, and he generally got his own way in the end. Spitshuker and Butler got on well enough on the whole, though Spitshuker's practically an Anglo-Catholic, and Butler was always complaining to the Dean and the Bishop about it, but it never had any effect. He bossed the minor canons about a bit, too. I don't know that there's much else. He seemed to get on all right with his wife and family"—Dutton paused—"at any rate until that Josephine business yesterday. She burned his manuscript, you know—the younger daughter, that is— then ran away round here, and he followed her and gave her the hiding of her life. I must say I think she deserved it."

"How long had he been here?" asked Fen.

"About seven years, I think. He may have had a living before that—I don't know. Anyway, he had pots of money of his own—or, rather, I think it came from his wife. He used to potter about the Continent from library to library—the whole family were in Germany for two years some time in the 'thirties. He was quite poor before he married—scholarship boy, son of a cobbler, or something like that—and I think the money rather went to his head."

An elephant-bell like an inverted sea-anemone, of Birmingham manufacture, summoned in the bacon and eggs; a malodorous alchemistic contrivance for the brewing of coffee was set in reluctant motion. These disturbances over, Dutton returned to his tale.

"Mrs. Butler one can't say much about: she's a little

unobstrusive woman without much character of her own. I think he used to bully her rather. Josephine's always been a wild, headstrong girl; she's likely to grow into the sort of woman who'll do anything for a thrill. She used to get some of the poorer kids in the neighbourhood together into gangs and fight round the neighbourhood—sometimes fight nastily and dangerously. But when it came to doling out responsibility she was always the picture of innocence and her father, who doted on her, would never do anything about it.

"Frances"—the young man paused and blushed faintly. "I don't know that I can say anything about her. She—she's a dear." Here, Geoffrey thought, is unassuming adoration; he was unsurprised, but obscurely the fact troubled him.

"Savernake?" asked Fen, piloting the conversation with laborious care over these quicksands. "What about him?"

"July's a pleasant chap—a bit stupid sometimes, that's all. He's—*was*—by way of being a protégé of Dr. Butler's. He's got the living at Maverley, a few miles out from here. Doesn't seem to spend much time there, though." There was a shade of disapproval in Dutton's voice; evidently he thought severely of such negligence.

"Leaves his sheep encumbered in the mire," put in Fen by way of apposition; then, seeing that the allusion wasn't recognised, became gloomy.

"I've an idea that relations between July and the Precentor were getting strained," Dutton went on. "July wasn't all that Dr. Butler expected him to be. Also"—he hesitated—"July's in love with Frances, and wanted to marry her. For some reason, Dr. Butler wouldn't hear of it—probably suspected he was after the money, or something." A thought struck him. "I suppose they'll be able to get married after all."

Geoffrey contemplated this prospect without pleasure. The possibility of serious rivalry had not hitherto occurred to him. Decidedly, it was disturbing. Dutton was saying:

"Peace I don't know anything about; it seems he's a successful psychoanalyst." He pronounced the word cautiously, as though fearing it might be too much for his auditors. "Spitshuker and Garbin . . . they're always arguing, but actually they get on very well together. Spit-

114

shuker's family's always been rich, and always connected with the Church; he's had an easy, placid life—never got married, he says because of his convictions, but actually I expect it's because no one would have him." He flushed with pleasure at this ingenuous exhibition of worldly wisdom. "Garbin's rather the opposite—a scholarship boy from a poor family with a personal and not a traditional inclination towards the Church. I've told you what he thought about the Precentor. Mrs. Garbin's a shrew—tries to run everything and everybody, including her husband. Curiously enough she hardly succeeds at all: interfering but ineffectual. He's always put up a solid show of passive resistance, and she's come to leave him more or less alone nowadays. She didn't like Dr. Butler, but then"—Dutton frowned in perplexity—"it's difficult to see that she likes anyone very much."

"Soured by a childless marriage?" said Fen.

"Oh, no: there are three children, two boys and a girl. Garbin wanted the boys to go into the Church, but they wouldn't. You know how it is." Dutton waxed philosophic. "Isn't it Anatole France who says that the opinions sons get from their fathers are identically opposite, like the cup moulded by the artist on his mistress' breast?" Suddenly confronted with the enormity of what he had said, Dutton blushed again, and shamefastly restored this treasure of analogy to the private quarters of his mind. "Anyway, the sons are in the Forces—I don't know about the daughter; I've never seen any of them." He hesitated. "Is there anyone else?"

"Sir John Dallow," Geoffrey put in.

"The Chancellor—oh, yes. He's rich, too, but as mean as Shylock." Dutton's discursion was beginning to be enlivened by literary allusions. "He hasn't an awful lot to do, nowadays, of course, though when there was a choir-school he was in charge of that. He's ordained, but he's never 'in residence' nowadays. He's been gradually unfrocking himself, as it were, over a period of years." Dutton waved his hands, to indicate a process of unobtrusive divestiture. "He's an expert on witchcraft, demonolatry —all that stuff. Another of these bachelors, too." From his tone it was evident that he regarded bachelorhood as *ipso facto* an evil condition. It occurred to Geoffrey that a flame of pure connubial idealism burned probably in the young man's breast.

Fen nodded sagely over his toast and marmalade. "That's the lot, I think, since the Bishop and Dean are away. And now one or two points about yesterday, if you don't mind. Brooks was killed at about six. Where were you then?"

"Out—walking."

"Alone?"

Dutton nodded. "I'm afraid so. I find it difficult to know what to do with myself now that music's forbidden me. I was on the cliffs—towards Tolnmouth."

"And last night—shortly after ten?"

"In my room, reading."

"Did you have the window open?"

Dutton looked perplexed. "Yes. It was a hot evening."

"And did you hear the crash when the slab of that tomb fell?"

"No. Not a sound."

Fen finished his coffee and got up. "Thanks very much," he said. "And now, alas! to work—dishonest, assuming work." Geoffrey and Dutton also rose. Shyness was again engulfing Dutton like a mantle. He hovered about, finally thrusting forward desperately a chromium cigarette-case. They lit their cigarettes. A silence fell.

"Well, I . . ." said Dutton. He shifted his feet. "I think I have some things to do in my room."

This palpable falsehood was received in stony silence Dutton became frantic, in a subdued manner. He tottered towards the door, paused and turned uncertainly; and, finally, saying "If you'll excuse me," in a low tone, made a dash for it and got out.

They sighed with relief. "How infectious embarrassment is," said Fen. And Geoffrey:

"He really is rather weird. But the life of a sub-organist is not a happy one. They never have the last word about anything, so they never get any confidence in themselves. Probably next to no money, either—poor as the proverbial church mouse. In fact," said Geoffrey reflectively, "now I come to think of it, Dutton *is* the proverbial church mouse."

"Natural shyness," said Fen, "is a superb disguise. And

shy people have a penchant towards cunning. They must, somehow, *act*, and since they daren't act in ways that people can see—in the open, as it were . . . What a lot of hooey I'm talking," he added moodily. "Sounds like the sort of stuff Peace turns out. Come on, we must go." He looked at his watch. "The Inspector out to be here by now. Thanks to Dutton, we know something about the people were're going to see. Did you notice rather an interesting thing in that account?"

"No. What?"

"About his not hearing the crash."

"Is that important?"

"I'm pretty certain it is."

Chapter Eight

TWO CANONS

"ITHA. *Look, look, master; here comes two rellglous*
 caterpillars.
"BARA. *I smelt 'em ere they came.*"

MARLOWE

"A PLEASANT MORNING."

The Inspector's voice thus greeted them as they passed
up the clergy-house drive towards the road. It held a hint
of complacency, as if the pleasantness of the morning
were somehow of his own contriving. And certainly it
was another glorious day, promising much heat and discomfort later on, but for the present as perfect as any
man could desire. Tolnbridge sunned itself, opulently and
lazily. Its colours took on a new freshness. The estuary
glittered—silver tinsel on a vivid blue—and the explosions
of the engines of the outgoing fishing boats proceeded
peaceably from it. Beyond them, a minute grey warship
lay at anchor. The cathedral itself achieved in the sunlight such grace and lightness that it seemed likely at any
moment to be transmuted into a fairy place and float
gently away into some Arcady, some genial Poictesme.
Decidedly, a pleasant morning.

It soon appeared, however, that the Inspector's comment
was less self-congratulatory than a propitiating gambit
in a difficult game. He had rung up the Yard, he said, join-
ing to this statement a good deal of devious rambling fantasy; they were sending a man down to-day; and—here
the Inspector's unease became acute—they considered
that unauthorised persons should be absolutely excluded

from any subsequent investigations which might be made.

"The boot," said Fen. *"Anathema sumus."*

"You see my position, sir," said the Inspector. Plainly he regretted the outcome as much for himself as for Fen. "As it is, they're not at all pleased that you know as much as you do. I suppose"—he stared at Fen unhappily—"I shouldn't have let either of you in on that radio business." He stared still harder, becoming acutely unhappy.

Fen's spirits, however, were normally raised rather than lowered by adverse circumstances. "Inspector," he said with evil glee, "I'll beat you to it. Bet you I get the murderer before you do."

The Inspector nodded pathetic assent. "Very probably, sir. You can't be much further off from it than I am at the moment. And, of course"—his eyes twinkled momentarily—"I can't stop you going round asking people questions if they're prepared to answer them."

"Have you," said Fen, "got any new information you can give us before the interdict comes into force? Or is it in force already?"

The Inspector peered anxiously about him; he appeared to be seeking for evidences of an ambush. Then, spectacularly lowering his voice, he said:

"I've had a go at that kid Josephine this morning. Would you believe it, the little devil still insists that message was given her by a policeman."

"Perhaps it was."

"No: she's obviously lying. But I'm darned if I know how to get the truth out of her. As far as I can see, if she chooses to stick to that story, there's absolutely nothing we can do about it."

"It's odd," said Fen. "I wonder why——?" He shook his head vigorously. "Anything else?"

"Nothing. The *post mortem's* this morning at eleven, and there'll certainly have to be an inquest. God knows what verdict they'll bring in—we can't help them. *Is* there any other way of violent death except murder, accident and suicide? They all look equally impossible."

"It was murder all right," said Fen with an exuberance unjustified by the nature of the statement. "Oh, by the way. You didn't, I suppose *trace* that radio in any way? There must have been a car to take it away. It occurs to me, too, that they must have been a fair time about it. All this whipping transmitting sets in and out of cathedrals must be quite a business. Surely there'd be aerials, or something?"

"Anyway, we didn't trace it," said the Inspector. It was evident that he was sinking to hitherto unplumbed depths of pessimism. "Nor was there anyone in the cathedral when we searched again this morning." He steeled himself reluctantly to action. "I must be off."

"Where are you going first? We don't want our interviews to clash. What a silly waste of energy," said Fen in a pained voice. "Interviewing everyone twice. We're going to Garbin."

"All right," said the Inspector. "Then I'll see Mrs. Butler. It doesn't seem to matter much what order one takes them in."

"I wish," put in Geoffrey, "that you could do something about the landlord of the 'Whale and Coffin.' "

"*Do* something, sir? Do what? Arrest him because he happened to know your Christian name? God love us," said the Inspector with feeling, "the things people expect one to do."

"Farewell, Inspector, and God 'ild you," said Fen. "We meet," he added grandiosely, "at Philippi."

"Colney Hatch, more like," said the Inspector.

Parting, however, was not to be yet. They were interrupted by the bustling advent of Canon Spitshuker, greatly out of breath.

"Wanted to catch Mr. Vintner," he gasped. "Music . . . organist . . . services." He paused to recover himself, and went on more coherently: "Since the terrible events of last night, the duties of Precentor have temporarily devolved upon me. Mr. Vintner"—he paused and wiped his forehead with a large purple handkerchief—"it will, in view of the circumstances, be *said* Mattins this morning——"

The Inspector interrupted. "Good heavens, sir," he said aghast, "you're not proposing to hold your service this morning as usual?"

"My dear Garratt, of course."

"But really, sir, after what has happened——"

A tinge of impatience came into the Canon's voice. "The Church does not *suspend* the worship of God on any

121

and every pretext. And if ever there was a time when our prayer and praise were needed, surely it is now."

"Praise!" The Inspector's voice was unexpectedly bitter.

"My dear Inspector, I have simply not the time to argue with your doubtless ridiculous notions about God allowing evil, and so forth. Now, Mr. Vintner——"

"But look, sir." The Inspector was mildly exacerbated. "There's the mess—the confusion . . ."

"That has all been cleared up."

"I beg your pardon?"

"Our cleaners have dealt with it. There is only the slab to put back."

"God have mercy," said the Inspector. "The things people do behind one's back."

Canon Spitshuker looked faintly puzzled. "I fear it was done on my authority. Surely . . . surely I have done nothing wrong?"

"You may have destroyed valuable evidence, sir."

"It could hardly be *left,* though, could it, Inspector? . . . Dear me." Spitshuker seemed perturbed. "And I never dreamed . . . Still, what's done's done."

"No use crying over spilt milk," put in Fen tediously.

"And now, Mr. Vintner: sung Evensong at 3:30, and the choir will be at your disposal at 2.0. Poor Brooks had his practices in the old chapter house—there is a good piano there. Now let me see." He felt in a pocket and produced a bundle of service sheets, among which he scrabbled unsystematically until he found the one he wanted. "For this afternoon we have down Noble in B Minor, and Sampson's *Come, My Way.* All quite familiar to the boys, I think." He thrust the sheaf at Geoffrey. "The music for future services is noted here. I leave it to you to make an alterations that you think fit." He made movements of hasty departure.

"One moment, sir." It was the Inspector. "Did you say you'd made arrangements to have the slab put back?"

Perturbation and alarm again appeared on Spitshuker's rubicund face. "I have, certainly, though if you think it will destroy evidence . . ." (Was there a hint of sarcasm in his voice? Geoffrey wondered.) "Still, it would hardly be desirable to hold Mattins with the tomb gaping open, would it?" He smiled innocently.

"If it hasn't been done already, sir, I should like to be present. There are certain tests I wish to make." The Inspector's manner was markedly stiff and official.

"By all means. By all means." Spitshuker looked agitated. "I promised to superintend the work myself." He glanced at his watch. "But we must hurry. Mattins is in less than an hour."

In the cathedral they found a group of men gazing at the fallen slab without enthusiasm, under the eye of the Verger. For the first time Geoffrey was able to examine properly the tomb of St. Ephraim. From the space beneath the spire, where the transepts joined the main body of the cathedral, a short flight of steps led up into the chancel; but the stalls of the choir, and of the cathedral officers, were placed some way further to the east, beginning just below the organ-loft. Beneath the Bishop's Gallery, hollowed from the wall, was the cavity of the tomb. The fallen slab normally filled it. In its edges were embedded iron rings, corresponding with others in the edges of the slab, so that when this was in position a large padlock could be passed through each pair to hold it firm. The cavity, though quite shallow, was about ten feet in length and six in height, and the slab was proportionately thick. Amid a good deal of premonitory groaning, it was hoisted upright, and eventually, with titanic efforts, lifted into its cavity. It fitted quite loosely, Geoffrey noticed, the lower edge between two and three feet from the ground, the upper some six feet higher. The Inspector had a chair brought and stood on it, motioning the men away with one hand and holding the slab in position with the other. Then with infinite slowness and caution he withdrew his hand. As yet unanchored by its padlocks, the slab swayed ever so slightly, delicately poised on its narrow base; but it showed no sign of falling, of its own accord. The Inspector grunted.

"Wouldn't take much to topple that out," he said. He got down from the chair.

Fen had been unwontedly silent and attentive during these proceedings. Geoffrey stepped back and spoke to him. "Explosive charge inside?" he asked. "Even though the slab doesn't fit exactly, the tomb would be pretty well air-tight."

Fen shook his head. "There'd be obvious traces. Any sort of mechanism's out of the question for the same reason."

Geoffrey glanced up to the Bishop's Gallery above. "Could it be pushed out, by a long pole or something, from there?"

Again Fen shook his head, and pointed. "That projection would stop it. And besides, think of the complications. Very unlikely. And you'd still have to account for how the person concerned got out of the cathedral. The wall between the Bishop's Gallery and the organ is solid brick, remember."

"I think I know," said Geoffrey, "how someone could have got out of the cathedral." Mentally, he fondled his cherished Idea. Fen gazed at him kindly.

"You mean Peace, of course. Just after the crash we find him wandering on the other side of the cathedral. Why shouldn't he just have come out, locking the door after him, and throwing away the key in case anyone should take it into his head to search him? Why indeed? The only snag is that it doesn't fit in with anything else we know about the case."

Geoffrey was peeved at having his thunder stolen; he made obstinate mental reservations, highly unwilling to have his Idea thus facilely disposed of. But he made no comment, since the Inspector was about to make another experiment. The group of men who had hoisted the slab into position, and who had been hanging about since exhibiting that gentle, inane interest in the goings-on of others which is one of the main-stays of the English character, showed as he explained his intentions stupefaction and gloom. He was proposing, in fact, to allow the slab to fall out again.

This, however, was a more difficult operation than at first appeared, chiefly because the slab rested quite flat in its cavity and offered no projection by which it could be pulled. Eventually the Inspector inserted a steel ruler into one side, and standing as far clear as he could, used it as a lever. Slowly the great stone moved, toppled. They watched in frozen silence. The fall at first was slow, rapidly gathering a tremendous momentum. Just before it reached the horizontal, Geoffrey noted, the lower edge came away from the shelf on which it rested. And the terrifying, stealthy silence of it! In a moment it lay flat on the ground, the chair which had been left beneath it crushed to splinters.

The noise of the impact was shattering, and yet . . . Somehow, Geoffrey thought, it was different from what he had heard the previous evening. The deadening effect of walls and doors might account for the disparity, but it was not exactly that. Perplexed, he watched the herculean heavings and groanings begin anew; perplexed, he saw the six padlocks inserted to hold the slab in position, and the remnants of the chair cleared away. The Inspector, apparently satisfied, made off on his own. Fen and Spitshuker, engaged in conversation, were walking towards the door. After a last look round Geoffrey joined them.

". . . A few questions," Fen was saying as they came out into the sunlight, "which I hope you won't regard as impertinent." The apology was conventional, and sounded it. "And I think you ought to know," he added, with an unwonted spasm of honesty, "that I'm no longer collaborating with the police."

Spitshuker clucked simultaneous dismay and assent. "But my dear fellow . . . of course. The police have thrown over your offer of assistance?" He made clicking noises with his tongue. "Scandalous, scandalous." This, too, seemed a trifle less than sincere. "Of course I will answer any questions. If you wish, I will walk with you towards Garbin's house. I am 'in residence' at the moment, so I have to say Mattins, but that is not for half an hour yet." He gathered his short coat about his portly little figure, and walked down the cathedral hill with them.

"Mainly about times," said Fen. "Six o'clock, and ten to ten-fifteen yesterday evening."

Spitshuker looked up quizzically. "You are trying to establish alibis," he stated with evident enjoyment. "I have none for six o'clock. I was alone in my room, working, at that hour. My housekeeper was in the house, but she cannot possibly vouch for me." He seemed to regard this as a matter for some pride. "Between ten and a quarter-past I was talking to the Inspector in the clergy-house drawing-room. About seven I had set out with Garbin to dine at the clergy-house, and after dinner, when

125

Dallow had given us the terrible news about poor Brooks, we held our little conclave—Dallow, Garbin, Butler and myself."

"Ah, yes." Fen was pensive. "I'm interested in this meeting."

"Unofficial. A purely unofficial affair. Of course the Dean and the Bishop have been communicated with, and are returning at once." The parenthesis confused the Canon, and he paused doubtfully. "The meeting was called when there was, as yet, no question of murder, merely this . . . accident which had occurred to Brooks, and which necessitated a little rearrangement among ourselves. We had intended, as it were, to clear the ground a little before the Dean returned. I fear that nothing very useful was said. The greater part of the meeting was taken up by a squabble between Dallow and Butler about the legal and financial position of the resident organist, and by some unavailing attempts at armchair detection on the part of Garbin."

"Not a very brotherly affair, in fact?"

"There was, perhaps, a slight undercurrent of unfriendly feeling." Spitshuker hesitated, himself somewhat taken aback, one fancied, by this flagrant understatement. "Nothing, of course, was decided—about anything." He smiled faintly. "The upshot of it was Butler's announcing that fatal intention of going up to the cathedral and stopping there alone. Had we not been in such a te—had we considered a little, I should say, we should probably not have allowed him to go."

"The meeting ended at what time?"

"About ten to nine, I should say. Yes, that would be it."

"And did anyone else in the house know of Dr. Butler's intention?"

"Everyone, I fancy. He met Frances in the hall, talking to Peace on some trivial matter, as he went out, and informed them. Dutton, I think, was lurking about, too."

"I thought he went early to bed," Geoffrey interposed.

"Dutton, I suspect, does not go to bed without extensive preliminary reconnoitring." Spitshuker nodded his approval of this cryptic comment. "At all events, there he was. I

126

remember noticing him when Butler was arranging to meet Peace up at the cathedral——"

"When *what?*"

Spitshuker was all mild-eyed innocence. "You didn't know? To discuss some business matter, I think it was. Butler suggested that Peace should follow him in about twenty minutes' time and Peace agreed, but I fear we sat so long talking together that it was close on ten o'clock before he——"

"Oh, my dear paws!" Fen exclaimed. "Oh, my fur and whiskers! I knew it. I knew something of the sort——" He checked himself, and asked urgently: "What happened to everybody after the meeting broke up?"

Spitshuker considered. "Dallow and Garbin, as far as I know, went straight home, Butler to the cathedral. I think Frances went to her room with a book. Dutton somehow faded out of the picture. I walked with Butler as far as the gate which leads from the clergy-house garden on to the cathedral hill. I thought he seemed moody, depressed, and a little nervous. I remember that as we stood chatting at the gate he picked a four-leaf clover to put in his buttonhole, which surprised me, because he was always inveighing against such superstitions. But as I say, he appeared nervous. Then I went back and talked to Peace."

"We know about all that," said Fen. "Savernake?"

"I've no idea. He disappeared immediately after dinner, I fancy." Spitshuker looked at his watch. "You must forgive me if I turn back now. I hope I have been of assistance." He smiled and, suddenly, was gone.

Fen seemed little inclined to talk as they walked on; conceivably he was reflecting on what he had heard. Geoffrey, too, reflected, but without much enlightenment, and fell to wondering at the general lack of extreme distress over the Precentor's death. If Spitshuker had been labouring under a burden of emotion, he had not shown it.

"Curious," said Geoffrey, "that all the Butler family should have been in Germany before the war."

"It has its interest," Fen replied. "But for all we know, *everyone* here may have been in Germany. Spitshuker was instructive, don't you think?"

Geoffrey frowned ponderously. "Possibly," he said with judicial caution. "He went off in a hurry. Were you going to ask him anything else?"

"One or two things," said Fen non-committally. "Whether he was an accomplished church musician, for one."

"Good heavens, why?"

Fen grinned. "That surprises you? It's half a shot in the dark, so I don't wonder. By the way, you might scribble down what people say they were doing at crucial times. It'll be useful for reference. I don't think it's much use trying to pry into alibis on the night Brooks was attacked in the cathedral. If people weren't in bed alone all night, then they ought to have been." He frowned puritanically.

Garbin's house and garden were pervasively humid and melancholy. The first characteristic, in view of the unexampled brilliance of the weather, it was difficult to account for; but no other word would describe the listless, damp impression made by the overgrown flowerbeds and drooping foliage which greeted Fen and Geoffrey as they turned in at the gate. In this riot of greenery, through which struggled an occasional misguided and feeble blossom in search of the light, Niobe must surely have wandered, all tears. Even the singing of the birds was without spirit, a mere dejected gurgle.

And the house was no better. Its grey walls seemed to sweat dampness. Large, Victorian and ugly, its windows stared upon the world with frank misanthropy. Were it not attached to his prebend, surely Garbin would not live in it. And yet a subtle affinity existed between the man and the house, a fundamental dull seriousness of outlook, and behind this a complacent if melancholy resignation to things as they were. So at least it appeared; but Geoffrey reminded himself that, here and now, no appearance could be trusted.

Mrs. Garbin opened the door to them, dressed in a suit of drab chocolate-brown. If she was surprised to see in Geoffrey her travelling-companion of the day before, she gave no sign of it. Her husband, she said, was working; not, one gathered from her tone, at anything that was ever likely to be the slightest use to anyone, even himself. No doubt he would be delighted to see them; it was one of the penances of a clergyman's life that he must always be available to anyone who chose to call; fortunately, he had nothing else to occupy him.

To this underhanded series of attacks, Fen replied monosyllabically. Before they were taken into Garbin's study he did, however, stop to say:

"You must feel Dr. Butler's death as a great loss."

The woman paused. "Of course," she said. "A very great loss indeed—to ourselves. It is possible that others may not be so greatly affected."

"A popular man, I thought."

"A man of strong personality, Professor. And you know what is commonly meant by personality—an obstinate blindness and lack of consideration. There were, of course, antagonisms."

"Serious antagonisms?"

"That, of course, it is hardly my business to say." She paused. "The Romish practices of Canon Spitshuker——"

"And the scholarly rivalry of your husband . . ."

She put a hand on the banisters. The pallor of her face was perhaps a little accentuated. "You had better go in now."

Garbin's study was a large room, unpleasantly panelled in dark pine. Massive mahogany furniture and bookcases added to the gloom. A dark brown carpet was on the floor. There were worn armchairs and a rack of pipes and a pallid bust of Pallas—or more probably of some dead ecclesiastic, since both sex and features were indistinguishable in the crepuscular light—in a niche above the door. And there, great heavens—Geoffrey felt the sense of unreality which one has immediately on waking from a vivid dream—was a raven. It perambulated the desk with that peculiar gracelessness which walking birds have, ruffled its feathers, and stared malignantly at the intruders.

"You're looking at my pet." Garbin rose from his chair as they came in, his tall, sombre form towering over the desk. "An unusual fancy, some people think. But he came to me quite by chance."

"Indeed?"

Garbin motioned them to chairs. A foreign sailor with

129

a tragic history sold him to me some two years ago. He is supposed to speak, I think, but I have never heard him do so. He is not"—Garbin paused—"a *companionable* creature, I admit. Sometimes I find his presence actually depressing. I have given him every chance to escape, but he displays only apathy." He stretched out a hand to stroke the bird's feathers. It pecked at him.

Fen, however, plainly was not moved by this recital. "We've come to talk about Butler's death," he said firmly. "There are some odd features about it, and I'm conducting a sort of unofficial investigation of my own." His eye strayed to the bird, and then hastily withdrew. "I don't know if you'd care to co-operate?"

Disconcertingly, Garbin regarded him in silence for a moment. Then he shifted in his chair, to indicate that he was about to speak. "Do you think it wise," he asked in his deep, slow voice, "to pry into these things? Surely the responsible authorities are capable of dealing with it."

"Possibly." Fen's admission was reluctant. "But I should hesitate to rely on them."

"I know you regard this sort of thing as a sport, Mr. Fen. Frankly, I cannot do so. The death of a man seems to me the poorest excuse for a display of personal ability. You will forgive my speaking so frankly."

Fen regarded him thoughtfully. "And you will allow me the same liberty, I'm sure. I shall say that the murder of a man is so serious a business that it concerns everyone who can possibly help in any way, and particularly those who, like myself, have had some experience of these things."

Garbin raised an eyebrow. "Your own vanity is not implicated in any way?"

Fen gestured impatiently. "One's vanity is implicated in everything, as Rochefoucauld pointed out. Action from pure motives simply does not exist."

"There are degrees of purity, none the less."

Fen stood up. "There seems little point in continuing this conversation."

"Please, please." Garbin waved a hand. "If I was offensive, I apologise. You must remember that I belong to a generation, and a calling, whose standards are strict. Rochefoucauld was not a Christian. Christianity maintains

130

that for a man to act from wholly disinterested motives is possible. Take that away, and the whole fabric of Christian morality falls apart."

"You did not consider it a disinterested action when Butler stole your ideas?"

"The inquisition has begun, I see," said Garbin drily. "No, naturally I did not. But it was forgivable, because Butler was no scholar—he hadn't the temperament. A *poseur* must plagiarise, or he can produce nothing."

"That's a harsh judgment, surely?"

"Perhaps so. God forbid that I should judge anyone. I should have said that—well, that what Butler undertook was beyond his capacities. His sail was too big for his boat."

"Still, you considered his thefts morally reprehensible?"

"Naturally." Garbin smiled slightly. "But surely you're not here to hold an enquiry into my moral standards. I bore him no lasting resentment, if that's what you mean."

The raven rose from the desk, and with a whirring of wings that sounded like a berserk mowing-machine, flew and perched on the bust above the door. Fen and Geoffrey eyed it in fascination. "A literary fowl," Fen murmured; then returned with somewhat of an effort to the matter in hand.

"Mainly," he said, "one wants to know about movements during yesterday."

"Ah, yes." Garbin put the tips of his fingers together. "At six o'clock, the time when poor Brooks was killed, I was alone here. Lenore was out to dinner and bridge——"

"*Who?*" The word burst from Geoffrey before he could stop himself.

"Lenore—my wife. So I have no alibi for that time. Between ten and a quarter past——"

Fen interrupted. "How about between nine and ten?"

The question evidently surprised Garbin as much as it did Geoffrey; he hesitated, slightly but visibly, before replying. "I left the clergy-house shortly before nine, after Butler had announced his intention of going up to the cathedral. I went for a walk along the cliffs."

"You overheard the arrangement Butler made to meet Peace up at the cathedral?"

"I could hardly avoid it. I fancy everyone did."

"May I ask what was said at the meeting?"

"I hardly think that concerns the death of Butler in any way."

"As you please. But did Butler by any chance say he had definite knowledge about the death of Brooks?"

"Since you ask—no."

Fen nodded. "It might have been necessary," he said, half to himself. "But that depends on the exact time the police guard left. . . . I must find out."

On its perch, the raven ruffled its feathers again. The branch of a tree growing outside the window scraped against the panes. Fen succumbed suddenly to the obsessing temptation.

"Surely," he said—"surely that is someone at your window lattice?"

Garbin glanced over his shoulder. "It's the tree. I am always meaning to have it cut down. It makes the room very dark." Plainly the allusion was lost on him. Geoffrey retired discreetly behind a handkerchief, and went red in the face.

"May I ask how long your walk lasted?" With manifest difficulty Fen had got back to the subject.

"Until about ten-thirty. When I arrived back here I made myself some cocoa, and sat reading by the fire."

"And each separate dying ember," said Geoffrey, "wrought its ghost upon the floor."

Garbin looked at him in mild surprise. "Exactly so. Shortly after eleven Spitshuker came in and gave me the news. We talked for some time."

Fen sighed. "Thank you. You're being kinder than your first words suggested. I wonder if, after all, you aren't anxious to get this thing cleared up?"

A shadow of evasiveness passed over Garbin's face. "Anxious. Most certainly I shall help the law in any way I can. But I cannot disguise from myself the fact that someone—that one of us who are connected with the cathedral must be implicated."

"What makes you think that?"

"It is a question of keys, is it not?"

"Ah, yes. I understand that virtually everyone had a key to the cathedral grounds."

132

"It seems pointless for people to have a key to the grounds, and not to the cathedral itself."

"Not at all. Suppose I had arranged to meet someone at the cathedral." Garbin paused. "As Butler arranged to meet Peace. I should unlock the gate into the grounds, and lock it again after me, to keep out . . . intruders. Then I should go up to the cathedral and unlock the door there. Anyone following me up there would thus require a key to the grounds, but not a key to the cathedral itself."

"That seems clear enough. Peace, I suppose, must have had a key to the grounds last night. I wonder whose he borrowed?"

"I'm afraid I can't help you there."

"And possibly Josephine as well."

"Josephine Butler?" Garbin's voice was guarded.

"She took a false message to the police on duty at the cathedral. But what time are the grounds locked?"

"At seven sharp. The sexton sees to it. There are only the north and south gates and that into the clergy-house garden."

"Is it absolutely impossible to get into the grounds otherwise than by the gates?"

Garbin shrugged. "Not impossible, no. Anyone who wished could manage it quite easily. The locking is chiefly a moral preventive."

"Ah, of course. To prevent the incontinent young from necking publicly on the cathedral hill."

Garbin made a gesture of impatience and stood up. This abrupt movement disturbed the raven, which emitted a hoarse, dyspeptic croak and began flying agitatedly about the room. Garbin beat at it ineffectually with his hands. Eventually it settled on the window-sill.

"I must apologise," said Garbin, "for my pet."

"Ghastly, grim and ancient raven from the night's Plutonian shore."

Garbin stared in bewilderment. "A little picturesquely put, perhaps. And now if there's nothing more——"

"One more thing. Are you interested in music?"

Garbin smiled wryly. "I know little or nothing about it; and care less. It always seems to me that it plays far too large a part in our services: there are occasions when the worship of God degenerates into an organised concert."

133

He bowed slightly to Geoffrey. "Please don't think me ungracious. And now, is there anything else?"

"Is there," said Geoffrey, "is there balm in Gilead?"

Fen hastily retired to make a close examination of one of the bookcases. "I see you have here"—he hesitated, and went on in a weak, quavering voice—"many a quaint and curious volume of forgotten lore."

It was at this point that the interview really got out of hand. Geoffrey was hardly able to contain himself, and Fen was scarcely better. The gravity and incomprehension of Garbin made matters worse. What he thought was going on it is impossible to say; perhaps he fancied Fen and Geoffrey to be engaged in some recondite form of retaliation for his earlier outspokenness. At all events he said nothing. Hasty farewells were made. At the door Fen turned to look at the raven again.

"Take thy beak," he said, "from out my heart, thy form from off my door."

"His eyes," said Geoffrey, "have all the seeming of a demon's that is dreaming." Then they went out, in some haste. At the front door, Fen recovered himself sufficiently to ask Garbin one more question.

"Do you know the poetry of Edgar Allan Poe?"

"I'm afraid not. I have no great use for verses."

"Not his poem, *The Raven?*"

"Ah. There's a poem about a raven, is there? Is it good? I know nothing about these things."

"Very good," said Fen with the utmost gravity. "You would find much in it to interest you. Good morning."

Chapter Nine

THREE SUSPECTS AND
A WITCH

"I'm not taken
With a cob-swan or a high-mounting bull,
As foolish Leda and Europa were;
But the bright gold, with Danaë."

JONSON

"POOR BROOKS," SAID FEN as they walked towards Butler's house. "He seems to have rather faded out of the
enquiry. But there's much less to get hold of in his case
than there is in Butler's.'"

"Didn't you think it rather odd that Spitshuker should
have cleared up the cathedral without consulting the police?"

"Possibly. Or possibly not. It depends on certain medical technicalities which I don't know about."

The sun was hotter now, but a light cooling breeze had
sprung up. A cathedral town, Geoffrey thought, is a delightful place—the most perfect practical combination of
church and laity in existence. Here one was comfortably
lapped about with the tradition and actuality of worship;
here, also, one's small vices and peccadilloes drew an
added zest from their surroundings. It occurred to him to
ask what Fen was doing in Tolnbridge.

"I came here," said Fen sourly, "to see the Dean, who
used to be at Oxford with me. He is not here—scandal-
ously inconsiderate. But I suppose he'll be back pretty
quickly now. I shall have to go in a few days—term starts
early next month, and I've got to lecture on William
Dunbar." He sighed. "I feel lost out of Oxford."

"You don't look lost."

135

"I wonder what sort of a term it's going to be. The undergraduates get more moronic every passing moment. But I believe Robert Warner's new play is to be on locally. In the meantime, I'm getting nothing done about insects. I shall go into this shop and buy a book on them."

This did not take long. "Insects!" said Fen loudly to an assistant, waving his hand impartially at customers and staff. He was found a tattered copy of Fabre's *Social Life in the Insect World*.

In the street they met Fielding wandering vaguely about in pursuit, doubtless, of some private delusive phantom of heroism. He had been reflecting on the case in all its aspects, he told them, but had come to no satisfactory conclusion. They gave him an account of what had turned up since the previous night, but it was evident that he was not enlightened by it. He expressed a vague determination to think things over, and to make what headway he could with the landlord of the "Whale and Coffin." Plainly he resented being excluded from the morning's interviews, but, as Fen said, with more forcefulness than tact, it was bad enough having one useless person hanging about all the time, without adding another. Fielding departed on his indefinite mission, which resolved itself in practice into his playing darts in a public bar.

Butler's house proved to be a substantial, overgrown affair sprouting little valueless wings, outhouses and potting-sheds over a large and untidy garden. At the gate Fen and Geoffrey met the Inspector, a sad and lonely figure plodding with pathetic hopefulness from one interview to another. He regarded them warily, wondering, it was evident, whether they were getting on better than he was. It was like one of those treasure hunts, Geoffrey thought, in which you have to hide the clues again after looking at them, and then, when someone else appears on the scene, put up an elaborate smoke-screen of nescience.

"We're getting on fine," said Fen, with deliberate malice. "The problem is practically solved. How are things with you?"

"I don't believe a word of it," said the Inspector. "*I* can't get anything that's any use out of anybody. What is the good of fussing away about motive and opportunity and so on when you can't even make out how the thing was done? But I shouldn't be standing here talking to you about it."

"Has the Yard arrived? How silly that sounds. But it's grammatical."

"It should be here after lunch some time." The Inspector was gloomy. "Then, thank God, I can shelve the responsibility for this thing."

"Inspector, Inspector," said Fen waggishly. "Is that a right attitude?"

"No, it isn't. But if you were as mixed-up as I am at the moment you wouldn't stand there carping."

"Carping?" said Fen, offended. "Who's carping? Carping," he added with more warmth, "your grandmother. I was trying to find out if anything new had turned up, that's all."

"Well, nothing has, except the details of why Mr. Peace went to meet Dr. Butler at the cathedral. And those I can*not* give you. That Josephine kid's as obstinate as ever—still says it was a policeman gave her that message. She's given about three contradictory accounts of when and where and how he gave it her, but on the central fact she won't budge. I don't like the look of her, either—nasty feverish gleam in her eye. Mrs. Butler's no help—she hardly *exists*. She's about as likely to know anything about the murder as you are to have climbed Mount Everest."

"I have climbed Mount Everest."

"That's a lie. Nobody has. You'd say anything for the sake of an effect, wouldn't you? Savernake's no use, either."

"Is he there too?"

"Staying in the house before he goes back to his parish. But I don't think he's got anything to do with it. For one thing, he was in London the night Brooks was attacked. I've checked on him *and* Peace *and* Mrs. Garbin, and as far as one can possibly tell, they really were there. Incidentally, I've also made enquiries round the hospital, to see if any of the front line of suspects turned up there about six yesterday, but it was hopeless. And I've discovered it's quite easy to get into the hospital by a back way, without anyone in the world seeing you."

"Ah." Fen was thoughtful. "One thing I wanted to ask:

137

do you know exactly what time the police left the cathedral last night?"

"As it happens, I do. The joltheads had just enough sense left to make a note of it. It was five to nine."

"Thank God."

"Why," said the Inspector with dispiriting jocosity, "are you involving the Deity in this affair?"

"Because if the time had been much earlier all my theories would have gone to Hades."

"You have theories?" The Inspector made it sound like a disease.

"Many theories, my good, my sweet Inspector. A whole —what is the collective noun for theories? A gaggle of geese, a giggle of girls, a noise of boys—of course: a thought of theories." Fen beamed with enthusiasm. That's it: a thought. Alliterative and expressive: shifting, insubstantial, delusive as a thought." He paused, overcome by this display. "And in return for your information, I'll give you some advice."

"No one ever took any harm from listening to advice."

"Don't platitudinise. I want you, as soon as the coast is clear, to make a thorough search of Peace's room."

The Inspector gaped in astonishment. *"Peace's* room? And what in heaven's name am I supposed to search for?"

Fen reflected. "The clergy-house key to the cathedral, perhaps. Oh, and a hypodermic, and a phial of atropine solution. I think that will be enough. You ought to find them all there."

"God pity us," said the Inspector, genuinely impressed. "If you're having me on I'll put you in gaol." He turned to go back through the gate.

"Not now. Let us get our bit of nagging over first."

"But there's no time to waste. He may move them."

"We'll keep him occupied and see to it that he doesn't."

"No, I must go back now."

"Really, Inspector, if I'd known you were going to be such a nuisance I should never have told you. You haven't got a search warrant, anyway."

"No," said the Inspector with a wink, "but we'll risk that, I think."

"If you go one step up that path I shall warn everybody in the house that you're proposing to make a burglarious and illegal entry, and we'll all get together and throw you out."

"You devil."

"It's hard," said Fen complainingly. "One gives the police a perfectly sound piece of advice—information almost—and that's the sort of thanks one gets."

The wraith of a smile passed across the Inspector's face. "All right," he said, "all right. Have your own way. I dare say it's all my eye, anyway. It can wait." He turned to go. "But my God, if this is a joke——"

"Don't threaten witnesses," said Fen. "Oh, one more thing—very important. Was there any trace of poison or bullets or knife-thrusts or anything at the autopsy? It is over by now, I suppose?"

"Nothing of the kind."

"Splendid. That suits me admirably."

"What a pity," said the Inspector with heavy irony, "that you've nothing more to find out. You must tell me when you make an arrest."

"Ah." Fen was pensive. "There's the rub. Means, motive, opportunity, all settled. The only trouble is that I haven't at the moment the least idea who did it."

They found Peace in the garden, extended fatly in a deck-chair and snoring up into the dappled foliage of the chestnut tree above his head. He had been little in evidence, Geoffrey thought, since the interview in the train; at dinner last night he had been curiously self-effacing, doing and saying nothing that could force itself memorably on the attention. And yet he *was*, in fact, the only person who could have been in the cathedral when Butler was killed, and it was conceivable that his "business talk" with the Precentor had provided him with an adequate motive. Geoffrey frowned. But a motive wasn't what was wanted—unless, as was quite possible, the phantom radio had nothing to do with the murder in the cathedral. Murder in the Cathedral. Would Butler, like St. Thomas, like St. Ephraim, be canonised now he was dead? Or Murder *ex cathedra*. Peace, of course, would have had time to get to the hospital from the station and kill Brooks; so would Savernake; so would Mrs. Garbin. But the murder of Brooks had depended, it seemed, on a knowledge of the

139

times at which he got his medicine; which none of these people would have had, since he had only been found, and taken to the hospital, the previous morning. Here, then, was a possible means of elimination. It was true that, since plainly more than one person was involved in the affair, a phone call to London earlier in the day could have given the necessary information, but this, surely, was too complicated and unnecessary a method of procedure to be plausible.

Peace still exuded his prosperous and professional air, even in sleep. Slumbering at ease, his face was composed and childlike. He snored, not thunderously, but with a faint and not unpleasant moaning, like the wind in a chimney. His well-cut suit, now creased and crushed, clung about his form unreticently, and his chubby hands lay upon his stomach. Beside him, on the grass, lay *The Mind and Society,* along with a tall glass and two lager bottles, one of them empty. This happy and idyllic scene conveyed no sense of tragedy—either that which had been already enacted or that which was now preparing. It seemed a pity to wake him.

Considerateness, and sensitivity to conventional atmospheres were not, however, Fen's strongest points. He advanced boisterously, making a formidable amount of noise. Peace jerked into alarmed wakefulness; then noticing the source of the commotion, heaved painfully to his feet and stood ineffectually brushing himself and blinking blearily and without enthusiasm about him.

"Awake, Æolian lyre, awake," said Fen, "and give to rapture all thy trembling strings."

"Rapture?" Peace peered at him anxiously. "Liar?" He paused dubiously. "That seems a little hard."

Fen settled himself on the grass. "And so," he said, "is the ground. Are there no more chairs? Phyllida and Corydon may have enjoyed this sort of thing, but not I." He rummaged in a dandelion root. "Ants," he said.

"The Arcadian myths"—the dominie in Peace became very evident—"are plainly sexual in origin. Always they concern pursuit. Pan is the incarnation of male desire, Syrinx the elusive, fleeting object of his lust. Almost one might say that the myth involves the whole contradiction

140

and antithesis of the male and female characteristics. Or possibly"—he became thoughtful—"not."

Fen grunted. "Do you ever get tired of rummaging about finding psychological parallelisms?"

"Yes. Very tired. But if one regards it as an amusing and preposterous game it can help to pass away a dull evening. The Faust legend, now: there's endless material in that—the stored dream-fantasies of a whole ethic division of humanity. And the principles of the game are so simple that, as they used to say about labour-saving machines, a child can operate it. Water is always the unconscious—I haven't the least idea why. If you dream about tumbling into the sea and swimming about underneath it means your unconscious has triumphed, or"—he paused—"that you're dyspeptic. Anything round or hollow is the womb, the feminine principle." He picked up the empty lager bottle and tapped the bottom of it. "This, for example—a mandala-symbol. Anything else is a masculine principle, in all probability. Also, there are primal old men with beards."

"It appears to me," said Fen gravely, "that we are in the presence of a radical breakdown of faith."

"Faith." Peace nodded. "That's it precisely. Not intellectual doubt, but a breakdown of faith. The witch-doctor loses confidence in his paint and headdress and amulets." He was silent.

Geoffrey sought for a means of turning the conversation to more relevant matters. "Did you," he enquired cautiously, "get any light from your conversation with Spitshuker last night?"

Peace glanced at him sharply; the ruse was transparent. "He offered to substitute his own faith for my own. He said it was at once much more rational and much less so and would consequently be twice as satisfactory."

"What do you think?"

"I suppose he's right. I confess I feel *drawn* to the Church in a way I've never experienced before. The transition shouldn't be difficult. It isn't *what* one believes that matters, it's the emotional need one's beliefs satisfy. Plainly I'm one of those people who need a faith—what kind doesn't much matter. Patriotism might do equally well."

Intellectually, Geoffrey thought, the man was stronger than he at first appeared to be; but that constituted only the surface of his mind. Where was the emotional centre? A woman? That was possible. A scientific passion?—but what he said conveyed little of that impression. Money? Creativity in some line? A man's life may be wholly bound up with a passion for basket-work. Or after all, was there no such centre? Was the shell really as hollow as it sounded? In himself, Peace was a perplexing problem. Somehow he lacked inwardness, lacked a self—the result, perhaps of constantly attending to the inwardness, the personalities, of others.

Fen, who was playing around with one of the lager bottles, said mildly:

"The *minds* of people, as such, are always less interesting, because more uniform, than the façade they present to the world. Dr. Butler, for example." He paused deliberately, to allow the change of topic to settle. "How little one knew about him."

Peace resigned himself. "He was a curious man. I knew little about him, for I saw him seldom. He disapproved, arbitrarily and without consideration, of my profession, which was one of the things that induced me to continue in it. For the rest, if you'll believe me (though it doesn't depend on that), he was entirely selfish. His calling required of him a certain show of charitableness, but it never went beyond the bare minimum of *bienséance*. And that was why I came down here."

"Oh?" Fen's voice deliberately lacked interest.

Peace leaned forward; he spoke slowly and emphatically. "My father died a rich man. There were only two of us children. As I was already on the road to prosperity and Irene, my sister, had nothing, he left his money to her—on the understanding that should my fortunes ever fail, half was to come to me for the benefit of my children. The capital, you realise, could not be touched." He paused and fingered his tie.

"That understanding Butler effectually wrecked when he married Irene. He persuaded her, in fact, that the whole of the inheritance should be left to their own children, and poor Irene, who never had a great deal of spirit of her own, was forced to agree. The man was a

142

bully, and I fancy he had an easy job of it." There was real feeling in Peace's voice now, Geoffrey noticed.

"Naturally, I want as good prospects for my children as I can possibly get, and just recently things haven't been going so well with me. People have had to draw in their horns a bit, and the war's induced them to stop fussing so much about themselves—which is a damned good thing. But just recently, too, Butler had been trying to get Irene to transfer the money to him, for better safety, as he said." Peace's lip curled contemptuously. "I knew once that happened there'd be no more hope for me and my family. Writing was no good, so I came down to talk things over with him. That's why I went to see him up at the cathedral last night. We'd had a few words about it earlier, when I first arrived, and he'd been pretty cool, I can assure you. Said he'd give me his final word later. *His* decision!" The man was agitated; he got up and paced restlessly up and down. "Well, he never did. But you see the injustice of it—the vile impertinence and lack of all moral decency. It isn't as if I'd wanted a lot; it isn't as if this understanding about the money were a fabrication of mine—I've got letters to prove it. And yet he—*he*, who had lived in comfort on that money for nearly twenty years—was going to 'give me his decision' as if I were a beggar, a poor relation soliciting at his door!"

Here was the man with a vengeance, thought Geoffrey: sincerity was plain in every word he spoke, a sincere sense of outraged justice, a sincere affection for his family; and it was hardly necessary to add, a sincere and plausible motive for murder. Fen asked:

"Was the reason for your visit here generally known?"

"He'd broadcast his own account of it pretty widely, you can be sure—the sponging relative."

"Ah." Fen was thoughtful. "And the money is very important to you?"

Peace grinned suddenly. "Very. I'm not quite so successful at my job as I made myself out to be to you, Mr. Vintner. I've done well enough, I suppose. But really I've always been a square peg. Most men fit their jobs, but I don't. I don't know what I should have been—an actor, I sometimes think."

Fen stirred himself. "How dreadful."

143

"And do you know, if I *had* found my proper place in the scheme of things, I don't think I should have bothered about this business at all, however poor I was."

Fen made vague signs of concurrence. "Dissatisfaction always breeds demands, even if they're not for the particular satisfaction that's lacking." He appeared rather pleased at this utterance.

"You see why I'm telling you all this." Peace sat down, something of his normal diffident good-nature restored. "I have, as far as I know, the best motive yet discovered for killing Butler, and obviously it's no use trying to cover it up. Also, I was the only person who could have been in that cathedral when he was killed. So I quite see that things don't look too good for me." He hesitated. "Personally, Mr. Fen, I know of you only as a literary critic. But I've been told that you've had a good deal of experience of these affairs, and that's why I put the facts before you. Not—heaven forbid!—in any frenzied attempt to prove my innocence, but in the hope that they may help to prove someone else guilty."

The man was so fool; very clearly he recognised his position. But, on the other hand, frankness and willingness to help might be an excellent pose; he might, in fact, be drawing attention to one motive in order to divert suspicion from another.

Fen cleared his throat, noisily and at great length. "You've told all this to the police?"

"Naturally."

"Of course, of course. The truth in all circumstances. I suppose you know they'll arrest you?"

Peace sat up. "Good God! Surely it's not as bad as that?"

"They're certain to get round to it sooner or later," said Fen with malignant delight. "Tell me about your movements."

"Movements? Ah, yes, I see. At the relevant hours. The train arrived more or less on time, and I came straight here. Characteristically, there was no one in when I arrived, but Irene and Butler turned up in about ten minutes—say at a quarter past six. No alibi for the Brooks murder, you see. Butler and I were both supposed to be going to the clergy-house for dinner, but he cried off at the

144

last moment. Couldn't stand the sight of me, I suppose. After dinner, when the meeting was going on, I sat in the summerhouse, but I got bored with that and went back shortly before nine. It was then that Butler arranged to meet me privately up at the cathedral, at about twenty past. I got talking to Spitshuker, and although I saw how the time was going, I thought it wouldn't do him any harm to wait. And besides, Frances was getting anxious about him. She said she was going out to look for you at the 'Whale and Coffin' and would I wait and let her walk up to the cathedral with me to make sure he was all right. The poor kid seemed really scared. Anyway, she was the devil of a time, so I set off alone just before ten—rather more than five minutes before you arrived—and I was just pottering about trying to find a door that was open when I heard that crash. The rest you know."

"Convenient," Fen murmured. "Extraordinarily convenient. The trouble is that one can't check the extra minute or two here and there which counts. Ultimately it doesn't matter, though."

Peace grimaced. "It matters to me."

"And what is the situation now about this money?"

"I suppose I shall get it now that Butler's dead. Which makes matters look worse. Do you think if I abandoned all claim——"

"Give up a lot of cash!" Fen howled indignantly. "Certainly not. Don't be so daft. No one ever leaves *me* any money," he complained darkly, "despite my frenzied efforts with rich old women. It's an extraordinary thing that the people who really deserve money——" He suddenly lost interest in what he was saying, and climbed to his feet. "Never mind that. I must see Savernake and the girl. Are they about?"

"Somewhere." Peace seemed indifferent. "But you haven't advised me what to do."

"Do!" exclaimed Fen. "If it were done when 'tis done, then 'twere well it were done quickly."

"What is that supposed to mean?"

"It isn't supposed to mean anything. It's a quotation from our great English dramatist, Shakespeare. I sometimes wonder if Hemings and Condell went off the rails a bit there. It's a vile absurd jingle."

Frances and Savernake were in another part of the broad, rambling garden, talking quickly and earnestly. Geoffrey wondered if Dutton had been right, and if after all they would get married now. Love imposes a sense of proprietorship; and though Geoffrey had no possible claim on the girl, he felt an active resentment at Savernake's easy air when he was with her. One should not, in any case, treat so much beauty with an easy air. Beauty, as Dr. Johnson remarked, is of itself very estimable, and should be considered as such. Geoffrey found himself disliking Savernake, and not entirely for reasons of jealousy —disliking his affectation, his evasiveness, his nervous jumpiness. As they approached, he stood twisting his long, thin fingers together, his sparse, corn-coloured hair meticulously brushed back and his grey eyes moving with great rapidity from person to person; just on the edge of downright shiftiness.

He opened the conversation unfortunately by a reference to Fen's butterfly-net. Geoffrey riposted with a feeble sarcasm, Fen being temporarily engaged in trying to catch hold of a dragon-fly. The atmosphere perceptibly worsened. It was not that there was any particular gloom about it. Frances quite candidly admitted that though she had been reasonably attached to her father, she was affected by his death more as something shocking than as something melancholy. But there was a tinge of what could only be called irritability in the air, a neurotic rather than an emotional reaction. Everyone was on edge.

"Poor Mummy," said Frances. "Daddy used to bully her rather, I'm afraid, but I think she's more affected now than anyone else. Isn't that always the way?"

She wore a light dress of plain black, with white collar and cuffs, which modelled her figure to perfection. Even Fen, who, being comfortably married, had some time ago, more from a sense of wasted effort than from any moral scruples, given up looking at girls' figures, was manifestly impressed. "O my America! my new-found-land!" he murmured; and despite an outraged glare from Geoffrey, who happened to know his Donne, continued to gaze in frank admiration. This inspection was, however, peremptorily interrupted by Savernake, who said insultingly, in the irritating drawl which unfortunately he did not always remember to assume:

"Is there anything in particular we can do for you?"

Now this was a mistake. Fen turned upon him a look of quite distressing vehemence. "Yes, you sheepshead," he said, forgetting the proper respect due to the cloth, "you can go and dance a rigadoon at the bottom of the garden. A nice thing, to be treated in that cool way when one comes along, bursting with sympathy"—Fen contrived to look suitably inflated—"to lend a helping hand. Apologise!" he howled in conclusion.

"My dear sir, I can only imagine you're mad."

"You fopling!" said Fen with great contempt. He was enjoying the scene. When not occupied with speaking, he beamed with enthusiasm and delight. "You numbskull!"

"Now look here——"

"None of that," said Fen sternly. "Either you answer my questions, or you don't."

"I don't."

"Oh." Fen seemed a little taken aback. "Well, in that case——"

"Oh, come on, you two," said Frances impatiently. "Don't squabble. Of course we'll answer any questions you like, Mr. Fen. Won't we, July?" She looked straight at the young man for a moment; then he nodded.

"I'm sorry."

"And so," said Fen without much conviction, "am I."

"Let's walk, shall we?" said Frances. "I can't bear standing about." They wandered across a lawn embryonically laid out for putting, towards the orchard.

The subsequent conversation, however, elicited little of value. On the monotonous problem of alibis, it proved that Savernake had one which, barring collusion, was virtually unassailable for six o'clock, having walked with Mrs. Garbin to the house where she was dining and playing bridge and stopped there some time with her. He had then gone straight to dinner at the clergy-house, only stopping to leave his bag at the Precentor's. After dinner he had walked—whither and with what purpose it was not clear. He had, however, met some local worthy and talked to him between 9.45 and 10.20, arriving home just in time to hear the news of Butler's death.

As for Frances, she had been down shopping in the town until just after six, when she had returned to the clergy-house to find the tail-end of the Josephine disturbance going on and to meet Geoffrey and Fielding as they came in from the train. She had gone to have a drink with them, as they knew, returned, got the dinner, gone to her room with a book afterwards, come down to deal with some problem or other of housekeeping in the kitchen and found the meeting breaking up, gone straight to the kitchen and done what she had to do, become a little anxious about her father, set out to find Fen, Geoffrey, Fielding and the Inspector and walked back with them; afterwards staying in the kitchen until Geoffrey had come to tell her of her father's death.

"Let's get the movements of this family straight," said Fen. "What exactly was your mother doing between five and seven?"

"She was out having tea with a friend, and got back about a quarter past six, meeting Daddy almost at the gate; they found Mr. Peace had arrived. By that time Daddy had found out about Josephine and his manuscript, followed her round the clergy-house, spanked her, and returned home."

"Does that mean," Geoffrey asked, "that your father was in the clergy-house when we arrived?"

"Yes. He must have left just after we set out for the 'Whale and Coffin.' "

"Ah," said Fen obscurely. "Is Josephine about? I must see her if it's humanly possible."

"She's somewhere in the house, I think."

"Good." Fen seized an apple from off one of the orchard trees, crunched it, and said indistinctly: "So far so good. And your account checks up with Peace's."

Geoffrey saw Frances exchange a swift glance with Savernake: so did Fen.

"Don't hedge," he said threateningly through a mouthful of apple. "I saw you."

Frances said: "Don't you think, Mr. Fen, that Peace ought to have had the decency to clear out when this happened?—and particularly since he and Daddy got on so badly together."

"I see." Fen's tone was guarded. "A business matter, wasn't it?"

"Business!" Frances' eyes blazed suddenly with indignation. "He was trying to sponge on Daddy."

"My dear girl," said Savernake with a sneer, "be more realistic. You must expect that sort of thing. Money attracts men of that type like wasps round a jam-pot."

Fen took another bite from his apple. "I think," he stated mildly, "that there's probably more than one side to the matter. . . . But don't let's talk about that now." Manifestly he was impatient to get away from the subject. "What really matters is that except for Dallow we've now got where everybody was, or say they were, at six o'clock last evening; to wit—

"Spitshuker was alone in his room, working—unchecked and apparently uncheckable;

"Garbin was alone in *his* room—ditto;

"Dutton was out for a walk—ditto;

"Peace was hanging about here—ditto;

"You, Savernake, and Mrs. Garbin were together;

"Dr. Butler was smacking Josephine at the clergy-house;

"You, Frances, were returning from shopping;

"Your mother was at a friend's for tea;

"Geoffrey and Fielding were walking to the clergy-house from the station;

"And I—what was I doing?" Fen frowned with concentration. "Yes, I have it: I was just going into a pub. I knew there was something familiar about six o'clock. If *everybody* had had the sense to go into pubs as soon as they opened their doors, this thing wouldn't have happened. Interesting lack of alibis, isn't there?" He finished his apple and threw the core at a bird. "Well, no more talking. I must see Mistress Josephine. She's in the house, is she?"

"Yes. July, be a dear and show Mr. Fen into the house and find Josephine for him." Savernake consented with an ill grace, and the two went off together. Geoffrey and Frances walked into the vegetable garden. Geoffrey felt that his moment had come.

Bachelorhood was engaged in a tour of his defences, but without much confidence in their efficacy; it re-

149

sembled more the last, sentimental walk round a long-familiar dwelling, now for ever to be abandoned. Staring with exaggerated interest at a row of radishes, Geoffrey meditated subtleties; and it was his inability to think of any rather than a sense of fitness which led him to ask at last, quite simply:

"Are you engaged to be married?"

She shook her head; the question seemed quite natural.

"Then would you marry me?"

She stopped and gasped. "But Mr. Vintner—Geoffrey . . . We've hardly met."

"I know," he said unhappily. "But I can't help it. You see, I'm in love with you."

The admission sounded so dismal that she burst out laughing. Geoffrey stared harder than ever at the radishes. Brutish roots! What did they know of the agonies of a middle-aged bachelor proposing marriage? He said, "I'm sorry," less because he felt it than because he could think of nothing else.

She stopped laughing quickly. "That wasn't very civil of me; I didn't mean to hurt you." Her eyes were soft. "But—well, do you think this is quite the time——?"

"No. I'm a tactless creature. I shouldn't have said anything."

"It's so sudden: that's the funny thing about it. I—well, it just took me aback."

"Will you think about it?"

"Yes," she said with real seriousness, "yes, I'll think about it. And"—hesitating a little—"I think you're sweet."

"No, I'm not sweet, really. You ought to know the sort of bargain you'd be getting." Bachelorhood was contriving rather a cunning oblique counter-attack. "I'm fussy and old-maidish and selfish, and fixed in my habits and disagreeable at breakfast and——"

"Don't!" She laughed a little breathlessly. "After all, I'm not such a prize-ticket as all that." She hesitated. "We must talk things over—soon."

"What about Savernake?"

"Oh, you know how it is: one drifts into an understanding without really wanting it. But don't worry. All that is —would be—my side of the business." She paused.

"Look, I must go in and see Mummy now, but let's walk —and bathe—to-morrow before breakfast. All right?"

"Lovely."

"I shall be sleeping at the clergy-house again, and I'll wake and bang on your door. We'll go really early, so that there won't be a lot of people about. Then"—she smiled—"well, we shall see."

They looked at one another in silence for a moment. Deepest, darkest, raven hair, blue eyes, red lips, and the body of a goddess. But banal! Our loves are separate and incommunicable; not all the poets who ever wrote begin to express what we feel. And yet it's only something pleasant and quite simple. And it doesn't cloud the vision, or how could one observe the radish-tops, caught in a momentary breeze, nodding their pygmy approval? Ecstasy is simplicity itself. Oh my America, my new-found-land!

Then she was gone, the glory departed. Even the radishes settled again to their vegetable loves, dull roots merely. Edible roots, however; Geoffrey pulled one out of the ground, wiped it clean, and ate it.

Fen and Josephine sat opposite one another in the big, gloomy library, he serious and not very talkative, she sullen and even less so. Her tousled hair fell over her eyes, unnaturally bright and with the pupils dilated. Beneath the black frock, her body was thin, and she trembled now and again, very slightly, crouching back in the armchair as though she were glad of its pressure against her back.

"Why did you burn the manuscript?" he said quietly. The child stirred. "I don't see why I should tell you."

"Nor do I really. But I could help you a lot if you did."

She considered; this seemed reasonable if it was true, but then it mightn't be true. "How could you help me?"

"I could get you the things you like."

"I don't know . . . whether it's one of the things I'm allowed to tell. I felt sick suddenly, and giddy, after I'd— after . . . My head went all sort of funny and I didn't know what I was doing. Then he beat me. I'd rather have died than let him lay a finger on me." She wiped her nose with the back of her hand.

"And who gave you the message?"

"A policeman." The reply was automatic.

"That isn't true."

"A policeman." She smiled suddenly and foolishly. "It was a policeman."

"Who gave it to you?"

"I'm not allowed to tell, or I won't be given what I want."

And that is?"

"I'm not allowed to tell."

Fen smiled, and with infinite gentleness and patience tried again. "Why did you mind so much having your father beat you?"

"It wasn't fair . . . I felt sick, I didn't know what I was doing." She suddenly buried her head in her hands.

"Poor kid;" said Fen. He leaned over and touched her on the shoulder, but she flared up at him.

"Don't touch me!"

"All right." Fen sat back again. "You ought to have had a doctor if you didn't feel well."

"I was told I wasn't to allow Mother to get a doctor. I had to pretend I wasn't ill."

"Who told you?"

"It was——" Her eyes suddenly shone with childish cunning; for a moment the extended pupils seemed enormous. "You're trying to catch me out. I'm not allowed to tell."

"Very well." Fen seemed indifferent. "But you still haven't said why you so hated your father beating you."

"It was a"—she struggled over the word—"a desecration. Only one man is allowed to do that sort of thing." The spasm of shivering caught her again.

"Who is that one man?"

"The Black Gentleman."

Fen sat up. Understanding was beginning to come to him. "Apollyon," he said.

"You know."

"Yes, I know" he answered. *"Maledico Trinitatem sanctissimam nobilissimamque, Patrem, Filium et Spiritum Sanctum. Amen. Trinitatem, Solher, Messias, Emmanuel, Sabahot, Adonay, Athanatos, Jesum, Pentaqua, Agragon . . ."*

"Ischiros, Eleyson, Otheos," she said, her voice rising

shrill above his own, *"Tetragrammaton, Ely Saday. Aquila, Magnum Hominen, Visionem, Florem, Originem, Salvatorem maledico . . . Pater noster, qui es in coelis, maledicatur nomen tuum, destruatur regnum tuum . . ."*

So the monotonous stream of foolish blasphemy went on, until at last there was a pause, and Fen said:

"You see, I'm one of you. You can trust me." He pulled a cigarette-case from his pocket. She looked at it greedily and he glimpsed her expression. "You'd like one?"

"Yes, give me one—quickly." She snatched a cigarette and put it in her mouth. He lit it for her, and watched in silence while she smoked, inhaling deeply. But after a minute she threw it away with a cry of disgust, almost of desperation.

"It's not the right kind!"

Fen stood up. "No," he said, and his voice was hard. "It's not the right kind. The Black Gentleman gives you the right kind, doesn't he?" she nodded. "I came only to test your faith. *In nomine diaboli et servorum suorum.*"

"My faith is strong." The child's voice was confident, but hysteria lay beneath. "My father died in the bad faith."

At the door Fen turned. "I am one of you. Tell me who is your director."

For a moment all hung upon a thread of gossamer. Josephine hesitated, shivered again. Then she looked up at him and smiled.

"I'm not allowed to tell."

Fen met Geoffrey at the gate, and his eyes were cold with rage.

"You've seen Josephine?" Geoffrey asked.

Fen nodded. "She has been systematically drugged," he said deliberately. "Probably with marihuana—a form of haschisch; at any rate with something in cigarette form. She must be taken to a hospital for treatment at once—I'm going to phone the Inspector about it now." He paused. *"And it's got nothing to do with the murders at all—* except that the same person is responsible: mere gratuitous devilry, corruption for the sake of corruption. And it's not only her body, it's her mind. There's something else."

"What?"

"She's a witch."

Geoffrey stared. "A witch!"

"In Tolnbridge, it seems, the old tradition dies hard. Yes, by ordinary definition Josephine is a witch. She burnt the book of Christian theology her father was writing. She wished to keep herself pure from his hands, for what beastliness we shall, I hope, never know. She told me he died in the bad faith. She has seen the Devil and taken the Black Mass."

Chapter Ten

NIGHT THOUGHTS

"Hatred and vengeance, my external portion,
Scarce can endure delay of execution."

COWPER

FOR GEOFFREY, the afternoon was spent first taking a choir practice, and then in playing Evensong. The choir was as well-trained, and the organ as excellent as he had expected, and no special difficulties arose. The moments of respite afforded by lessons and collects he occupied in considering the account Fen had given him of his interview with Josephine. Even at second-hand, it seemed an appalling business. And Fen had said it was actuated by pure malice and had nothing to do with the murders—though how he could know this Geoffrey was unable to imagine. There remained Dallow to be seen—the affected, slightly epicene little Chancellor who was an expert on witchcraft. What was it Frances had said?—"takes rather more than a scholarly interest in the subject." There should, at all events, be something of interest and importance here.

Dinner was over before they set out for his house. Fen had spent the afternoon meandering about the countryside in search of insects, and was in high spirits. He walked at his usual exhausting pace, talking incessantly all the while. Josephine had been taken away from Tolnbridge for expert treatment, he said, out of harm's way.

"She'll recover all right," he added. "Though she won't

155

enjoy herself for the first few weeks. But I shall be interested to discover which of all these people has the sort of mentality which regards the systematic drugging of a child of fifteen as an entertainment."

Sir John Dallow lived in one of the new, large, expensive villas overlooking the estuary. And no sooner had the servant opened the door than the extreme and depressing fastidiousness of the man became apparent. There was something more, too: the study into which they were shown exhibited tastes so depressingly morbid as to be almost incomprehensible outside a madhouse. A repellent little vampire-sketch by Fuseli hung on one wall; beyond it, an alaborate drawing by Beardsley of the fifth circle of the Dantean inferno; and dominating the whole room, over the fireplace, a meticulous, distorted painting of a torture-scene by an early German master. A bad reproduction of Dürer's *Melancholia,* which completed the decorations, did, however, contrive to lend his miniature chamber of horrors a respectable, even a conventional air. The bookshelves were loaded, and as Sir John had not yet put in an appearance, Fen and Geoffrey inspected them fairly thoroughly, and with a growing sense of depression. Certainly there was an almost unparalleled collection of works on witchcraft: the *Daemonolatreia* of Nicholas Rémy in the original edition of 1595; a modern private printing of the *Malleus Maleficarum*; Cotton Mather's *Wonders of the Invisible World;* the *Sadducismus Triumphatus*; and inevitably, all the standard text-books on the subject. But there were also other books which suggested a propensity to enjoy as well as to study the night-side of Nature: Toulet's scabrous study of sadism, *Monsieur du Paur*—de Sade's *Justine,* and many other recondite volumes of perverted semi-pornography. Fen regarded them thoughtfully.

"At least he doesn't keep them in cupboards," he said. "And I somehow fancy that people who enjoy that sort of thing in books never do much harm in real life. The fact that they go to books at all suggests something very like impotence. Still, one never knows."

In another minute Dallow minced into the room, his wispy white hair straggling chaotically all over his head. "My *de-ear* Professor! And Mr. Vintner! But this is

156

charming! And I *can*not apologise too much for my disgraceful negligence in not being here to greet you. I have been toying—*toying*—with the most depressing cheese *soufflé* you ever saw. Nothing more important than that. My foolish woman didn't tell me you were here. But you must make yourselves at home."

The furniture was modern and luxurious. Geoffrey sank with some relief into an armchair. Dallow gabbled on:

"But you've no idea the life I lead here—so lonely. Visitors are really a treat to me. Mr. Vintner, how did you find the choir?"

"Admirable, thank you," said Geoffrey. "No difficulties at all."

"Good. Good." Primly, Dallow folded his hands. "The boys are *not* what they were in the days when there was a choir-school, of course."

Probably not, thought Geoffrey, with a headmaster whose reading was de Sade; but perhaps Dallow had been different then.

Fen roused himself from a sort of stupor to say: "We're making an unofficial enquiry into Butler's death. Would you care to co-operate?"

"But of course—*delighted*." None the less, Dallow's tone was more guarded now. "How can I help?"

"It's about your movements."

"My *movements*." Dallow giggled foolishly, crossed and uncrossed his legs, and unnecessarily straightened his tie. "The good Inspector has already examined me on the subject, so you see, I have my story ready. I have an alibi, my dear Professor, for six o'clock. I was *here*, and talking to my servant, at precisely that hour. But at ten-fifteen—no. I left that foolish meeting and went straight to discuss some business with a local contractor. Unhappily, he was out, and I had my long tramp for nothing. I arrived back here at, I suppose, half past the hour."

"What hour?"

"But *ten—of course*." Dallow twisted his lips into a thin phantom of a smile. "I dined about seven, alone here. At five-fifteen I went down to the hospital to visit Brooks, but they wouldn't let me see him. That must have been about the time he recovered his reason. It was then, by

157

the way, that the excellent Inspector gave me the clergy-house key to the cathedral to bring back."

"Ah, yes, there's a point there. To whom did you return it?"

"Strictly, I suppose, to dear Frances. And *she* put it back in the vestibule, where normally it hangs. I saw her do it."

"That seems clear enough. Have you any ideas about Butler's murder?"

"None," said Dallow definitely. "Except that it was a blessing we had not dared to hope for."

"Blessing?" Fen stared. "You disliked him, then?"

"If we are to be candid, my *de*-ear Professor, I disliked him intensely. The man was a fool—neither scholar, nor artist, nor priest. More accurately, he was nothing, devoid of all talent and interest. And besides, he threw contempt on my studies. Human vanity being what it is, the last is the obvious motive for my detestation of our lamented friend." Dallow was slightly and absurdly flushed with annoyance.

"And Brooks?"

"Ah, Brooks I liked. He was a musician to his fingertips. He made those boys sing as I have never heard boys sing before. *He*, my *de*-ear Professor, was an Artist." Dallow got up and paced lightly about the room. *"O ces voix d'enfants,"* he exclaimed, *"chantant dans la couple!"*

But Fen waved this Mallarméan ecstasy a trifle brusquely aside. "Why should anyone murder Brooks?" he enquired.

The Chancellor paused to finger one of three huge orchids in a Chinese vase. "I dare say," he murmured, "that Butler was responsible."

"No."

"As you say." Dallow resumed his pacing with an elaborate shrug. "Brooks had no enemies that one knew of, Butler, on the other hand, had a great many, myself included. But as to who killed them, I haven't an idea."

He was at least frank, thought Geoffrey. But oh, the permutations of frankness and deceit—the double, triple, quadruple bluffs that were possible! Moreover, Dallow was quite intelligent enough to put on an act. The *poseur* so successfully hides his real self that he makes falsehood difficult to detect; where there is no apparent truth, there can be no obvious lie.

Fen, however, who had little of the traditional persistence of the investigator, was becoming bored. He shuffled his feet impatiently about and shifted the conversational ground. "Is St. Ephraim a revenant?" he asked.

Dallow stared, for the moment uncomprehending. "St. Ephraim?"

"I gather there have been rumours locally about the curious method of Butler's murder—the tomb."

Dallow's face lit up with understanding. He suddenly clapped his hands with childish glee. "I see! No, St. Ephraim has never, as far as is known, disturbed the peace of the living. The most active spirit in the neighbourhood is, of course, Bishop John—that excellent ghost."

Outside, a soft warm rain had begun to fall. Beads of water gathered on the window-pane, joined, parted, joined again. Fen stared abstractedly out at the garden.

Geoffrey looked perplexed. "I wish I knew something more about it."

"Spitshuker," said Fen, "told us you could give us some information about the Bishop. The bare fact that he caused a number of unfortunate young women to be burned, we know. But his spirit, it appears, rests uneasily in his odd tomb, and seems likely to be more uneasy still after having it desecrated."

Dallow was plainly delighted at the turn the conversation had taken. "So the people believe," he said. "I have heard rumours of it already—and very possibly it is true. The story of why he chose to be buried in Bishop's Gallery is curious. It seems he could not bear the idea of being, in death, completely enclosed—a sort of posthumous claustrophobia." Dallow giggled. "The Gallery provided, as it were, an outlet into the world—and not one person, but many, have seen him hovering behind its parapet. He—and a woman."

The rain-clouds were obscuring the light, and the room was darker now. Geoffrey shifted uncomfortably. This was a waste of time, and yet . . . And yet not for all the world would he have missed hearing more about Bishop John Thurston. He scented mystery. And he was not mistaken.

"The tale," said Dallow, "is an interesting one. The Bishop was only twenty-five when he came here in 1688. As was so often the case in those days, such positions were obtained by influence, and the suitability or experience of the candidate hardly canvassed at all. Certainly that must have been so in his case. He was a curious problem of a man—an inconsequent mingling of rakehell and Puritan. His father had been one of Cromwell's men, and had made a late marriage with a woman of good position in a Cavalier family. And there was something of both parents in the boy: the father's severity and dull moralism; and the mother's light-headed looseness of character. He went to Eton and then to King's College, Cambridge, and entered the priesthood at the age of twenty-three. He remained, as was normal in those days, unmarried, but when his parents died and left him considerable means, he was able to buy his sexual pleasures out of a glutted market, himself in any way. Such, in brief, was his history when and there seems little reason to suppose that he restrained he arrived here. I ought perhaps to have said that he was no fool—that he was, in fact, a man of considerable education and ability."

Dallow was absorbed; his affectation and self-consciousness were gone. It occurred to Geoffrey that he was probably a born romancer; except that this was not fiction. . . .

"Curiously enough," Dallow went on, "it was not from Thurston that the persecution of the witches began in the first place, but from the townspeople themselves, who saw, or fancied they saw, the black art being carried on in every hole and corner. And there seems little doubt that several covens were operating in the district. Why, one wonders? Why at one particular time and in one particular place? Why in Salem? Why in Bamberg? Why in Tolnbridge? And yet it was so. And recusant priests of the diocese were involved, as it is said they must be, in the celebration of the Black Mass. That brought the ecclesiastical authorities, chief among them Thurston, to the centre of the persecution. Suspicions and accusations multiplied, because the best defence against suspicion of oneself was to accuse another. There's no evidence that the Bishop, in the first instance, particularly encouraged or enjoyed the proceedings. But soon there came a change." Dallow paused. Fen was lighting a third cigarette from the end of the second; he seemed more than usually thoughtful.

"You must know," Dallow continued, "that it was the custom to torture witches in order to extort confessions from them—though it often happened that they confessed without torture. And it was necessary, at least, that the confession should be reaffirmed without torture. But there was slow, methodical flogging and the hot witch's chair, and thumb-screwing and leg-crushing and hoisting by weights. And it came to be observed that Bishop John Thurston was more frequently—though always unobtrusively—present at these scenes than his office warranted. He was present, too, at the executions, and it was said that it was he who had instituted the custom of burning as opposed to hanging the malefactors. Certainly some extraordinary legal quiddity must have been involved —though I have never succeeded yet in properly discovering what the legal position was—because elsewhere in England witches were invariably hanged and not burned. And one has no means of telling whether or not the imputation was correct. At all events, Bishop John was beginning to read Glanvil, and the *Malleus*. And one sees how this ready-made, well-sanctified moral issue would appeal to his underlying Puritanism—and how the methods used in dealing with it would appeal to his sensuality. For many of the women were young, and some beautiful. So it was in 1704, the year before he died."

Dallow went to the cupboard, and took from it one of several thick, leather-bound books. Reverently he opened it, and turned over the pages.

"Here," he said, "is the Bishop's personal diary, for the last months of his life."

Even Fen showed signs of intelligence at this.

"It is," Dallow continued, "one of the most complete first-hand records of a haunting in existence, and there seems no doubt of is authenticity. The Bishop left orders that the diary was to be destroyed at his death—unread. But such is human curiosity, and so extraordinary was his account of the last months, that it passed into the keeping

161

of the then Chancellor, and so came to me. Mr. Vintner"
—Dallow crossed to Geoffrey's chair—"perhaps you
would care to look at it—to read it to us, even. I never
tire of hearing the story. And the diary itself gives the
whole thing, without any need for commentary. You are
not in a hurry, Mr. Fen?"

Fen shook his head, and Dallow gave the book to Geoffrey. It was heavy, and the writing was neat, large, and
fastidious. Leaning over Geoffrey's shoulder, Dallow
turned the pages, and at last pointing to an entry:

"You might perhaps begin here. . . ."

So Geoffrey read, as the rain hissed softly on to the
garden, and the yellow, veiled light of the sun came and
went, cloud-driven, across the stiff, thick pages.

"27 Febr. A° 1705. We are advis'd in one of those
Sermons of Dr Donne of St. Paul's that have so justly
been rever'd as sound Doctrine, that the pleasures of the
Senses are right to be employ'd insofar as they interpose
no veil between the soul and its Maker; that is to say,
moderately employ'd. Yet Donne himself was a notorious
Rakehell in that earlier part of his life that preceded his
reception in the bosom of the Church of Christ, a man of
great profligacy and extravagancies, an associate of London whores and conycatchers. If therefore in Youth a man
may overtop the limits of moderation and yet be due to
Repentance and Charity later defy the pains of Hell, why
should I being yet in ye flower of mine age and full of
natural energies be hinder'd through exercise of my Holy
Office from the relaxations that are everywhere enjoy'd
by common men? It is written that even the Sons of God
lusted after the daughters of men. True it is that their
Desire was Impiety by the disparity in Kind between the
Angelic Substance and the bodies of those Jewish Women;
but let there be no such disparity, and where is the sin?
If we believe, our crimes are expiated as soon as committed.

"Often upon my pillow I think of my youth in London,
of the Playhouses and those comedies of Mr Wycherley,
and the darkness and the smell of the women's hair and
the gleam of their naked throats; and take out sometimes
the *Ars Amatoris,* to read that Passage that concerns the
wooing of a woman in the Playhouse (thus inaccurately

162

paraphrased by Mr Dryden.) These things for me are past by, but I desire them still. Here I am among Bumkins, having neither Wit nor Grace of body or mind. Their women are like sacks.

"See that this be regularly lock'd away, after perusal.

"*4 Mar.* Have seen her come twice this week into Mattins, most modestly veil'd; but was able to perceive the extraordinary Texture and richness of her Hair.

"*6 Mar.* I have found that she is nam'd Elizabeth Pulteney, being niece of a woman burn'd last year by my order as a Witch. Her bodily perfection and Grace of carriage argue a higher origin than in that low station to which as I am assur'd she belongs. She is devout, yet there have been accusations against her. Four Women were burn'd this week. The crowds grow less continuously.

"*21 Mar.* Return'd from the flogging of a woman to extort confession. It was not long. She was stripp'd and beaten with triple knotted thongs of leather. The screams were unusually piercing. I took no pleasure in it, as I should do, were I properly concern'd with the chastening of Satan through this punishment. My thoughts were continually elsewhere.

"*26 Mar.* Spoke to her this morning for the first time. Her Skin is remarkably soft and fine. She is meek and reverent. I have offer'd her regular spiritual Guidance. She will come to me often now. To chasten that Submissiveness into active pain! But these are idle Fancies."

(Here Geoffrey omitted a number of entries dealing with the work of the diocese. The next reference to Elizabeth Pulteney was dated April 23rd.)

"Tonight her fourth visit. I stress'd to her the need of Absolute submission to those set in Authority over her, and set her the test of unclothing straightaway before me. She demurr'd greatly and it was long before I persuaded her (by various Means) to do it. Her modesty excited me beyond all caution. Learn'd she is but seventeen years of age, but remarkably well-inform'd, and the tresses of her Hair coiling long and golden about her . . . Milton, in his great religious Poem, tells of the naked beauty of Eve and of her hair. So also Donne in that Elegie.

"She realis'd my purposes early, and seem'd afraid. I

163

twisted the Hair about her throat and pretended to be about to kill her. She is a foolish child, with her talk about being the Bride of Christ. As I said to her, is not the Church Itself that? But the threat of Persecution as a Witch silenc'd her.

"Feel unusually depress'd. The house is over-silent, and it is not good to be alone. Must get to my bed and drive these thoughts and scruples away with recollections of the Pleasure I have had. But first to lock this away downstairs. The house has echoes, and I have always hated the dark. I dare not leave it here. The Servants have long since retir'd. _

"*13 Aug.* All goes well, and I have not had sufficient Leisure to write in here previously. Since I must to myself be honest, I have fear'd to face the doubts which have lain about me. I have reason'd with my self and see no cause for fear in my actions. If I have chasten'd her body, there is Authority and Precedent enough, as in the history of the early Church. She grows very silent and unresponsible, and my interest dies. I shall not see her again. Why do I feel so continuously the enormity of my acts, when Reason itself does not condemn them?

"*15 Aug.* The worst has happen'd, and she is with child by me. But the threat of burning will keep her silent.

"*16 Aug.* Met her this day secretly, in the coppice beyond Slatter's Close. She is recalcitrant, and will own the parent of her child. It seems that even the Threat of torture as a Witch does not deter her. But there is no other course. Her Ravings against me will be held the evidence of demoniac Possession. She is resign'd, as it seems, to penitence and Expiation. Oh, the Follies of these religious women! I would spit upon their hateful Piety.

"*23 Aug.* The Danger is pass'd. Her accusations against me were as I had anticipated an added condemnation of her self. It was Madness ever to fear that she would be believ'd. Today the thumbscrews to extort Confession. When that fail'd, hoisting by weights. The Confession greatly Circumstantial, led me to suppose her in fact a Witch. And what more likely than that the Devil through her employ'd his arts to surprize my steadfastness? I am convinc'd that this is the Truth.

"Throughout her eyes fix'd upon me, though she no

longer spoke against me. I do not like the Memory of that.

"*29 Aug. Deus misericorde me.* Today she burn'd. I thought it might last for ever. Her hair was first shav'd, and burn'd separate. There was some Cavill and Murmuring in the crowd, that the Sergeants were forc'd to employ their Authority in the maintenance of a due silence and respect. Adjur'd to confess publickly, she kept obstinate silence, only as she came by me saying 'Keep fast you doors against those that will wish to visit you.' Then was hurried to the Stake, bound, and the Faggots kindl'd. She seem'd little more than a Child.

"I know not what she mean'd by this, but the house is cold, and I were better in bed. Without doubt I acted rightly, and she was a Witch.

"*4 Sept.* We are cruel punish'd for our Follies, and I, most miserable sinner, with hardest stripes. As I lay in bed last night, the curtains of the bed drawn upon three sides, and the fourth open to admit the light of the candles set upon my table, that fourth curtain (no Person being in the room) was drawn sudden in upon me, when I was left in the darkness. And some Creature of the Night, moving without, seem'd trying to crawl beneath the curtains, and plucking at the bedclothes, so that I scream'd out loud, and one of the Servants came running, but nothing was there. Had him stay with me the remnant of the night, in great fear and perturbation of mind, with every light burning. Shall see that all doors be fast lock'd but I fear 'twill make no difference. I dare confide in nobody. But, Christ the Lord will protect me against the consequence of my Evil.

"*5 Sept.* Today went about the house, setting the Pentagram upon the sills and thresholds, after repeating the rite of Exorcism. With these cares, I shall live long and happy. She shall not filch from me the time to expiate my sins. Though the Autumn is cold and windy, the house grows uncomfortably warm. Being just come in from Mattins, ask'd one of the servants if he had notic'd this, but he said no. Seeing he seem'd surpriz'd at my appearance, ask'd him the reason. 'Why sure,' said he, 'I thought your Grace was in the Studdy, for not ten minutes hence I heard someone walking to and fro there.' When I went up no one was there.

"10 Sept. I have seen It for the first time, and pray I may never again. God have mercy on my Soul, and rescue me from the horror. Hell is not Anguish, but Fear, such as this. Tonight late in going to my Chamber, pass'd by the Studdy door, and there saw one of the serving-maids (as I thought) bending to make up the fire. I went in to reprove her for not being retir'd to her own quarters, when the Thing straighten'd suddenly and put its arms about me. I fell to the floor in a Faint, but one of the men happening to be by, came to my assistance, but saw no thing. I cannot write more. Christ, have mercy on me.

"13 Sept. There is Whispering in the town that all is not well here, and Whispering against my own Person. Seven of the servants have left. Burning coals found scatter'd about the library, though there was no fire there. The warmth grows insufferable.

"19 Sept. A servant to-day found all the hangings of my closet ablaze. The conflagration was hard to extinguish.

"2 Dec. Praise be to God for all His mercies! Two months gone and no Incident, and the heat likewise evaporated. That Devil's minion Elizabeth Pulteney sent at last to her right Account. Virtue can command even the Powers of Hell. My mind is at last at rest, and I can apply my self with renew'd vigour to the affairs of the Diocese. God has allow'd this as a Testing of my Faith, and I am emerg'd triumphant. The evil Phantasms are gone.

"3 Dec. I shall not see Christmas. This morning enter'd one of the Sextons to tell me that a woman would see me by the North Transept of the cathedral. Poor fellow, he knew not what manner of thing it was bade him fetch me forth. As I stood looking about me for the Woman, I saw it crouching in the shadow of a buttress. The skin is like parchment, peeling from the Skull, that shows through in white patches. There are no Eyes. The Hair is still beautiful, beautiful. But I must not see it again . . ."

The writing trailed away. Geoffrey turned on; the rest of the book was blank. There was a long silence. Geoffrey looked enquiringly at Dallow.

"The night of the twenty-fourth," said the Chancellor softly, "was cold and windy, and on Christmas morning

166

there was snow. They found Bishop John Thurston lying in his bed. There were burns on his face, and he had died of suffocation. There was no sign of a struggle, but his mouth was full of hair."

Geoffrey closed the book and put it on the table beside him. He made no comment.

"An ugly, frightening tale," said Fen, who had let his cigarette go out and was now relighting it. "The history of Tolnbridge Cathedral is evidently more lurid than I'd imagined." He turned to Dallow. "Is there devil-worship in Tolnbridge now? I've reason to believe there may be."

To Geoffrey's surprise Dallow nodded. "A singularly childish cult of demonolatry exists—in no sense, you understand, a continuation of the tradition, but merely a trumped-up, unspontaneous affair. It appears to give certain people a mild *frisson* of excitement."

"I think," said Fen, who was beginning to fidget and shuffle his feet, "that it may have some remote connection with the murder of Butler. You don't run it yourself, I suppose? From the contemptuous way in which you referred to it, I should imagine not."

"You imagine rightly, my *de*-ear Professor. I have been once or twice to the Black Mass, but much of it was always so incompetent and—if I may use the word— uncanonical, that I have recently discontinued my attendance."

"You never thought of reporting it to the police? It is illegal, you know."

"But so *harm*less! If you could only *see* the poor dears——" Dallow stopped, glanced at his watch, and suddenly beamed. "Half-past eight. And yesterday was Thursday. Now, does Friday come after or before Thursday? *After,* isn't it?"

"Why?" Really, thought Geoffrey, this amiable posturing was a little much.

"Because I think it is on Fridays that they devil-worship. Every Friday—just like a *churchwardens' meeting,* my dear sirs. If we were to go to their place of resort we might find them at it. Would you like that?" Dallow might have been organising a Sunday School treat.

"It seems a good idea," said Fen. "Let's visit them. But first tell me more. Who runs the racket?"

"My *de*-ear Professor, I haven't—I really haven't—the least notion."

"You don't *know?*" Geoffrey exclaimed.

"It may be the Bishop him*self*." Dallow giggled irritatingly, and balanced himself on the tips of his toes, looking for a moment like a drawing by Edward Lear. "Both celebrants and participants are masked, you understand. Identification of your neighbour is made virtually impossible. And that reminds me that we too shall have to be masked." He went to a cupboard, and took three weird contraptions from it. "Animal masks, you see. Rather beautifully designed. They are of Hindu origin. They will do." The masks were of a pig, a cow, and a goat.

Fen put on the cow's mask. His pale blue eyes stared disconcertingly from the eyeholes. Geoffrey took the pig, and Dallow the goat. They surveyed one another without enthusiasm.

"You both look pretty silly," said Fen. He mooed experimentally, and then, seeming pleased with the sound, did it again. He continued to moo all the way to their destination. There were times when Fen could be very irritating indeed.

The Black Mass proved to be in progress in an old wooden Scout hut, situated in a deserted spot a little way off the road from Tolnbridge to Tolnmouth. It still bore traces of its former occupancy, in the shape of cardboard beavers, otters, and other amorphous-looking fauna pinned to various parts of the hall, and which stared down at the goat, pig and cow which came and settled themselves at the back. They looked very absurd, but no one took any notice of them.

There were quite a number of people present, all masked, and mostly women. Two masked and black-robed figures pottered ineffectually about by an improvised altar. There was no talking. Presently the business of the evening commenced, and very dull it was. It consisted, as far as Geoffrey could judge, of the ordinary Latin Mass, with the *Confiteor* and *Gloria* omitted. Geoffrey, Dallow and Fen made no attempt to communicate, and no one seemed to expect them to. There were no diabolic ecstasies—but then, Geoffrey reflected, there were seldom any noticeable ecstasies at the Divine Mass. There was no human sacrifice, or obscene ritual. Geoffrey had seldom spent a less interesting half-hour. Fen became very fidgety indeed, and could scarcely be restrained from stalking out. Geoffrey wondered how it would end; perhaps they would play God Save the King, or the Doxology, upside down.

Eventually, however, things seemed somehow or other to come to a stop. The Celebrant and Acolyte departed to a room at the back of the hut, and the participants, after a little whispering and sniggering together, melted away into the growing dusk.

"I thought they always had an orgy after the Mass," complained Fen, removing his mask.

"An orgy." A trace of humour appeared in Dallow's voice. He waved a hand at the surroundings. "Hardly the right *milieu*, do you think? One would require to be very determined indeed to have a satisfactory orgy here."

The hall, except for themselves, was now completely empty. Geoffrey went to the altar, and examined the Cup and the Host. The latter, he found, was a large section of turnip painted black, apparently with creosote.

"That is traditional," Dallow explained. "I expect they got it out of a book," he added contemptuously.

The Cup proved to be a revolting concoction with a basis, it seemed, of quinine.

"Keep them healthy, anyway," said Fen cheerfully. "I'm going to interview the priests of these rites," he added, making for the door into the back room.

"Then I shall leave you," said Dallow pleasantly, "to your investigations. I think you may have difficulty. The rule of secrecy is very strictly observed, and—for obvious reasons—particularly by the Celebrant. However, I wish you luck. You may catch me up—I am a slow walker. In case not, a very good evening to you, with a murderer behind every door." He giggled, and with a limp wave of the hand left the hut.

Fen turned the handle of the door, and pushed it open. It was ill-fitting and scraped on the floor. They found themselves in a room structurally identical with the one they had just left, only much smaller. It was unfurnished, except for a single cheap table and chair.

169

The Acolyte had gone, but the Celebrant was unrobing, his back turned towards them. When he heard them come in, he replaced his mask unhurriedly: then faced them.

"Well, gentlemen?" The voice was clearly disguised. But Geoffrey found it impossible to identify the original.

"We hoped to be able to make your acquaintance," said Fen.

"I'm afraid that that's impossible. Absolute anonymity is the rule. You yourselves should be masked."

"That's rather absurd."

The Celebrant made a gesture which might have been humorous resignation. What he actually did was to take an automatic from beneath his robes and fire it at Fen.

Chapter Eleven

WHALE AND COFFIN

*"Why, what a disgraceful catalogue of cutthroats
is here!"*

OTWAY

By SOME MIRACLE, the shot went wide. Looking back on
it afterwards, Geoffrey thought that the Celebrant's arm
became entangled in his robes; and there was no doubt
that he was extremely nervous. Fen, who had fought in
the Great War, fell flat on his face, with well-drilled precision. Geoffrey, who had not, remained immobile, gaping in frank stupefaction. And the Celebrant was seized
with panic. There was no logical reason why he should
not have killed both of them there and then. But he
hesitated, and as he hesitated, there came a sound of
running footsteps outside; someone had heard the shot.
Grotesque in his robes and mask the Celebrant rushed
to an outer door, flung it open, and vanished. Almost at
the same instant someone pounded across the hall, and
came in through the door by which they themselves had
entered. It was Dallow, dishevelled and alarmed. More
automatically than courageously, Geoffrey followed the
Celebrant out. As he went, he was aware of Fen climbing
to his feet and grumbling quietly to himself.

The Celebrant had a good start. Like some fantastic
crow, with his black robes flapping in the wind, he was
running across the wet fields into the gathering dusk.
Grimly Geoffrey set off in pursuit, though with no very
clear plan of action in mind. The chase proved abortive,

for before very long the Celebrant stopped, turned, and fired his automatic at Geoffrey. As an offensive measure this was perfectly useless, since the shot must have fallen at least a hundred yards short. But as a deterrent it was good enough. Geoffrey slowed down, stopped, and stood watching as the figure plunged on and was eventually lost to view in a small clump of trees. Then he returned to the hut. It was not heroic, but it was sensible.

"I don't know what good you expected chasing him to do," said Fen peevishly when he re-appeared. "I am covered," he added with more concentrated malevolence, "in bruises."

He inspected himself tenderly.

"I lost him," said Geoffrey rather obviously.

Dallow, who apparently was now acquainted with the situation, moaned faintly in deprecation. "I confess, my de-ear Professor," he said, "that I lingered, fearing trouble of some kind. But this I did not anticipate."

Fen pressed himself experimentally, and let out a sudden howl.

"Perhaps you might tell us," he said when the noise had subsided, "why you were so anxious."

The Chancellor had his answer ready—almost too ready, it seemed to Geoffrey. "In the first place," he pronounced, with the air of one embarking on a lecture, "there were ritual considerations. In the second, the compelling need of anonymity in this business. I suspected your intrusion would not be welcome, though I never thought . . ." He stopped, not even pretending to simulate incoherence.

Fen grunted. He inspected the place where the bullet had buried itself in a wooden joist, and then the room. It contained absolutely nothing beyond the table, the chair, a quantity of dust, and themselves.

"Useless," he exclaimed disgustedly. "Let's go."

"You will perhaps allow me, my de-ear Professor, to accompany you as far as my house?"

Fen gave a grudging and uncivil permission. They set off, walking moodily and in silence. It was the measure of Fen's absorption that he passed by three dragon-flies, a golden beetle, and a nest of flying ants without even deigning to notice them. Geoffrey thought, rather unintelligently and quite fruitlessly, about the case. What Dallow was thinking it was impossible to tell, but he appeared to be reciting sections of *The City of Dreadful Night* to himself at brief intervals. It was only when they were nearing his house again that Fen exclaimed:

"Oh, my dear paws!"

Dallow was not aware of Fen's recourse to the White Rabbit in moments of high excitement. He looked round with mild surprise.

"What a fool I've been," said Fen.

"I know this stage," put in Geoffrey. "You tell us you know who the murderer is, we ask you, and you won't inform us, though there's no reason in heaven or earth why you shouldn't."

"Of course there's a reason why I shouldn't."

"What is it?"

"Because," said Fen solemnly, "you did it yourself."

"Oh, don't be so daft."

"All right, I know you didn't. But seriously, there is a good reason why I shouldn't. An all-important reason. You'll know it finally."

"Are you certain you know what you're talking about?"

"Logically certain. I can't think why I didn't see it before. Unfortunately, there isn't a shred of material proof —nothing that would hang the person concerned. For that reason I've got to go warily. (It's the Butler murder I'm talking about, by the way.) But the identity of one person concerned is as certain as anything on this earth. Or rather . . ."

"Well?"

"There's one snag." Fen was very thoughtful. "Just one. And it depends on something I must ask Peace. At least——" He hesitated. "Yes, it must depend on that."

"You mean Peace isn't guilty?"

"Certainly not."

"But he's the only person who could have been in that cathedral. . . ."

Fen groaned. "I know, I know. But just the same, he's *not guilty*."

"He had the best motive."

"Don't be so foolish. We know perfectly well what the motive was. And it wasn't money. I should have thought you would have known how Butler was murdered, if anyone did."

Geoffrey was blank. "Me?"

"Certainly."

"But didn't you say that the police would find incriminating evidence in Peace's room?"

Fen sighed and shook his head, like one dealing with a particularly backward child. "Oh, Geoffrey, Geoffrey. . . . Perhaps this will give it to you. Peace left to go up to the cathedral before we got back to the chapter-house last evening, didn't he?"

"That was what Spitshuker said."

"Well?"

"Well what?"

Fen shook his head again. "Never mind. You ought to know, and so ought everyone else. I expect we shall find Peace at the police station. They'll have found the stuff in his room by now, and either arrested him or detained him for questioning."

"I don't see how you knew anything would be in his room."

"No," said Fen rudely. "You wouldn't."

At this point the argument ceased, as they had arrived at Dallow's house. The Chancellor bade them an affected good night, and went in. They continued down the hill into the town.

"It occurs to me," said Geoffrey, "that this Black Mass business might, if suitably handled, and with the help of drugs, be a very good way of getting military information out of the wives of people in the know—they were mostly women there."

"Yes, that's true. In spite of the horrid boredom of the whole business, I really believe the majority of those people must have thought they were doing something wicked and exciting and important."

They walked on in silence. Thanks to the rain-clouds, it was considerably darker now than it had been on the last evening, when they had gone up to the cathedral and found Butler dead. Looking at his watch, Geoffrey was surprised to see that it was only half-past nine.

"Still time for a drink," said Fen laconically when informed of this fact.

174

"Why didn't you want to tell me who the murderer was?" asked Geoffrey. "Was it because Dallow was with us? Is he in on this business?"

Fen frowned in perplexity. "He may be. That's just what one doesn't know. There must be more than one person concerned—perhaps three even, though I doubt if there are likely to be more. All I know is that one person was quite definitely concerned in the murder of Butler, and *may* be the brains of the whole business."

"You say *concerned* in the murder. . . ."

"Well, there must have been more than one of them in the cathedral when Butler went up there, in order to get that radio away." Fen paused. "Geoffrey, are you very famous as a composer?"

"No. Church musicians would probably know about me. Very few other people. Why the change of subject?"

"I was thinking about the landlord of the 'Whale and Coffin' knowing your Christian name. He might just be a knowledgeable music-lover, overwhelmed at being confronted by you in the flesh." (Geoffrey glared.) "But it doesn't seem very likely." (Geoffrey snorted crossly.) "We must tackle him on the subject. They're occasionally inefficient, these people. But I've no doubt the same idea will have occurred to them, and they'll be ready for us. Anyway, we must see Peace first."

They found the Inspector standing on the steps of the police station, smoking a cigarette and gazing blankly and purposelessly up the street. He brightened somewhat when he saw them.

"Ah, here you are, sir," he said to Fen. "You were right about that stuff in Peace's room. We found it easily enough, under the traditional loose floor-board: the clergy-house key to the cathedral, a phial of atropine solution and the hypodermic."

"Any finger-prints?"

"Not a thing. They'd been wiped clean."

"Yes, I rather expected that. What have you done about it?"

"Arrested him. Or rather the Yard people have. He's here now, but we haven't got a thing out of him more than he told us before."

"Oh," said Fen. "So the Yard's come, has it? Appleby?"

"No, unfortunately." The Inspector looked uneasily over his shoulder, and lowered his voice. "A couple of great churls, they are. Most unco-operative. They think they've got the whole business cut-and-dried, now they've arrested Peace. Won't do anything but sit in the station playing rummy and smoking foul pipes."

"It seems to me," Geoffrey interposed, "that they'll have to make up their minds which motive to go for. If they think it was the radio. . . ."

"The point is, sir, that they regard the money motive as simply a cover for the real one."

"Is all that money business a fake, then?"

"No, it isn't: and that's what worries me. We've checked on it, and things are exactly as Peace said, even to the fact that Butler was trying to get his wife to transfer the dibs to himself. Now it's all very well to say that's a cover for the spy business. But it seems to me the crisis over the money came up pretty conveniently just at the time when the murder was necessary. Somehow, it doesn't really seem plausible. Not that they haven't got a pretty good case without that."

"For instance?" queried Fen.

"Well, the stuff that was found in his room."

"Could have been a plant. The fact that there were no fingerprints suggests it, in fact."

"That might have been only an additional precaution. But I agree, mechanically speaking it *could* have been a plant. I've checked times, access to Peace's room, and so on, and you can take it from me that *anyone* remotely connected with the case could have put the things there. But there's other things, the chief being that only Peace could have been in that cathedral when Butler was murdered. They had it in for me, I can tell you, for not searching him for the key immediately afterwards." The Inspector stared aggrievedly. "Not that he couldn't have hidden it somewhere, and recovered it afterwards."

"The point is," said Geoffrey, "that one can't see why he kept it at all. He could quite easily have put it back in the clergy-house or left it where he'd hidden it. He didn't need it again."

"Exactly, sir. That's another point in his favour. But there's more to it yet. According to his own account, Peace got to Dr. Butler's house at five past six, and was there till a quarter past, when Dr. Butler and Mrs. Butler returned. Now, the poison was put in Brooks's medicine at six o'clock, and we've no proof at all that Peace didn't go straight down there from the station and *then* back to Dr. Butler's house, since there weren't even any servants in to receive him. Mr. Vintner, you didn't happen to notice which way he went when he left the station?"

"I didn't, I'm afraid."

"Well, there it is. It's possible, though it doesn't seem to me likely."

Fen, who had been shuffling his feet and showing other signs of impatience, now demanded:

"But what about the first attack on Brooks—in the cathedral? I thought it was quite certain Peace was in town that night. And why should he have the *hypodermic* in his room?"

"Yes," said the Inspector, scratching his nose thoughtfully. "If your theory about a plant is right, that was a serious mistake. Even those ruffians from London"—he pointed a thumb at the interior of the police station—"admit that he couldn't have been responsible for that. But then, we know there's more than one person concerned, don't we? And the evidence against Peace on the other two accounts is pretty black."

"Except," said Fen, "for the business about the key and the mixed motives. But I suppose there are ways of getting round that."

"The trouble is, sir, that I don't know where else to look, even thought I'm inclined to agree with you that Peace isn't guilty. They're mainly concerned with the spy business, mind you, and of course that's quite right. But they think they can get at it through Peace, and they're hardly bothering about anything else."

"Can I see Peace? There are a couple of rather important questions I want to ask him. If I get the answer I want to the first of them, I think I shall be on to something at last."

"I don't see why you shouldn't, sir. I shall have to ask

those churls' permission, though. And they'll probably want to be present."

Fen nodded, and all three passed inside. As they went, Fen asked if Josephine had been got away safely.

"Nasty business that, sir," said the Inspector. "What decent person'd want to do a thing like that to a little kid? It was clever of you to tumble to it. Yes, we got the doctor to look at her, and she's been sent to a private nursing-home up north for expert treatment. Mrs. Butler wanted to go with her, but we headed her off. She was in a rare taking when she heard about it, I can tell you. I don't think she had anything to do with it, though."

"No. Still, it was wiser not to let her go. Did you get anything more out of the girl?"

"No, the doctor wouldn't let us ask any questions."

The churls were, as the Inspector had predicted, playing rummy and smoking foul pipes. He went over and engaged in a muttered colloquy with them, while Fen stood with a poker-faced expression which made him look like something loose from a mental home, but which was evidently intended to be noncommittal. After a while they all set off to Peace's cell, which was small and comfortable-looking. Peace was sitting on the bed, smoking a cigarette and reading *The Mind and Society*. He seemed pleased to see them.

"Ah," he said, "you've come to visit the condemned man. Have you been hearing about the case against me? It all sounds rather unpleasant. And as I keep telling these people, I'm damned if I know how those things got into my room." His tone was light, but Geoffrey sensed great strain and anxiety behind it.

"You'll be out of here in no time," said Fen. "That is," he added minatorily, "if you give the right answer to a question I'm going to ask you."

"Well?"

Fen hesitated. Even Geoffrey, who had no idea of what Fen was getting at, felt somehow the importance of the moment. Even the churls took their pipes from their mouths.

"What time," Fen asked, "did you leave the clergy-house to go up to the cathedral and meet Butler?"

"It was"—Peace paused—"just before ten."

178

Fen turned to the Inspector. "According to Spitshuker, five minutes before we got to the clergy-house." The Inspector nodded; Fen turned back to Peace.

"Now this is the point." He leaned forward and spoke with emphasis. "When you left the clergy-house, did you go straight up to the cathedral?"

Peace stared. "Yes—I . . ."

"Damn!" Fen began pacing about the room. "No, it can't be. I can't be wrong. Think again. Think, man, think. Didn't you delay at all? Everything depends on this."

Again Peace hesitated. "No, I—wait a minute, though. I did."

"Well?" There was a fury of impatience in Fen's voice.

"I went straight out on to the cathedral hill. Then I stopped for five minutes to look at the burning-post. I was thinking about the psychological impulses which go to make witches and witch-burners. . . ."

"Only five minutes?" Fen broke in. "Are you sure?"

"I'm sorry," said Peace helplessly. "It couldn't have been more than that. If as much."

"That would mean you got up to the cathedral at five past ten—at the latest. It was 10.15 when we arrived and heard the crash. What were you doing in the other ten minutes?"

The two Yard men looked at one another. "It seems to me, sir," said one of them, "that you're just doing our work for us. In that time we have reason to believe that he went into the cathedral, knocked Dr. Butler out, dropped the slab on him, and slipped out, locking the door behind him. Then he met you as you rushed round."

"He did nothing of the sort," said Fen offensively. "And don't interrupt."

"Actually," said Peace, "I wandered round the cathedral trying all the doors. I couldn't make out why Butler didn't hear me."

"*All* the doors? On both sides?"

"Yes, of course. Several times."

Fen took out a handkerchief and mopped his brow; Geoffrey had seldom seen him show so much emotion. "Thank God!" he said. "It *is* possible, then. Or rather"—he became suddenly anxious again—"it's possible provided we can find out what that innkeeper was doing all evening."

"Harry James?" enquired the Inspector.

"Yes. There's a third conceivable snag, and that is that none of these people we're thinking of had anything to do with it at all. But no, that's impossible. It must have been someone connected somehow with the cathedral, for reasons we've discussed. One more point," he added to Peace. "What key did you use to unlock the gate between the clergy-house garden and the cathedral hill?"

"I borrowed Spitshuker's."

"Good. Well," said Fen, recovering something of his normal boisterous manner, "we shall have you out of here in no time. Try not to get into any mischief," he adjured Peace with tedious facetiousness. Then he nodded farewell, glared at the Yard, and marched out, accompanied by Geoffrey and the Inspector.

They paused on the steps, and the Inspector remarked: "I didn't quite see what you were getting at, sir."

"No," said Fen rudely; "you're too stupid. And let me tell you another thing: I have to report an attempted murder."

The Inspector stared. "What? Attempted murder of who?"

"Of me."

"Good heavens." The Inspector stared even more. "But how? . . . why? . . ."

Fen explained about the Black Mass, and what had followed.

"Black Mass!" the Inspector exclaimed. "Holy God, what shall we be having next? Here, you'd better come in and make a formal statement about all this."

"I haven't time," said Fen shortly. "They'll be closed in half an hour. Besides, I've got to write things down on pieces of paper, to clear up my ideas a bit. If it's devil-worship you're worried about, then you can take it from me that's not likely to crop up again after this evening's *fracas*."

"But what about you?"

"I'm all right," said Fen irritably.

"They'll try it again."

"No, they won't. That was just a panic impulse, because the fellow thought we'd find out who he was. Very silly. Come on, Geoffrey, we must go."

"Just as you like," said the Inspector with theatrical resignation. "It's your own funeral. But you might tell me what this idea of yours is. It won't be much good to us if you're bumped off without telling anyone."

"You go and think up an idea of your own," Fen replied. And without more ado he strode off towards the "Whale and Coffin."

"Seriously, though," said Geoffrey when they were out of earshot of the Inspector, "why don't you tell him?"

"Because, my dear Geoffrey, he'd insist on at least detaining the person concerned, and that's the last thing I want. They're not quite such fools that they won't have provided against the contingency of arrest. Whatever work they have to do will be done in any case. By far the best thing is to leave them free, imagining we don't suspect them, and then see if we can't somehow ferret out what their methods are. But it's going to be difficult. Damned difficult."

The public bar of the "Whale and Coffin" was crowded, and they went round to the lounge, where it was still possible to sit; not, however, before collecting Fielding, whom they found playing darts. A spasm of remorse seized Geoffrey as he realized that he had not once thought of Fielding during the past few hours; after all, the man had twice saved his life. He seemed as dejected and purposeless as ever. Geoffrey resolved to make amends for his past neglect.

They discovered the innkeeper, Harry James, and Fen questioned him. He seemed quite ready to reply, and suspiciously prompt in his details. Last evening, he said, he had been in the bars uninterruptedly from opening time (six o'clock) to closing time (10:30). From 9:30 to 10:30, he said, he had been talking to three regulars, whose names he was prepared to give. (Geoffrey noticed with surprise that Fen heaved a sigh of relief at this intelligence.) Fen asked if he had himself opened the doors at six o'clock. He said he had, and that several customers who had been waiting outside would bear him out. It was all very natural, and not unexpected, but Geoffrey found himself disliking more and more the little man, as he stood there with his small eyes blinking through the thick lenses of his glasses, and fingering incessantly his watch-chain. There was something almost physically repulsive about him.

"I was wondering," Geoffrey put in, "how it was you came to know my Christian name last night."

"Why, Mr. Vintner"—James smiled, and his glasses flashed, as he turned, in the electric light—"I know of you as a composer of Church music. I'm afraid you must be too modest about your reputation."

"You said at the time that you were thinking of someone who was dead."

"I didn't wish to embarrass you," James replied smoothly. "I deplore the habit of pestering well-known men."

"You're interested in Church music, then?"

"Very much so. I've made it a life-long study."

Geoffrey simulated interest with, he secretly thought, a good deal of success. "It's unusual to find a layman who knows anything about it. We must have a talk some time. What is your favourite setting of the evening service?"

James smiled again. "I'm a Presbyterian myself, so I'm not well acquainted with settings of the Anglican service. But of those I've heard, I have a sentimental liking for Noble in B minor."

"Personally I prefer Stanford in E flat." Geoffrey waited breathless for the answer. But James only raised his eyebrows and said:

"In E flat? I've never heard of it. The B-flat is delightful, of course, and the less-known G."

Geoffrey cursed inwardly; the man had the better of him. Aloud he remarked:

"You should come to Mattins at the cathedral tomorrow. We're doing Byrd's eight-part setting of *In Exitu Israel*."

"Ah." James beamed, and Geoffrey's spirits rose. "I'm afraid the only one I know is the Wesley." Geoffrey's heart sank; his ruse had failed again.

"May I before I go," James was saying, "thank you for your own delightful Communion Service. The Creed is particularly fine, with that recurrent rising crotchet fig-

182

ure in the accompaniment. . . . Well, gentlemen, if I can't help you further. Jenny!" He called to a passing waitress. "These gentlemen are my guests for the evening. A glass of the special whisky for Professor Fen here. A very fine liqueur whisky," he added confidentially to Fen. "You'll like it, I'm sure. Good night to you all." He beamed at them, and was gone.

"Whisky!" said Fen with great satisfaction. None the less, he tasted it circumspectly when it came.

"Flummoxed," said Geoffrey in disgust. "Amazing what a day's intensive study of the text-books will do."

"Personally," Fen remarked, "I like Dyson in D. It's a battle of religion and romance, of Eros and . . ." He checked himself abruptly. "Never mind that. I've got what I wanted to know. Let's get down to work now."

He produced from a pocket a number of grubby, crumpled sheets of blank paper, and from another an assortment of blunt, stubby pencils. Then he and Geoffrey settled down to work out individual timetables for each of the persons likely to be concerned in the case, Fielding proffering valueless conjectures and advice the while. Eventually, after some acrimonious argument and mutual accusations of defective memory, the following list was produced:

Garbin. At 6.0 p.m. was alone in his house (unconfirmed); about 7:30 arrived at clergy-house; stayed to meeting after dinner.

Left the clergy-house shortly before 9.0 and went for walk along cliffs (unconfirmed). Arrived home at 10:30.

Spitshuker. At 6.0 working in his room at home (unconfirmed). At 7.0 set out with Garbin for the clergy-house, arriving towards 7.30.

Vouched for from then to the end of the meeting (*circa* 8.50). Walked to the clergy-house gate with Butler.

From then till just before 10.0 talking to Peace. Met on the point of leaving, at 10.0; by Geoffrey, Fielding, Fen, Frances, the Inspector.

From 10.5–10.15 talking to the Inspector.

Dutton. At 6.0 out walking (unconfirmed).

At 7.30 returned to dinner.

After dinner retired to his room, but was seen about when Butler was arranging to meet Peace at the cathedral.

Remained there for the rest of the evening (unconfirmed).

Dallow. At 6.0 talking to his servant at his house. Had an early dinner, and went down to the hospital to see Brooks. Then returned to clergy-house, arriving about 8.0. Stayed to meeting, left about 9.0, and went to see a local contractor on business; found him out, and returned home about 10.30 (unconfirmed).

Savernake. At 6.0 was walking with Mrs. Garbin from the station to the house where she was dining, and stayed there for some time. Returned direct to dinner at the clergy-house, only stopping to leave his bag at Butler's house.

After dinner went for a walk (unconfirmed). Talking to one of the aldermen between 9.45 and 10.20. Returned home just in time to hear the news of Butler's death.

Peace. At 6.0 had arrived from the station at Butler's house and found no one there (unconfirmed), but met Butler and Mrs. Butler when they returned at 6.15. Dinner at the clergy-house at 7.30. After dinner sat in the summer-house (unconfirmed) but went back shortly before 9.0. Arranged with Butler to meet at the cathedral at 9.20. Stayed talking to Spitshuker till just before 10.0, then set off for the cathedral. Found outside the cathedral at 10.16.

Butler. At about 6.0 was smacking Josephine at the clergy-house.

Returned home at 6.15, arrived at clergy-house about 8.0.

Left meeting to go up to the cathedral about 9.0. Was found dead at about 10.20–10.25.

James. From 6.0 to 10.30 in the "Whale and Coffin."

Frances. At 6.0, shopping down in the town (unconfirmed). Returned to clergy-house, meeting tail-end of Josephine disturbance and Geoffrey and Fielding at about 6.10. Got dinner, went to her room with a book afterwards, reappeared as the meeting broke up

(8.50). Did some work in the kitchen (unconfirmed), set out for a stroll, met Fen, Geoffrey, Fielding, the Inspector at about 9.50 and returned with them to the clergy-house, subsequently going to the kitchen (unconfirmed).

Josephine. At 6.0 was being spanked by her father in the clergy-house. Subsequent movements uncertain, but took a false message to the police at the cathedral at 8.55.

Mrs. Garbin. At 6.0 was walking with Savernake to a friend's for dinner and bridge. Remained there till 11.0.

Mrs. Butler. Returned at 6.15 from tea with a friend, accompanied by Dr. Butler. Remained at home for the rest of the evening, with Dr. Butler till shortly before 8.0, after that alone (hence unconfirmed) until Spitshuker brought her the news of her husband's death.

At the bottom of the last sheet Fen had scribbled:

(1) The police left the Cathedral at 8.55;

(2) The implications of the tomb-slab—unpremeditated;

(3) The plant in Peacc's room—mistake about the hypodermic;

(4) The cathedral grounds are locked in the evenings, but anyone who really wanted to could easily get in without a key (Josephine did).

On the point about Geoffrey's Christian name, and the lasso, James may be involved; one other may be involved.

From the evidence of the timetables and the points listed above, *one person was quite definitely involved in Butler's murder, may have been the murderer, and is almost certainly the brains of the spy-ring.*

Fen looked at Geoffrey and Fielding. "Do you get it?" he asked.

"No," said Geoffrey.

"Nincompoop," said Fen.

Chapter Twelve

LOVE'S LUTE

"O Love's lute heard about the lands of death!"
SWINBURNE

THE NEXT DAY BROKE in a haze of fierce, shimmering heat. Geoffrey's night had been uneasy, beset with dreams which were just on the edge of real nightmares. He had woken, restlessly slept, woken again. And when towards morning he did sink into a deeper sleep, he was disturbed almost at once (as it seemed) by a light tapping on his bedroom door. He opened his eyes a little way, perceived without enthusiasm that it was quite light, and uttered that choking, miserable sound which those newly conscious employ to indicate their ready comprehension of what is going on around them. From behind the door, Frances' voice said:

"I've finished with the bathroom. For the Lord's sake don't be too long, or we shan't have time to really do anything before breakfast."

Geoffrey looked at his watch, saw that it was only shortly after six, shook his head at the lack of veracity of womankind, and succeeded eventually in getting out of bed.

When he arrived downstairs she was waiting for him, dressed in an open-necked check shirt and a pair of dark blue slacks. He wondered afresh at the dark beauty of her hair, the unblemished milk-white skin, just relieved from pallor by, here and there, a touch of red, the breath-

187

taking perfection of her body. This morning she looked, somehow, almost a child; and the sparkle in her eyes, and her impatience to be away, added to the impression. He wondered just what she felt about her father's death. And as if reading his thoughts, she said:

"You think it's rather shocking that I should be going out to enjoy myself when my father's been killed."

"I don't think so a bit."

She smiled, a little sadly. "I suppose it is shocking, really. But . . . Well, damn it all, one can't *force* oneself to feel sorry when one doesn't."

"Weren't you fond of him?"

"Yes, I was. That's the funny part. But only in an aloof sort of way. I mean . . ." She laughed suddenly. "How absurd that must sound! I don't know how to express it, really. Of course it was a horrible shock when . . . when you came and told me, but somehow it didn't last long. None of us ever knew much about him, really. He was always shut up with his work."

They went out of the house and through the garden, taking the road which led up to the cliffs between Tolnbridge and Tolnmouth.

"I hope nobody sees us," said Frances. "I really *oughtn't* to be gadding about."

"No one in his senses will be up at this hour."

She turned to look at him, and grinned. "You really are an old maid."

"Yes, aren't I? I think that's why women don't like me. They like a man to be a man—large, hairy, masterful. A sort of D. H. Lawrence gardener or pit-boy."

"What utter nonsense. All women like different things about men. Don't make specious generalisations like that. Men who generalise about women simply show that they don't know anything about them."

"*I* don't know anything about them."

"I know. That's partly what makes you so nice to be with. A man who's really shy about a woman is a lovely change."

"Is Savernake shy?"

She looked at him quickly. "You would drag him into it."

"It's because I'm jealous."

"Are you really? How nice. Well, he isn't shy, if you want to know. He's bumptious."

"Are you still engaged to him?"

"Yes." She answered shortly, almost hurriedly.

"Frances . . . I meant what I said yesterday. . . ."

She put a hand quickly on his arm. "Please, Geoffrey, I don't want to talk about that. Not now, anyway. Later, perhaps."

He felt an irrational tinge of resentment; she seemed to sense this.

"We'll discuss things later."

And, after all, he thought, I've only known the girl less than forty-eight hours. I've no right to try and burst into her personal life like this. Perhaps no right to do it ever. Perhaps I don't even want to do it. To marry her would mean giving up a lot of things I don't want to give up. But then I don't know whether she'd want to marry me.

Almost, he wished he had not come. She was beautiful, she was desirable, but if he committed himself. . . . He wanted more time to think. Then he cursed himself for an idiot and a coward, and, his sense of humour suddenly reasserting itself, he laughed out loud.

"What are you laughing at?"

"My own absurdity."

"I suppose you are rather absurd. Let's not talk for a while."

They walked on in silence. The sun, still low in the heavens, burned hotter, its edges ragged with fire. They turned from the hot, dusty road and climbed a path which led over a steep ramp into a wood hanging in the hillside. In the wood it was cool, a green, liquid coolness. Dying bracken, and brambles were twisted together between the trees. There were one or two wild roses, and some sour-looking small blackberries. The path, which led up the hillside, was narrow, and sloped at the edges, like a trough. The centre was full of stones, and yellow mud still wet from the water which flowed down it, so that once or twice they stumbled as they went on upwards.

Coming out of the wood was like emerging from a cavern. They found themselves on a wide expanse, dotted with rough stones and encircled with gorse. Overhead the gulls glided, their wings stiff, in long, immensely rapid flights. Their harsh shouting was the only sound except for the distant murmur of the sea. The young ones were ugly, speckled with brown. One came so low that they could see its throat throbbing with the sound.

In another moment they stood above the estuary-mouth, looking out to sea. Below them stretched the brown cliffs, with a strip of sand at the bottom strewn with the wreckage of a disused quarry: a rotting wooden landing stage; two lopsided trucks; rusted rails, broken and uneven, leading to nothing. The grass was short, hard, coarse, and brown with drought. A faint wind, brushing the surface of the sea into rows of tiny corrugated wavelets, played about their faces. Frances stretched out her arms in sheer animal pleasure.

"Lovely!"

They went on along the cliff path, towards the sea itself. Tiny fishing-boats, blue and brown and red, with little triangular sails at the stern, chugged along below them, convoyed by gulls. After a time Frances beckoned to Geoffrey, and they both went to the very edge of the cliff. Beneath was a wide stretch of clean, almost white sand, a cove where the water ran out clear as glass as far as the eye could reach.

"That's nice," said Geoffrey rather prosaically.

"Come on."

"Good heavens! I can't climb down there. It'd be mad. We'd break our necks."

"There's a way down," she said, "if you know how. I do. It's quite easy."

"It doesn't look easy to me."

"No one else knows about it. Or next to no one. You can always rely on getting it to yourself."

"I should like my coffin to be of lead, if there's anything recognisable to put in it."

Tant bien que mal, by a series of hair-raising athletic feats, they achieved the climb.

"Lord," said Geoffrey, panting, when they reached the strand, "I hope we can get back again."

"It's much easier to climb up than down." Frances performed a couple of tiny dancing steps on the sand. "Isn't it wonderful? We're quite alone. Let's have a bathe."

"But I haven't got any things."

"It doesn't matter. Nor have I."

He stared at her. "Do you think we've really known one another long enough? . . ."

She laughed infectiously. "Oh, Geoffrey, don't be a prude. Wouldn't you *like* a swim?"

"Yes, but . . ."

It was too late. She had already begun to take off her clothes. Apprehensively, Geoffrey followed suit. When they had finished, they looked at one another for a moment in silence; then simultaneously burst out laughing.

"Don't *stare* so!" she said with mock indignation. "It's rude." They raced each other into the water; it seemed to Geoffrey very cold.

Frances swam quickly out, with a swift, competent crawl. Puffing slightly, Geoffrey followed her.

"It's a pleasant sensation," he said, "but I feel very immoral." In the clear water, fathoms beneath their feet, they could see one or two small fish going about their esoteric affairs.

When they had come out, and were drying themselves on some rocks, Geoffrey put his arm round her shoulders, but she pushed him away.

"Not till I've got some clothes on." Geoffrey suddenly and unexpectedly blushed.

Then, as soon as they were dressed again:

"Frances."

"Well?"

"You know I'm in love with you?"

"Yes: I think I'm in love with you, too." He was almost troubled at the sincerity in her voice.

"I should like to marry you."

For a long time she was silent. Then she said: "Geoffrey, I'm sorry, but . . . I can't."

"Why?" He took her almost fiercely by the arm.

"Don't. You're hurting me."

"Why?"

"It's Daddy. I've been thinking, and after what's happened I can't leave Mummy. You do understand, darling?"

"Yes, but you've got your own life to live. And besides, all that can be got over. Your mother can live with us—"

and Josephine as well." He made the offer with a certain gloom.

"That's sweet of you, but I mustn't promise anything—just now." She laughed. "Promise—as though I was conferring some kind of privilege. It does sound vain."

"You're not refusing because of Savernake?"

"No. No." The denial was quick and eager. "I shan't marry him in any case."

"You did say you were fond of me."

"I am. Oh, my darling, I am. I love you so very much. But don't you see . . . I'm confused. It's all so quick. We can wait, can't we?"

"I don't want to wait."

"We must. All that's happened. . . . Oh, darling, what *did* happen to him? Was it an accident? It must have been an accident. Surely not even Peace. . . ."

"They've arrested him."

"I know." It was like a shadow between them. "Has Professor Fen discovered anything?"

He put his arms round her. "Don't bother about all that. Other people will look after it." He tried to put his lips to hers, but she pulled her head away. He stood back. She looked at him with eyes in which there was a hint of tears.

"Let's go home."

But when they were again at the top of the cliff, she turned and pulled him to her and for a moment kissed him warmly. Then they walked back, in silence.

Thus began the third day.

Geoffrey afterwards looked upon it as the day when, quite suddenly and as if at a signal, the talk ended and the final struggle began. Hitherto they had dealt with characters single, isolated from one another, mere waxworks lined up for questioning. When they had turned their backs one of those figures had moved, and there had been killing. But now some sixth sense told him that the end was near, that the pretence could no longer be kept up. He felt that they stood at a cavern-mouth, waiting for some creature to spring at them from the darkness, and yet not knowing what kind of thing it would be.

And there was no more time for conjecture now; they were committed, at last, to fight.

When he had played Mattins, he set out with Fen and Fielding to a little pub on the outskirts of the town, where Fen was proposing to put some plan of action before them, since there they were less likely to be interrupted or overheard there than at the "Whale and Coffin." Fen carried a large map of the district, which he persisted in opening as they walked along and refolding the wrong way, so that it became crumpled and torn.

"I don't think," he said, "that these people can possibly be operating from the centre of the town exclusively. It would be too dangerous. I've been trying to find out if there are any likely hideouts nearby—a pretty impossible business."

"Did you discover anything about the wireless messages they sent out?" Fielding asked.

"I'm going to ring up the cipher department, but I don't expect they've decoded the stuff yet. That sort of thing takes time. But the trouble is," he added waspishly, "that it's all so vague. Ten to one nothing will turn up at all."

At this point there was an interruption. They were going down a narrow path, flanked by high yew hedges, which skirted the churchyard. And from the other side of one of these hedges they suddenly heard a voice.

"*You may seek it with thimbles,*" said the voice informatively, "*and seek it with care, you may hunt it with forks and hope . . .*"

Fen stopped dead. "I know who that is," he said gloomily.

"*You may threaten its life with a railway share,*" pursued the voice, "*you may charm it with smiles and soap. . . .*"

"Charlemagne!" Fen bawled suddenly. The voice stopped, and there was a scraping sound on the other side of the hedge.

"That, I fancy," said Fen grimly, "is the Regius Professor of Mathematics."

A gruff, hairy, little old man put his head over the hedge.

"What are you doing here, Charlemagne?" asked Fen minatorily.

"I am holidaying," said the head, "and it was impolite of you to interrupt a total stranger in that ungentlemanly way."

This made Fen so indignant that he uttered a little shriek.

"Don't you know me?" he said irritably. "Don't you know me, you stupid old man?"

"Yes, I know you," said the head. "You are the New College buttery boy." It then disappeared.

Fuming, Fen rushed on to the next gap in the hedge. The Regius Professor of Mathematics arrived there simultaneously.

"*But oh, beamish nephew,*" he chanted, wagging his finger at Fen, "*beware of the day if your Snark be a Boojum! For then*"—he lowered his voice to a bloodcurdling whisper—"*you will softly and suddenly vanish away, and never be met with again! It is this, it is . . .*"

"Stop all that," Fen commanded peremptorily. "It's nothing but affectation. You know perfectly well who I am. I'm Gervase Fen."

"You might be," said the R.P.M. "I remember a much younger man."

"Oh, it's no use talking to you," said Fen. "Come on, you two."

"Where are you going?" said the R.P.M. He said it with such suddenness and severity that they all started.

"That's no business of yours," said Fen. "But if you must know, we're going to have a drink."

"I shall come too."

"Oh, no, you won't. We don't want you."

"I shall recite you *The Hunting of the Snark.*"

"We'd rather do without that, thank you."

"I shall accompany you," said the Professor with such firmness that even Fen was daunted.

"Are you quite sure you want to?" he asked feebly.

"I am sure of nothing," said the Professor, "except the differential calculus. And I'm not as good on that as I used to be."

Fen moaned and shrugged his shoulders, and they all set off. "He's all right, really," Fen said to Geoffrey in a penetrating whisper. "Only he's dishonest. He steals things. But I don't think it'll hurt to have him with us.

And I don't see," he added with more venom, "how we'd get rid of him even if we wanted to."

Beside them, the Professor placidly continued reciting Lewis Carroll.

The public bar of the "Three Shrews" was empty when they arrived there, apart from the landlord, who stood polishing glasses in the detached, other-worldly manner of his kind. They ordered beer, for which Fen prodded the Regius Professor of Mathematics into paying. Then they all sat down at a table, listened patiently to the conclusion of Fit the Seventh, and began to talk.

"It seems to me," said Fen, "that our general strategy has got to be (a) to try and find out where these people's headquarters is and (b) when we've done that, to discover precisely what their plans are."

"As simple as that?" said Geoffrey. Fen glared at him.

"Well, if you can suggest anything else," he grumbled, "you suggest it. It may not be as difficult as it sounds. What we must *not* do is to start arresting them right and left without knowing what arrangements they've made for just that contingency."

"No."

"Very well, then." Fen opened the map. "I've been making enquiries about deserted buildings in the neighbourhood." He pointed at a section of the map, and Geoffrey, glancing idly at it, caught the words "Slater's Wood." "And I've come to the conclusion that apart from the Scout-hut, there's only one . . ."

It was at this moment that Fielding interrupted him. And before many hours had passed, Geoffrey was bitterly to regret that interruption.

"I don't see how you know," said Fielding, "that it's anywhere *out* of the town at all."

"I know," said Fen severely, "or I *think* I know, because I've been making discreet enquiries about the general activities of the person chiefly concerned in all this. And I've discovered that that person has had a habit of taking frequent jaunts in the surrounding country, and always in the same direction. They may have been pleasure trips, of course. But I rather doubt it."

Here the landlord, who had momentarily vanished on

some obscure mission, returned with an envelope in his hand.

"Excuse me," he said, "but is any of you gentlemen named"—he stared at the envelope—"Gervase Fen?"

"Me," said Fen ungrammatically.

"I just found this note for you on the mat. Heard it slipped in through the letter-box."

With this pronouncement he returned to polishing glasses. Fen tore the letter open; it was type-written.

"Clever of you to find out who I am. But you won't have me arrested, will you? There's not sufficient evidence. And I have enough deputies to look after things if you do. Let us have a talk some time: I shall be about this afternoon as usual. (And my apologies for that foolish shooting at the Mass: of course it wasn't my doing.) My best regards."

"But this is *fantastic!*" Fielding exclaimed. "Criminals just *don't* write letters like that."

"I rather agree," said Fen thoughtfully. "There's something half-phoney about it. But the impulse to swank is quite genuine, I think. I wonder . . ." he mused. "Oh, Lord, I wish I knew what to do. The trouble is, that letter's quite right. There really isn't enough material evidence—cigarette-ash, footprints and so on—to convict the person concerned; just times, and an odd method of murder."

"They don't seem to be worrying very much about anything you can do," said Geoffrey.

Fen looked at him queerly for a moment. "No, they don't, do they?" he said slowly. "And after all, what can I do? Threaten them with a revolver? They'd give me no information, and I should get arrested myself."

"We might whisk them away and torture them," put in Fielding hopefully.

"I can't help feeling that if we tried that we should end up with bullets in our backs."

"Dear, dear," said the Regius Professor.

"Oh, shut up, you," said Fen. "But what I *am* going to try and do is ring up the War Office and try and find out if they know anything yet about the radio messages.

McIver's the man. Now, what on earth's his number? White-hall something."

"Look it up in the Directory."

"It isn't there. And enquiries won't give it you, either. It's a national secret. But it's got a five and a six and an eight and a seven in it. 5-8-6-7; 7-6-8-5; 7-8-6-5 . . . Nothing sounds right."

"We'd better work out all the possible combinations," said Fielding, "and try the lot."

"That's going to take a time."

"I'll work out the combinations," said the Regius Professor of Mathematics eagerly. He grabbed hold of a pencil and a piece of paper.

"Couldn't you try someone else?"

"He's the only man I know. No one else would listen to me."

"Well, come on, then."

The Regius Professor laboured for five minutes. Then he gave them the complete list of possible combinations. Geoffrey looked at it and said:

"You've forgotten 5687."

"Impossible," said the Professor. "I worked it out by the factorial four."

"Well, you've still forgotten 5687."

The Professor gazed at the list intently. "That's funny," he admitted.

"Oh, come on," said Fen impatiently. "I'll do it. You see, you put each number first, in turn. . . ."

"Try the ones you've *got*," said Geoffrey. "Look at them. Does any of them strike a chord?"

Fen looked at the list for a long time, and finally said: "None."

"Let's go, then."

"There's a telephone in the passage outside. I saw it when we came in."

Fen finished his beer with a disgusted expression, and they all trooped out. The pub still seemed completely deserted. They put Fen in the telephone box and he got in touch successively with the offices of a Warden in Lunacy, a large undertaker's, a theatre, the Prime Minister, and Mr. James Agate at the Café Royal (something must have gone wrong with the mechanism at this point).

They all turned out their pockets for coins, and rushed to and fro procuring change from the bar. Eventually, and rather to everyone's surprise, he got the number he wanted.

"Hello, is that you, McIver? This is Fen. . . . I don't *care* if you're busy; you just pay attention for a minute. . . . No, I am not drunk. Listen."

He explained the circumstances. There was a prolonged crackling from the other end.

"Information about military and naval dispositions," said Fen. "Yes, I was afraid of that. Well, it'll be all your fault if we lose this war. You'll wake up to-morrow with Himmler in the chamber pot. . . ." He turned to the others. "Go away, all of you. I'm going to gossip." Obediently they trooped back to the bar.

There they ordered more beer, and consumed it. The day was already drowsy. Geoffrey lay back in a pleasant stupor. Flies buzzed on the window. Somewhere in the distance a car started up and drove of. The landlord polished glasses with wearisome persistence and no appreciable result. Geoffrey looked at the note which Fen had just received. The amiability of the wording was hateful. He remembered that whoever wrote it had helped to drug a child of fifteen, to drive a man mad and then poison him, to crush another man to a blood-flecked jelly. . . . Despite the warmth of the day, a shiver of sheer repulsion seized him. He handed the letter to the Regius Professor of Mathematics, who was sitting drinking his beer and staring blankly in front of him.

"I haven't the least idea what all this is about," said the Professor, "but I agree there's something wrong about this letter. The tone is so indifferent. Almost as though it were intended to lull someone into a sense of false security. . . ."

Geoffrey and Fielding sat up. The same thought flashed across both their minds.

"Fen's taking a devil of a time over that call."

Almost in one bound they were at the door, sick apprehension in their hearts. The passage was empty, and the door of the telephone-box stood open. There was no one there. But the receiver hung, swaying gently, at the end of its wire, and a faint smell of chloroform sweetened the air.

The Professor, who had followed them out, paused by the empty booth.

"He has softly and suddenly vanished away," he said gravely. "The Snark *was* a Boojum, you see."

Chapter Thirteen

ANOTHER DEAD

"An intellectual hatred is the worst."
                                        YEATS

THE FIRST THING TO BE DONE was obviously to rush out into the road and discover if anything was to be seen. But even as he went, Geoffrey remembered the car he had heard drive away, and knew it was useless. There were wheel-marks in the gravel court, but they lost themselves in a fringe of macadam adjoining the road, and it was impossible to tell which way the car had gone. For the rest, not a soul was about. As a kidnapping it was not only daring but flawless.

Then there was the Inspector to telephone. The language with which he received the news fitted in well with Geoffrey's mood. He promised to use what resources he could in tracing the car, and suggested that Geoffrey and Fielding should come down to the station at once to discuss a plan of action. They set off, leaving the Regius Professor of Mathematics drinking gravely and peaceably on his own, and never saw or heard of him again.

But while they walked, Geoffrey realised the utter hopelessness of what they had to do. For Fen had not told them the name of the criminal, and they could not find him in that way. He felt none of the excitement of the chase—only a nausea, a dull despair, and a sense of bitter self-reproach. What a perfect trap that note was, and what a blind imbecile he had been not to see through it!

The Inspector listened with a glum expression to what they had to tell him, and seemed devoid of constructive ideas. The churls from the Yard, it appeared, had returned to London early that morning with a view to making certain investigations into Peace's past career. Fielding asked rather irritably what Peace could have been supposed to have had to do with it, since he was locked up in his cell when Fen disappeared, but even Geoffrey saw the logical flaw in this: they were dealing, after all, with a gang. The only slender clue they had to go on, as the Inspector pointed out, was the possible complicity of Harry James, the landlord of the "Whale and Coffin." Certainly a search-warrant could be produced, to enable them to look at his premises; but equally certainly, that move would have been anticipated. The Inspector had had one or two fresh pieces of news since they saw him last, but all of a negative kind: the case which had been dropped on Geoffrey in the train could not be traced; nor could the man who had dropped it; and nor could the assailant in the shop, who had made his escape through one of the other departments in the general confusion. But these, at the moment, were matters of very secondary importance. The Inspector had thought that he might be justified in pulling James in for questioning. Now that Fen had been kidnapped, however, he was less certain of the wisdom of this. If he was not dead already (Geoffrey turned sick inside), such action might simply precipitate his murder.

In the end, Fielding persuaded them that as a resident of the "Whale and Coffin" it would be easier for him than for them to do a little unobtrusive snooping. Neither Geoffrey nor the Inspector seemed very willing to leave this to him alone. The "Whale and Coffin" was, after all, their only chance. It was finally decided that while he was investigating Geoffrey should be stationed in the bar, as a second line of defence; and that, as a third, a constable should remain unobtrusively outside, ready to summon more help if necessary.

And so it was that a quarter of an hour later, with a quick-beating heart, Geoffrey stood once again in the crowded little public bar of the "Whale and Coffin," waiting. Fielding's plan of action had simply been for a general search, as far as that was possible: and it had been agreed that if he did not return within twenty minutes, the place should be turned inside out. Geoffrey sipped whisky, and saw the minute-hand of his watch crawl through aeons of eternity from four to five, from five to six. . . . All about him, the serious business of drinking continued tranquil and unregarding. It was impossible to suppose that their enemies had not anticipated this move, that they were not conscious of what was going on. Geoffrey became more nervous every second, and was profoundly grateful that he was surrounded by a crowd. The landlord was nowhere to be seen. He wondered what Fielding was doing.

In point of fact, Fielding had already found what he was looking for. He found it at once, and the chance nearly cost him his life. He had set off from his own bedroom down the narrow, panelled corridor, bending his head to avoid the low beams, and feeling slightly less enthusiastic about secret service work than usual. As it happened, he was gifted with a fairly high degree of physical courage, but it had occurred to him, as to Geoffrey, that they were hardly likely to take whoever they were looking for unawares, and the reflection not unnaturally depressed him. Experimentally he tried the first door along the corridor on the right. It was not probable that criminal evidence would be lying about in such a public spot, but one had to be methodical. The door yielded, and he could himself in a low white-panelled sitting-room, well-lighted and pleasantly furnished in chintz. It was empty, but from a closed door on the other side came the sound of voices. He tiptoed towards it, and put his ear to the keyhole. Fragments of conversation reached him.

". . . tell you there's never been a conger caught on this coast longer than twenty feet."

". . . you get them bigger in Cornwall."

"The trouble is, the local men haven't got the pilchard to bait the lines. And there's so little good eating on a conger . . ."

This sounded unpromising, and he was about to creep away again when he thought better of it. If the people in there were guests of the hotel he could easily apologise. If not . . . Gently he turned the handle, opening the door a fraction of an inch. From within, a surprised voice called out:

"Hello! Who's there?"

So there was nothing for it but to go in. He opened the door wide and stepped across the threshold. There were two men there talking. One was Harry James, and the other . . .

Savernake.

They sat at either side of a table, with beer in front of them. The room was a rather smaller replica of what he had just left. Apart from a few books which, his eye passing rapidly over them, Fielding recognized as being textbooks on Church music, it gave no sign of permanent habitation. Savernake said cheerily:

"Fielding! How pleasant to see you. I'm sorry we haven't been able to see more of one another since you arrived."

James said:

"Well, sir! Anything I can do for you? You're quite comfortable, I hope?"

Savernake said:

"Join us for a drink. I very rarely do this, myself—one has one's reputation to look after—but I like to have a talk with Harry about fishing now and again."

He got up and put himself between Fielding and the only door, that by which he had entered. Fielding saw that the one large window was heavily barred, looking out on to a deserted courtyard at the back of the inn. He realised he had to fight. The two men were looking at him queerly. He felt suddenly helpless, and tried to speak, but the words stuck in the back of his throat.

Then he pulled over a table, and kicked a chair at the innkeeper. James stumbled momentarily, then righted himself. Neither he nor Savernake made any other movement. Fielding fell back slowly into a corner, scraping his left shoulder against the wall.

"Why, Fielding," he heard Savernake say, "whatever's the matter?"

Sick fright closed about his heart. For an age it seemed to stop beating. Then he filled his lungs to shout.

The room turned suddenly to blood. He was vaguely conscious of an explosion, a sudden tearing jolt which spun him hard against the wall and drove him fathoms down to a smashing concussion with the floor. Lying there, he struggled frantically both to keep consciousness and to suppress (biting his tongue) the terrible panic of the mind at the first realisation that a part of the body has been destroyed. Obscurely he knew that he must keep consciousness, in case they said anything that would help him to find Fen; he must make them think he was dead. . . . The lights of a million roundabouts whirled and pirouetted before his eyes; the pain was just beginning. Echoing strangely through mile-long tunnels and labyrinths, their voices came to his ears.

"What did you want to shoot for, you fool?" James was snarling. "That's the second time playing about with that gun has nearly finished us. Do you want the whole neighbourhood in here?"

"No one will have heard it. Please remember that I am in charge here. I shall do what I think best."

"Sweet Fanny Adams. What are you going to do now, Mr. Clever? You know Vintner's downstairs and a copper outside the door?"

"We must get out, of course. Destroy the stuff and get out. If we can reach Scotland . . ."

"*If* we can reach Scotland! That's pretty."

"Go and dope Vintner's drink. We can put him in a back-room and leave word that he was taken ill. That will give us a little more time."

"You bloody, over-educated bungler. . . ."

"I should not have the slightest compunction about using this gun again—on you. In fact, it would make my own departure a good deal easier."

"Listen. Someone's coming. . . ."

"No, they're not. No one heard that shot. Get out, will you, and fix Vintner's drink."

"And Fen? What are you going to do about him?"

"He'll be dead by now."

"I don't think. Not with the trickle of gas you let out of that tap, and the room not properly sealed. Your blasted little bit of sadism's going to fix us properly. We ought to go out to the old asylum and finish him off."

"*There's no time, you f—— swine. Go out and fix that drink.*"

205

James went, and Fielding, unable to hold on any longer and incapable of warning Geoffrey, fell into a dead faint. In five minutes the landlord was back—five minutes during which Savernake paced about, wiped the perspiration from his long, thin face, smoothed back his corn-coloured hair, and twisted his fingers nervously together. His narrow upper lip was quivering slightly, with fright, and a muscle twitched continually in the corner of his right eye.

"Took it like a lamb," said James briefly. "I've left word what's to be done with him when he passes out." He turned and inspected Fielding. "He's not dead. If you can't kill a man at that range, you'll better leave that gun alone."

Savernake produced the gun again.

"No, you don't," said James. "We were lucky first time —nobody downstairs heard—but we mayn't be again. There are quieter ways of finishing him than that. Here, give me a hand."

Together they dragged Fielding over to the gas-fire. It was of the movable kind, attached to the tap in the wall by a length of flexible tubing. James removed the tubing from the fire, and inserted the end into Fielding's half-open mouth. Then he took a roll of surgical tape from his pocket, and plastered up Fielding's nostrils and the corners of his mouth. He turned the gas-tap full on, and they stood back for a moment, listening to the gentle hiss, and watching the blood from his wound spreading slowly on the uneven floor.

"That'll fix him," said James. "Now let's shoot. If we once get to Bristol, G. will have a plane to take us to Scotland, and we can snap our fingers at the lot of them."

"I'd better look through his pockets."

"For Jesus' sake, hurry. If you aren't down in five minutes, I'll take the car without you."

"I'll be down."

James went out, slamming the door behind him. Savernake bent over the recumbent body.

But Geoffrey was not doped. With a perceptivity unusual in him, he had observed that the last whisky he ordered was not drawn from the bottle suspended above the bar, but brought in from outside by the woman in charge, on the excuse of its being a better brand. He saw, too, that there was someone watching him through the chink of a door marked "Private" beside the bar. With an ostentatious gesture he turned his back and pretended to drink, actually pouring the doped whisky down his collar inside his shirt. It felt extremely uncomfortable, but his buttoned coat hid the broad stain, and fortunately none of the other customers had noticed, or shown surprise at, this unusual manoeuvre. Wiping his mouth, he turned back to the bar, put his empty glass on it, and with some facetious remark ordered another. The woman went off to get it, and Geoffrey leaned idly on the bar until, out of the corner of his eye, he saw the door by the bar softly close, and knew that for a moment he was safe. He knew, too, that Fielding had been caught, and what he must do.

He strolled carelessly to the door leading on to the street, and standing there for a moment, whistled a bar or two of "Widdicombe Fair." In response to the prearranged signal, the constable moved gently away; but once out of sight of the windows, he ran. It was only five minutes' walk from the "Whale and Coffin" to the police station. Geoffrey calculated that in little more than ten the place could be surrounded.

He turned back to the bar, and pushed his way through to the lavatories. From them, he remembered, there was a second exit into the hotel proper. But once there, where to start looking? The place was an absolute warren of rooms and passages, in which the unknowledgeable might easily get lost. He considered, as well as he could. He knew at least where Fielding's room was, and it was by no means unlikely that he had started his search from there, working outwards. Also, it was plain that he had not had time to search far. The upshot of it was that in another minute Geoffrey was entering that outer room which Fielding had entered a few minutes before.

As he stood on the threshold, the door leading into the inner room opened, and Savernake came out, shutting and locking it carefully behind him. Savernake! But Geoffrey did not pause to consider. He would not have paused to consider if it had been the Archbishop of Canterbury. He performed a sort of flying leap across the room, and landed on top of Savernake before the clergyman had even become aware of his presence.

Like most struggles, it was a hazy, chancy, unscientific business. But Geoffrey had the advantage of surprise, and Savernake was unable to get his gun out of his pocket. Moreover, Savernake was smaller, weaker and less wiry than Geoffrey. The end of it was that he fell, smashed his head against the skirting-board, and lay there, dazed and moaning.

Geoffrey was not waiting to make sure of him, however; the smell of gas from the inner room was becoming too insistent for that. He burst in, turned off the gas, tore the tape from Fielding's mouth and nostrils, and applied what methods of first aid he could think of. Fielding was still breathing. Somewhere below Geoffrey heard a car start up and drive off. Then in a little time other cars drove up, and the police were on the stairs. Geoffrey pulled Fielding from the inner room to the other. He found Savernake had gone, and wondered momentarily if it had been he who had been in that car. But no; there would not have been time for him to get downstairs and out.

The Inspector had brought with him a doctor, who set about applying restoratives to Fielding, and dressing his wound. Geoffrey explained what little he knew.

"Savernake!" the Inspector exclaimed. "So that was it. Though I still don't see . . ." He checked himself. "Never mind that. We'll get him."

"I think James must have left in a car."

"We'll get him, too. I'll telephone the county police and the military authorities, and we'll arrange for a cordon." He disappeared abruptly from the room.

"He's coming round," said the doctor. He pillowed Fielding's head in his arm. "Someone ring the hospital and tell them to send an ambulance."

Fielding opened his eyes and was violently sick. He groaned and struggled to speak.

"Keep quiet," said the doctor. "You'll be all right. I don't think the wound's serious," he added to Geoffrey. "It must just have missed the right lung."

". . . James . . . Savernake . . ." Fielding said. His speech came slowly, broken by long, retching gasps, and

his face and finger-nails were blue with cyanosis. "Fen
. . . gassed . . . in . . . in . . ." His voice became incoherent. Geoffrey leaned forward.

"Yes?" he said. "Yes?" His whole body was itching
with impatience.

Fielding tried again, but only succeeded in retching
air. Then he fell back, with his eyes closed.

"For God's sake," said Geoffrey to the doctor. "For
God's sake try and bring him round somehow. He knows
where Fen is . . . Fen's life depends on it. . . . You must
bring him round."

"My dear sir," said the doctor with a touch of irritation,
"you're demanding the impossible. That is . . . Well, I
could try, but it would be infernally dangerous. It would
probably kill him."

"He'd want you to do it."

"Perhaps," said the doctor drily; "but that hasn't got
anything to do with it."

"I should say it had everything to do with it."

The doctor looked at Geoffrey steadily for a moment.
Then he said:

"All right. I shall get struck off the register, and probably had up for manslaughter into the bargain. My wife
and children will starve. But I'll try. Give me that bag."

Fen had awoken from a dream in which he was being
pursued by a gigantic praying mantis down the steep
slope of a railway cutting, to find himself constricted in a
large white contraption which he only slowly recognised as
a strait-jacket. After trying to sort out the implications of
this unusual situation for a moment, he devoted himself
to being quietly sick. Then he looked up to see Savernake
and James, who were standing silently watching him.

"Hello," he said with as much cheerfulness as he could
muster. "You look pretty silly."

Savernake sneered. "Not as silly as you do, I assure
you. There's a certain appropriateness about your surroundings, don't you think? This is the old lunatic asylum,
you know."

"Indeed," said Fen briefly. He made experiments with
his limbs, and found that his legs also were tied.

"Don't bother to try and get free," said Savernake. "It will be a waste of energy."

"Why did you kidnap me?"

"To be able to kill you quietly and conveniently."

"Thanks so much. . . . Excuse me, gentlemen, but I'm going to be ill again . . . your blasted chloroform. . . ."

"Do."

When he had finished, Fen said: "And what now?"

"We shall be obliged to dispose of you."

"Do talk English," said Fen with a touch of acerbity. "And try to stop imagining you're in a book."

"My dear Professor, I am the last person you are ever going to speak to. You might pretend to be civil."

Suddenly Fen laughed. "How old are you, Savernake?"

"Why?"

"I just wanted to know."

"I'm twenty-six.'" Fen laughed again, and Savernake snarled: "What the devil's so funny?"

"It's only that I know your type of undergraduate so well. It's always existed in Oxford—over-clever, incapable of concentration or real thought, affected, arty, with no soul, no morals, and a profound sense of inferiority."

Savernake stepped forward and kicked Fen in the face. After a minute:

"That hurt," said Fen mildly, "and you've knocked out one of my teeth." He spat it on to the floor. "Why do you conspire against your country?"

"That has no relevance at present, and I am not prepared to discuss it. I find a certain charm, however, in the fact that Nazism muzzles the fools, the public-bar wiseacres, the democratic morons."

"It kills a lot of people."

"That does not matter."

"No, I suppose it wouldn't to you. When you're being killed it will, though. You'll find it most unpleasant, and at that moment you'd give your soul to spend the rest of your life listening to public-bar wiseacres."

"Like all democrats, you are a sentimentalist."

"I think killing people is a bad thing, that's all," said Fen, still mildly. He sighed. "Well, what are you going to do with me?"

"Turn on the gas."

"The gas?" Fen was surprised. "But I thought this place was deserted. It'll be off at the main."

"It's being taken over by the military authorities the day after to-morrow," said James. It was the first time he had spoken. "The gas has been very conveniently put on again."

"Where is this, anyway?" Fen asked.

"Five miles out of Tolnbridge," Savernake replied, "a mile from road or cottage in every direction. If your nerve fails and you scream, as you very probably will, no one will hear you. But we shall gag you before we leave, just in case."

Fen thought for a moment. Then: "I think," he remarked, "that I'd rather have a quicker death than gassing."

"Very well," Savernake's voice was totally indifferent. "Shoot him, James."

James took a revolver from a shoulder-holster, opened the magazine, and shut it again.

"Do hurry up, man," said Savernake in the same lifeless tone. "We can't stop here all night. And for God's sake put your glasses on. You might not do it properly first time, and we don't want a filthy mess."

James nodded, without speaking. He drew a case from his pocket, opened it, took out the glasses, polished them carefully and put them on. Then he cocked the pistol, pointed it at Fen's head, and tightened his finger on the trigger.

Fen abruptly changed his mind. "I think I'd rather be gassed," he said very rapidly, and added, as James with a shrug lowered the gun: *"Plutôt souffrir que mourir, c'est la devise des hommes."*

"Oh, we'll try and arrange for you to suffer," said Savernake. He went over to the gas-jet in the wall, and experimentally turned it on. There was a sharp hiss.

"Admirable," he said. "But that would make it rather too quick." He turned the tap down to the lowest possible point. "Now, let's see. The windows are closed, but the room won't be properly sealed, so there'll be some escape. I should say that with the gas at that strength it will take about an hour and a half."

"That seems bloody foolhardy to me," muttered James. "Suppose someone finds him before the time's up?"

"No one will. How can they? And we must leave him a little time to meditate, mustn't we?" To Fen: "I'm afraid we must gag you now. We'll make it as comfortable as possible." Then, when it was finished:

"Goodbye. I won't say that I'm sorry to have to do this, because it delights me. Come on, James."

Fen, being incapable of other utterance, nodded his head in dismissal. They went out, locking the door behind them.

Fen found the silence a relief. He bent his head towards the jet, which was on the other side of the room, but the issue of gas was so weak that it gave no sound. Then he did a little struggling, without other effect than to accentuate his cramp and send spasms of sharp pain through his limbs. The strait-jacket made him extremely hot, and he soon desisted. The room offered no promise of assistance, being large and totally devoid of furniture—the warden's office, he judged. Germans, he reflected vaguely, seemed to have a neurotic obsession about mad-houses—there was *The Cabinet of Dr. Caligari,* for example and *The Testament of Dr. Mabuse.* But these were Nazi agents, and the Nazis had driven out Wiene and Lang. . . . He pulled himself together. These vague meanderings would not do. He was conscious of an insistent regret at the prospect of dying.

Fielding's eyes were still closed. The doctor put his things back in his bag and looked up at Geoffrey. "Sorry," he said. "No go. I can't bring him round."

"Oh, God. . . . He isn't worse, is he?"

"No. He'll pull through all right. Is that the ambulance? About time we got him out of here. I'll let you know the moment he utters a word."

Geoffrey stood helpless, irresolute. "If they only catch James or Savernake. . . . No, it's hopeless. Fen'll de dead by then."

"They're swine, aren't they?" said the doctor simply. It was more comforting than an elaborate assumption of concern.

Fielding was taken out on a stretcher. He seemed hardly to be breathing. The doctor followed. Geoffrey cursed viciously and racked his brains. Where had they put Fen? What way was there to find out? He sought desperately for a clue, but none came. Gassed . . . a tap in a wall . . . gas, gas . . . gasometers . . . gas company . . .

He emitted a sudden yell. "Idiot!" he shouted to the empty room. "Idiot!" It gave a surprised and slightly mocking echo. Geoffrey rushed like a lunatic down the stairs.

He met the Inspector coming away from the telephone. "So far, so good," said that worthy, blandly unaware of Geoffrey's pressing desire to communicate with him. "The cordon's out, and I don't think that car'll get through it. Savernake must be on foot, or on a bike. I'm going after him . . ."

"Never mind all that," Geoffrey interrupted him excitedly. "Get back to that telephone!"

The Inspector stared.

"The Gas Company!" Geoffrey bawled. "The Gas Company . . ."

Five minutes later, beneath some four thousand lunches in the last stages of preparation, the gas flickered and went out. The supply for the whole district had been cut off at source.

Three times already Fen had been violently sick, and twice he had only just prevented himself from going under. There must be a good deal of gas in the room by now, he thought, and his mind was by no means clear. What the time was, and how long had passed since James and Savernake had left, he had no means of telling. His face hurt badly, but the gas had a little anaesthetised the pain. He found he could no longer focus the room properly. He sighed inwardly, and devoted himself to meditating on the First and Last Things.

A quarter of an hour later, he found to his surprise that he was still meditating on the First and Last Things. The shock was sufficient to clear his brain a little, and to allow him to observe that the sun was appreciably higher than it had been when he had last looked. Moreover, the room was coming back into focus, and his face was hurting more. A mood of mild curiosity seized him. Perhaps there was something peculiar about his lungs which made him immune from gas. The thought amused him so much

213

that he made himself sick again trying to laugh at it, and to be sick with a gag in your mouth is not a pleasant experience. He calmed down a bit.

But two hours later still, when Geoffrey, the doctor, and two constables broke into the room, he was feeling lively, irritable and obscurely aggrieved. The first thing he said, when they had taken the gag out of his mouth and he had painfully forced his jaws into working order again, was:

"I'm immune from gas."

"Don't be silly," said Geoffrey. "It was turned off hours ago at the main. And oh, you old devil, how glad I am to see you again."

While they helped Fen down to the car, Geoffrey explained what had happened. "Eventually," he concluded, "I remembered that when we were in the 'Three Shrews' you pointed to some place on the map which you said might be the gang's centre of operations. Then Fielding interrupted you, and we never heard what it was. But I noticed a name near where you were pointing. I *couldn't* remember what it had been—you know that sort of complete mental blank—but I knew it had something to do with the ghost story and Thurston's diary. I rushed round to Dallow's house, and looked at the diary again. There it was—'met her to-day secretly, in the coppice beyond Slater's Close.' Of course—Slater's Wood. The police knew there was only one empty building near there—this one. So here we are."

"Ah." Fen was unusually laconic. "Well, it was a pure guess on my part, but a lucky one. Thank heavens for all of you." After a while he said grandiloquently: "I have saved the country." He went on saying this for some weeks afterwards, but as no one took any notice of it, he finally gave it up.

They drove back to Tolnbridge, to the police station.

But when they got there, the cupboard was bare. Which is to say that the Inspector and most of his men were out on the search for James and Savernake. From an excitable Sergeant left in charge, his head evidently full of heroic deeds and high responsibility, they learned that Fielding was going on as satisfactorily as could be expected; that it was almost certain James was still in the area, since the cordon had been quickly and tightly organised; and that no sign had been discovered of Savernake, who it was supposed had gone to earth in some part of the town. They decided to wait in the hope of getting some news. It was now nearly teatime, and a constable brewed them a thick oily concoction of tea. They went and saw Peace—still in his cell, still reading *The Mind and Society* —and told him everything that had happened. He seemed bewildered.

"Well, I never liked Savernake," he said. "But I shouldn't have thought he had the mentality to organise a thing like this." He embarked on an account of psychological types, to which nobody paid much attention.

Meanwhile, the Inspector pursued his ways, alone and full of a righteous indignation. He had organised the men at his disposal so as to cover the places at which Savernake was most likely to be found, and had chosen, for himself, to return to Dr. Butler's house. Savernake, he reminded himself, had frequently stayed there, and might at least have looked in to collect money or belongings. In this he was proved to be right. Frances met him in the drive, pale-faced and frightened.

"Thank God you've come!" she exclaimed. The words tumbled over one another. "It's July—Savernake. He's been here with a gun. What's been happening? Is Geoffrey all right? Did July kill my father? He disconnected the phone and we couldn't reach anyone, and we didn't dare come out of the house, in case he was still about. He took all the money we had."

"How long ago was this?"

"About ten minutes."

"Do you know which way he went?"

"No. We didn't see. Mummy's in a terrible state."

"Listen," said the Inspector. "Will you do something for me?" His normal easy-going manner had vanished, and a brisk, formidable coldness taken its place.

"What?"

"Go down to the station and tell them what's happened. They'll know exactly what to do."

"I . . . I daren't. I'm frightened." She hesitated. "And I'm afraid to leave Mummy here alone."

"Take her with you. You've nothing to worry about.

215

Savernake's too busy trying to get away to bother about you." He looked at her steadily. "Will you do it?"

"I . . . All right."

"Good girl."

The Inspector ran back to his bicycle and mounted. From the gate he shouted:

"Was he on foot?"

"Yes. I think so." He left her standing forlorn and slightly helpless in the drive.

There were three ways Savernake might have gone. One was back into the town—a wholly foolhardy undertaking, unworthwhile even for the sake of bluff; a second was down to the waterfront, which he must have anticipated would be guarded; and the third was along the estuary and round the cliffs to Tolnmouth. Here it might just be possible for a man on foot to elude the watchers, and the Inspector decided it was his best chance. He would, of course, make an admirable target, on his bicycle, for a stray shot from copse or thicket by the roadside; but that had to be risked. The Inspector, normally a peaceable, easy-going man, kind to his wife and family, fond of books, genial in his enforcement of the law and very generally liked in Tolnbridge, had now become a formidable machine, practically insensible to ordinary fear. He recognised, wryly, that he would probably be a good deal less bold running with the hare instead of hunting with the hounds. But he remembered also the many unamiable characteristics of his quarry, and deliberately stifled that pity for the defeated which springs up infallibly in the English mind. He liked England, without thinking very much about it, and he objected, with more intensity than he would have admitted, to people who tried to interfere with her. Moreover, he liked to think of England as standing solidly against her enemies, not buffeted by treachery from within; that offended his sense of symmetry. *"Je hais,"* he might have said if he had known enough French, *"le mouvement qui déplace les lignes."*

He was glad to have his gun with him. The only time he ever gave himself wholly up to resentment and dislike was when engaged in target practice. At such times he vaguely felt himself to be engaged in destroying some undefined power of evil; the target became his personal enemy, and he fired at it as though it represented some amalgam of the forces of oppression—Capitalism, Fascism, Bolshevism (he seldom particularised further)—incarnate in shadowy, insubstantial, infinitely menacing figures. It was the only form of day-dreaming he allowed himself, but it made him peculiarly dangerous when he had his gun and something legitimate to shoot at.

In the meantime, it was exceedingly hot.

In a quarter of an hour he had arrived at the top of the cliffs, near the deserted quarry which Geoffrey and Frances had seen on their walk that morning. It was possible that he had missed Savernake on the way. But he knew that half a mile on there were guards, and he decided to climb up among the gorse-bushes on a small knoll and discover if anything could be seen. And it was just as he was laying down his bicycle—no longer practicable on the rough track—that he saw Savernake.

He was working his way quickly, silently, and apprehensively through the bushes only about fifteen yards away, and by a lucky chance had not observed the Inspector's approach. It was possible to see the sunlight gleaming on the sweat which poured from his brow, and the limp, tousled condition of his corn-coloured hair. The Inspector sighed his satisfaction as he crouched out of sight: it was too simple. He waited until Savernake, glancing nervously about, had arrived in the open and turned his back to go further, and then drew his revolver and stepped out after him.

"Stop and hold up your hands!"

Savernake stopped, stiffened, but did not turn. Then he began in a sudden fury of desperation to run, doubling back away from the direction he had been going, and the guards. The Inspector went after him, but he was the heavier man, and Savernake was impelled by panic fear. The Inspector stopped and aimed his gun.

Twenty yards now separated them, and the shot was a difficult one, with Savernake in swift, dodging flight. He staggered for a moment at the impact of the first bullet, but still went on—more slowly now, tripping on stones and gorse-roots, and clutching at the spines for support. The Inspector fired again; missed. A third time, and Savernake fell. But he went on crawling away, still alive,

as a chicken will run about a farmyard with head severed.
Perhaps he was remembering what Fen had told him
about his own death, only three hours before; no one ever
knew. For the Inspector also was remembering things—
the killing of two men, the dreary blasphemy of the Black
Mass. He fired a fourth time, and the shot smashed Savernake's backbone as he crawled. He stopped, seemed to
be trying to get to his feet, and then fell hard on his face
and lay still. So he was dead.

Fen and Geoffrey walked back from the police station
to the clergy-house. They had grown tired of waiting, and
when Frances had arrived to announce that the Inspector
was on Savernake's track, had made up their mind to return. It was with a full heart that Geoffrey saw Frances
again; he realised now that he had never really expected
to. But a hand-press and a smile were somehow all he had
been able to manage.

Of James nothing had so far been heard. The guards
were positive that his car had not been able to get
through, and thought it extremely unlikely that he had
succeeded on foot. But Geoffrey was only too willing to
leave the job of finding him to the police, and so, it
seemed, was Fen. Although now doped and patched by
the doctor, he had grown noticeably more bilious, irritable and depressed. He refused to indulge in any expla-
nations, merely saying:

"I'm going to my room to lie down until dinner. I'm
ill," he added severely. "You think things out on your
own." He tramped upstairs, while Geoffrey settled down
in the drawing-room to think.

Harry James got up from the armchair in Fen's bedroom as Fen flung open the door and strode in. His eyes,
small and black as a pig's, glistened behind the thick
lenses of his glasses, and the hand which held his revolver
trembled slightly. His clothes were dusty and dishevelled.

"Come in, Professor," he said softly. "I was waiting for
you. Close the door quietly and don't try to shout."

Fen did as he was told. He felt very tired.

"You were mad to come here," he said. "And you certainly won't get away."

The innkeeper's hand was trembling more. "I know

that. But I decided I wanted to settle things with you first. If you hadn't been so bloody interfering, we should have been all right. . . . No, keep your hands up."

"It's uncomfortable," Fen complained.

"Never mind. It will only be for a minute."

Fen thanked heaven, with perhaps more fervour than was normal, that he was standing behind a chair, with his feet and legs out of sight of James. He blessed the inefficiency of the housekeeper, who had left a small pebble lying there, where he had dropped it yesterday when emptying out what he had imagined was a praying mantis, but which proved to be a deformed grasshopper. The only other problem was of not betraying in the upper part of his body the movement of his leg—that and getting the pebble in the right direction without moving his eyes from the man with the gun. Of course, the chance was so frail as to be almost ludicrous, but there was no other, and he had at least the advantage that James was in a highly nervous state. His glance strayed to the full-length cupboard set in the door; it had been convenient because of its lack of a keyhole. He hoped the damned things hadn't all killed one another by now. It was a pity he was not near enough to James to risk a leap at the crucial moment, but that couldn't be helped.

Aloud he said:

"What I can't fathom is why the hell a man like you gets mixed up in a business like this at all."

"Don't try to gain time. It won't help you." James' finger tightened on the trigger.

"For heaven's sake give me a minute or so."

"So you want to know why I joined the Nazis, do you?" It suddenly occurred to Fen that for James, too, every minute of life was now precious; the thought encouraged him.

"Then I'll tell you, Mr. clever-bloody-professor. I joined 'em because they pay well, see? A fat bloody lot I care what government there is. That doesn't affect men like me. But I can tell you one thing: if I'd had the running of this business things would have turned out very differently. . . ."

Now, thought Fen, now: no use putting it off. His eyes fixed unwaveringly on James, he kicked the pebble. His

219

heart almost stopped until he heard the slight tap and clatter as it hit the cupboard door. Inwardly he vowed libations to the gods; outwardly he gave a slight start, and ostentatiously paid no attention. From now on it depended on acting.

James had heard. He stepped quickly back to bring Fen and the cupboard door simultaneously within his range of vision. Then he jerked his head towards it.

"What's through there?"

"Nothing," said Fen rapidly. "It's only a cupboard. Why?" (Oh, the strain of not over-acting one's acting!)

"I think you know very well why. There's someone behind there." (So the trick *had* worked.)

"Nothing except my suits, I assure you." Fen kept glancing rapidly and with heavily concealed expectancy at the door. James' nerves were getting worse, and he also was unable to keep his eyes off it. The problem now was to keep his mind off the realities of the situation. From his point of view, it hardly mattered if the whole Devon constabulary were behind that door; he had chosen to make his own escape impossible, and he would still be able to carry out his purpose of killing Fen. At the same time, he evidently had no wish to die at once, which would almost certainly happen if there were someone behind the door, and besides, the motive of curiosity is a very powerful one. Fen was relying on these two factors. And it was therefore with intense dismay that he heard James say:

"But is doesn't matter, does it? It doesn't make any difference to our little quarrel."

It seemed to have failed. But still the curiosity and the fear must remain, waiting to be aroused again. And plainly James did not suspect the origin of the noise, for the pebble was a small one, and moreover had bounced out of sight. Fen noted with slight satisfaction that if James moved to the door he would be in range of a quick jump; but the difficulty was to get him there.

"I wonder if you'd mind," said Fen, "if I got something out of that cupboard . . . in a pocket of my suit . . ."

"Don't try that on me . . . and don't move." The trigger-finger was tense again.

"Perhaps you'd get it: a photograph . . ."

"And perhaps I wouldn't." James' eyes were uneasy again. The sweat was beginning to trickle down his cheeks, and his glasses were misting over—an added advantage, Fen thought, as he dare not attempt to wipe them. Suddenly he burst out:

"You leave that bloody cupboard alone! How do I know it's not a door with one of your fine friends behind it?" Anger, and fear, had triumphed, and Fen felt a moment's real hope. But it rapidly faded. The innkeeper recovered his self-possession. His nerves had come very near breaking-point, but they had not broken. He was breathing quickly and heavily now, as a man breathes whose heart is beating too quickly.

"I've had about enough of this," he snarled. "I'm going to finish you now, before you can get up to any more of your tricks." Again his finger grew tight.

Fen was desperate. He must get the man's attention back to that door, or perish. A start in that direction? It would have to be very carefully judged. Too little, and it would be ineffectual; too much, and James' already overstrained nerve might break, and the fatal shot be fired. But that must be risked.

For a fraction of a second Fen resigned himself to eternity. No explosion came. But now James could stand it no longer. The sweat was literally dripping on to his collar, and his hand shook almost uncontrollably.

"How do I know it isn't all a bloody trick!" he shouted suddenly. "How do I know that! There's no one there! I'll prove it! And by Christ, I'll make a mess of you when I have!"

He strode towards the cupboard door. Fen closed his eyes in gratitude. He had done all he could. It rested with them now. New anxieties seized him. Perhaps they had fought and killed one another. Perhaps the darkness had made them torpid. Perhaps . . . He calculated distances, and braced his muscles for a jump.

A faint drowsy murmur, the murmur of a hayfield in summer, filled the air. James backed towards the cupboard, stood pressed against the wall, felt for the latch, lifted it, and, after a moment's hesitation, half opened the door.

It was enough. Out of it, like the battalions of hell,

poured a seemingly unending swarm of bees, wasps, and hornets, assembled there by Fen for the purposes of experiment, and maddened by their dark and prolonged imprisonment. Since James was the nearest animate object, they attacked his face with the utmost ferocity. It would have needed a superman to keep his head in such an extraordinary situation, and James' nerve was already gone. His attention was diverted just long enough for Fen to take a running kick at the gun in his right hand. It went off, smashing three fingers of his left. The insect horde turned its attention to Fen. When Geoffrey, startled by the shot, came racing upstairs, he found James babbling and moaning on the floor and Fen beating fiercely but unavailingly at his vengeful collection.

Since Fen was rather badly stung (though not as badly as he made out), they put him to bed, swearing terribly and crying for whisky.

Chapter Fourteen

IN THE LAST ANALYSIS

"Here she comes; and her passion ends the play."
SHAKESPEARE

FROM AMONGST A MASS OF BANDAGES which the doctor was now unwinding, a bleak, pale blue eye glared at the assembled company. "I'm not well enough," said a familiar voice from beneath the bandages. "I am not well enough to be unwound yet."

"Nonsense," said the doctor in the brisk, heartless manner of his kind. "You're perfectly well. The swelling's practically gone—you must have a skin like leather. And you can't go about for weeks looking like a mummy."

"You're most unkind," said Fen, feeling his restored features tenderly. "I have been gassed, bludgeoned and attacked by the third plague of Egypt. But does anyone sympathise? No. They stand about jeering." He sat up in bed and scowled.

It was the following evening, and they were all gathered in Fen's bedroom, which only the prolonged exercise of Flit had succeeded in clearing of insects. Geoffrey thought that the occasion had the solemnity of the unveiling of a monument. Frances, Garbin, Spitshuker, Dallow, Dutton all stood or sat about the room. Various formalities had prevented Peace's being released yet, but he would be out shortly. And the Inspector, who as Fen told them was superintending the final break-up of the cordon, had promised to look in a little later.

Of course they wanted an explanation, and after a good deal of grumbling, Fen consented to give it.

"The motive for the murders of Brooks and Butler," he said, "was obvious from the start—as was the whole of this business," he added with some vehemence, "to anyone with even a speck of brain."

"Control yourself," said Geoffrey.

After a mild fit of the sulks, Fen went on:

"That motive was, of course, the wireless hidden in the Bishop's Gallery in the cathedral—an admirable hiding-place, blamelessly public and yet easily available for use at night to anyone with access to a cathedral key. Brooks found out about it—how, and how much, we don't know, but enough to make it necessary to put him out of the way. The first attempt, after the choir-practice, failed; the injection of atropine wasn't fatal. So he was murdered in the hospital before he recovered sanity enough to tell what he knew. But in the meantime the cathedral had been put under guard, and it was imperatively necessary to get the transmitting set away to some spot less under the eye of the law. The only time to do it was during the hours of service. The organist was dead, and the deputy organist temporarily out of action; it would be possible to burrow discreetly through to the Bishop's Gallery from the organ-loft, concealing the hole behind the big music cupboard which stands against the partition. Apparently they hadn't contemplated the possibility of another deputy coming at once; so when your arrival was announced, Geoffrey, it gave them a bit of a shock. They tried to put you off with threatening letters and they tried to put you out of action. No good. Another way had to be devised."

"Then it was Savernake," asked Geoffrey, "who put that letter on my seat in the train?"

"Almost certainly."

"He must have written it and had it ready in case of emergency. But I suppose it was the merest chance that I happened to get into his compartment."

"I think so. If you hadn't, he would have got it to you just the same. As to his writing it . . ." Fen's blue eyes glanced easily round the gathering.

"Well?" Geoffrey felt a sudden, unaccountable tension in the air.

"Apparently it hasn't occurred to any of you," said Fen, "that if Savernake had the brains to run a spy-ring, he hadn't the personality; and if James had the personality, he hadn't the brains. What's more, Savernake could not have systematically drugged Josephine, since he was out at Maverley most of the time; and for James it would have been nearly impossible."

They were silent.

"And there's another thing," said Fen, "which doesn't seem to have suggested itself to any of you. *Both James and Savernake had alibis for the murder of Brooks.*"

Geoffrey felt a sudden sickening premonition. Nobody made any movement, or said a word.

Fen nodded slowly. "No, you're quite right. We haven't got them all yet." He paused and leaned back against the pillows.

"The murder of Brooks provided no handle. Someone—one of a number of people without alibis—knew of the arrangements at the hospital, slipped into a room and rang the bell for the nurse who was bringing his medicine punctually at six o'clock. Then, evading the nurse as she came up, went down and put atropine in it. There were no fingerprints on the bell; there was no clue of any kind, any more than there was in the first attack on Brooks, in the cathedral. But the death of your father, Frances, was different."

Again Fen glanced at them. Again nobody moved or spoke.

"There were two features in that which no sane man could stomach for a moment. One was the method—the tomb-slab; and the other was the fact that Butler quite unexpectedly announced his intention of going up to the cathedral, and must have arrived there only five minutes after the police guard left.[1] Do you see the point?"

"No," said Geoffrey. "For God's sake get on and tell us." His voice sounded strained and harsh.

"We heard the slab fall at 10.15—nearly an hour and a

[1] See pp. 138 and 183.

225

quarter afterwards. The purpose of getting the police away was to remove the wireless. Do you suppose they'd wait an hour and a quarter to do that? Of course not. They'd get on with it at once, which would mean they must have arrived just before, or simultaneously with, or just after Butler. So what was he doing during that hour and a quarter? Looking on and giving helpful advice?"

Dallow cleared his throat, a little nervously. "Surely, my *de*-ear Professor, it is possible that he was himself involved?"

"I considered that. But other evidence, which I'll come to in a moment, went against it. No, the plain fact is that he must have been killed almost as soon as he arrived in the cathedral."

"Then the slab was a decoy!" Geoffrey exclaimed. "No, wait, you can't *counterfeit* a noise like that. And, anyway, how was it got to move? There was no one in the cathedral, and no one except Peace could have got out. How was it toppled on top of Butler?"

"I will interrupt the classic perfection of my narrative," said Fen severely, "to digress on that point. It's more or less guesswork, and it has no relevance to the identity of the . . . person with whom we're concerned. But you should have realised, Geoffrey. What was the one part of the cathedral we paid no attention to, thinking it could have nothing to do with the affair?"

"The organ loft," Garbin put in. His deep voice momentarily startled them.

"Precisely. And you remember there's a thirty-two-foot stop on the pedals which literally shakes the cathedral . . .[1]

"Good God!" Geoffrey exclaimed.

"You remember how delicately that stone was poised once the padlocks were out. Two notes played together at the bottom of the pedal-board would topple it out in a moment. You remember, too, that you noticed a difference between the crash we heard and the Inspector's experiment. The first crash was preceded by a marked vibration, the second by absolute silence.[2] That alone made

[1] See p. 12.
[2] See pp. 98 and 124.

me pretty certain I was on the right track. And you must recall how little attention we paid to the organ loft. It would have been perfectly possible in the general confusion for anyone to get out *that particular* door.

"But that didn't really matter." Fen waved the point indifferently aside. "What did matter was why this elaborate business had ever been contrived. Butler was dead a long time ago, you understand. Probably he was thrown over the edge of the gallery immediately over the tomb, and the idea was improvised on account of his position. To move him about would leave dangerous traces. Some pretty quick thinking was done. But why?

"It was not to falsify the *manner* of death, since the autopsy found no trace of weapons or poison. So it must have been to falsify the *time* of death. The slab had three advantages: (*a*) it produced the same physical results—crushed and broken bones—as the fall from the gallery; (*b*) it made medical assessment of the time of death impossible; and (*c*) it made the devil of a noise. The plan must have been improvised at lightning speed—that was why I emphasised all along that it was never intended. But still—why?

"It might have been to create an alibi; it might have been to incriminate someone else; or both. Before long it became plain that it was the second possibility that mattered. To supply a personal motive for the murder might still divert attention from the spying (they knew nothing about the C.I.D. radio van). So I hunted about for likely personal motives, and, of course, the most glaring was Peace's money.

"Now I began to understand things—with a vengeance. I remembered that a number of people knew that Peace was going to the cathedral to meet Butler at 9.20. *But in fact he didn't go then; he went at 10.0.* Now imagine the mental processes of the criminals. Butler is dead. They have removed the wireless and locked the cathedral, throwing the key away somewhere, to be found later and used as evidence against Peace. But no Peace appears. *Rigor* is setting in, and if he does not come up to the cathedral soon it will be impossible to connect him with the crime, on medical evidence alone. Someone returns to the clergy-house and finds he has an infallible alibi, talk-

227

ing to Spitshuker here. What they decided to do, you know. They decided to drop out the slab and create a false impression of the time of death."

Fen paused, and lit a cigarette. Geoffrey saw that Frances, crying a little, had crept out of the room. He felt a pang of pity, but worlds would not have moved him from the spot.

"So far I got," Fen was saying. "And then for a long time—like a fool—no further. Even when Dutton told me that he hadn't heard the crash of the slab from the clergy-house—right on the edge of the cathedral grounds—I didn't properly realise its importance. Even when I learned that those grounds were locked at night, so there would be no casual wanderers, I didn't see what it meant. And then, suddenly, I realised.

"Someone *had* to hear the slab fall."

Fen glanced quizzically around. "Someone had to be got up to the cathedral at about the right time—when Peace was up there. Some reliable person—you, Geoffrey, or myself, or Fielding, or even the Inspector. Perhaps all four of us. . . . The crash wouldn't be heard outside the grounds, and there would be no lovers to listen, since the grounds were locked. . . .

"Do you remember who we saw, when we came back from the 'Whale and Coffin'? Spitshuker, of course, but he had an alibi for almost the whole evening. And Fielding—but if he was involved, why did he prevent you, Geoffrey from being put out of action at a time when it was essential you should be? There was only one other person to decoy us to the cathedral. That person expressed great anxiety about Butler, and asked us to see that he was safe. That person learned that we were going up to the cathedral on business of our own—very satisfactory information. . . ."

"Stop!" Geoffrey almost shouted the word.

Fen turned to him. "I'm sorry, Geoffrey," he said quietly. "Yes, I'm very sorry. Of course it was Frances."

What Geoffrey thought in that moment he never afterwards remembered. It was too turbulent and too vilely painful. But he left the room at once and went downstairs and out of the house. There he saw Frances again.

She was walking rapidly towards a car which stood in the drive, a small attaché case clutched tightly in her hand. She swung round as she heard him, and a small automatic was in her other hand.

"Don't interfere with me," she said briefly. "Our sentimental relationship is now at an end. A one-sided affair, I'm afraid, but I enjoyed my little piece of acting. If you make the slightest attempt to move, to stop me, or to shout, I shall shoot you without hesitation. One more fool dead will be no loss to me or to anyone else."

She got into the car. He stood silent, watching her drive off. There was no movement from inside the house.

Of course the cordon had not been removed. She drove into the barrier on the Exeter road at seventy miles an hour. They said afterwards that there was no point in even attempting to shoot. A piece of jagged metal tore open the carotid artery in the left side of her neck, and before they could get her out of the wreckage she had bled to death.

Chapter Fifteen

REASSURANCE AND
FAREWELL

*"Should she to death be led
It furthers justice, but helps not the dead."*
DRAYTON

A DAY MORE, and both Fen and Geoffrey were packing to leave Tolnbridge: Geoffrey with an elaborate, old-maidish care, Fen chaotically. Dutton had been pronounced by the doctor fit to take on the services again until a new permanent organist should be appointed, so Geoffrey was no longer needed; and Fen had to attend an educational conference in London before returning to Oxford.

Geoffrey's mind was numb. The three days he had been in Tolnbridge had produced so many shocks that he was incapable of assimilating them. And the death of Frances . . . For a long time it would be in his dreams. But he knew that sooner or later it must go. It would take months, perhaps, but in the end he would forget. He knew now, too, that he could never have loved her, being what she was. Perhaps it had never been more than an infatuation: love, he remembered, was supposed to triumph over all the defects of its object. But not that; not that. He trembled involuntarily. But it would be all right in the long run. Bachelorhood, with returning confidence, surveyed with new pleasure the green and smiling expanses of his demesne.

He found the manuscript jottings for his Passacaglia and Fugue, and his spirits lightened somewhat. There was

231

always work, and his cats, and his garden, and Mrs. Body. . . . He snapped the case shut, and after a brief glance round the room to make sure that nothing had been left, went in to see Fen.

He found the Inspector, Dallow and Peace with him, Peace newly released, and bearing as ever *The Mind and Society*. Fen's ruddy face, still swollen slightly and blue from Savernake's kick, glowed with effort, and spikes of hair stuck up obstinately from the crown of his head. He was smoking a cigarette, throwing things wildly into a suit-case, striding about the room and drinking whisky. Geoffrey marvelled at his powers of recovery.

". . . So James confessed," the Inspector was saying, "as soon as he heard Miss Butler was dead. And confirmed pretty well everything you said. It was he who made the first attack on Brooks in the cathedral, and injected the atropine after knocking him out; but it was Miss Butler who put the poison in his medicine at the hospital. And Butler *was* toppled over that gallery—by Savernake, with Miss Butler looking on. They tried to knock him out and kill him more quietly, but he put up a fight, and it was a near thing that Savernake didn't go with him. They were expecting him, of course—as soon as she heard he was going up there, she pretended to go to her room, but actually slipped up ahead of him to warn Savernake. James had taught him to use the lasso, you see, and it was he who was deputed to get the wireless out. Well, Butler was killed, and Savernake took the wireless off, while Miss Butler waited in hiding for you, Mr. Peace, having conceived the idea of pinning the murder on you. But you didn't come. She slipped back to the clergy-house and found you talking to Spitshuker, so the second plan—the tomb-slab—had to be improvised."

"I suppose," said Peace to Fen, "that you thought of the plant in my room as the obvious sequel of the attempt to incriminate me."

"It seemed likely," said Fen mildly. "To leave the hypodermic was a mistake, though." He shook his pyjama-trousers free of a wasp. "But you see why I was so interested in two things: whether James had an alibi for the time of the faking (he had) and whether Peace had gone straight up to the cathedral when he left Spitshuker. Savernake, of course, I didn't know about at that time, but there was a certain amount of reason for suspecting James. Anyway, it was obvious that he couldn't have been concerned in the murder of Butler or the faking. Then I remembered that Peace left the clergy-house to go up to the cathedral *before* we returned there with Frances. To my mind that meant either that it *wasn't* Frances who played about with the organ and made the tomb-slab fall out, or else that you, Peace, somehow delayed on your way up to the cathedral, and enabled her to get there ahead of you. (I was a bit worried about whether it was *her* key you borrowed to get into the grounds, but fortunately it wasn't.) Of course, she must have got a frightful shock when she got back to the clergy-house with us and found you'd already gone; because you promised to wait and walk up with her when she got back. That was simply a means of keeping you *in situ* until she'd collected her witnesses. Savernake, of course, imagined when he left with the wireless that you were going to be there at 9:20 according to your arrangement with Butler, and so never returned. He just disposed of the wireless and provided himself with an alibi for the rest of the time. So she had to do everything herself. That was what made me think she must be the leader—no subordinate would have taken that amount of responsibility."

"It was an extraordinary chancy affair," said the Inspector reproachfully, as though Fen were somehow responsible for this.

"Certainly it was," said Fen a trifle irritably. "It was a rapidly improvised emergency scheme. Ten thousand things might have gone wrong. We might never have gone up to the cathedral at all. As it happened, it went more or less right. But, of course, it was the merest idiocy to attempt to incriminate the good Peace at all. I think something like personal malevolence may have been involved, to judge from what she said about you the other day in Butler's garden. Because there was no earthly reason why she shouldn't have left Butler lying where he was. As an accidental fall, it would have appeared improbable, because the parapet of the Bishop's Gallery is high, and because of what had already happened to Brooks. But it

233

would have left the murderer in complete obscurity. It was the fatal desire to round things off by incriminating you, Peace, which did for the scheme—a plan much too hastily conceived not to have loop-holes all over it.

"Actually, the loop-holes made it all the more confusing. And I admit that (but for one point) my own processes of deduction were chancy, too. When you're dealing with a gang of unspecified dimensions they have to be. That's one reason why I hope this affair won't go into the Chronicles of Crispin.[1] Still," Fen went on indignantly, like one accused of some disgraceful negligence, "they weren't as chancy as all that. Once one had grasped the reason for the use of the tomb-slab, and the fact that someone had to be about to hear it fall, it became pretty clear. Spitshuker couldn't have been involved. Nor could Fielding, because he rescued you, Geoffrey, from being knocked out when it was most desirable that you should be. And that left Frances. She had no real alibi for the crucial times. She tried to make certain that you, Peace, didn't leave until she got back with us—another point. And the last confirmation was when I found out from McIver that there weren't more than three agents working here in all. I saw Savernake and James with my own eyes when they kidnapped me, suspecting I already knew too much. Both of them had alibis for the time of the faking, so that, again, left Frances."

"Some supplementary questions," put in Geoffrey. "Was the wireless found?"

"It had been taken to bits, sir," said the Inspector, "and hidden in various parts of the 'Whale and Coffin.' One of the women in the bar there, by the way, knew something was going on and co-operated with James, but didn't know what. We pulled her in. The stuff they used, materials for making keys to the tomb, atropine, radio parts and so on—must have been smuggled over here from Germany before the war." He gestured, as though in apology for making so elementary a point.

"That's another thing," said Geoffrey. "Why make keys to that tomb?"

"I got that from James," the Inspector replied. "In case

[1] Vain hope.—E. C.

of an invasion, it was to be filled with explosive and the whole cathedral blown sky-high, as a signal. Nasty, isn't it? You see, they had to get the stuff in there beforehand, since it had to be ready at a moment's notice, any hour of the day or night. But they hadn't started on that when the attack on Brooks was made, and afterwards, with the police guard and so on, it was impracticable." He smiled grimly. "The whole business is a very pleasant commentary on the celebrated German efficiency. A flop."

"You might remember," said Peace, "that I was nearly indicted for murder."

Fen took a cardboard box and emptied the dead bodies of a number of insects out of the window. "I've finished with these nasty things," he said. The butterfly-net, forgotten and unused, stood in a corner. He glared at it for a moment, then broke it across his knee; subsequently he deposited *Social Life in the Insect World* in the waterjug. "Like Prospero," he announced, "I have broken my staff and drowned my book." He looked round complacently, but no one was paying much attention.

"One thing more," said Geoffrey, "and that's about Josephine and the Black Mass."

"James disapproved of all that," the Inspector explained. "The devil-worship business was a private toy of Miss Butler and Savernake. Of course, sir"—turning to Fen—"it was Savernake shot at you—in a panic, more or less."

Fen nodded. "I thought so. A recusant priest is supposed traditionally to celebrate the Mass."

"As to drugging that kid," the Inspector went on, "and initiating her into their filthy goings on, I confess I can't understand it. Of course, she was useful as a tool—as in taking that message to my men at the cathedral—but it seems to me most of it was just sheer devilry."

"The manuscript had nothing to do with it, then?" Peace asked.

"No," said Fen, "I think that was probably just a fit of blind rage at being deprived of the stuff too long. It was given her in cigarette form, you know. Marihuana generally is."

Peace sighed. His plump, red face was creased with worry, and his grey eyes were sad. "It's going to be a busi-

235

ness looking after Irene," he said. "She wasn't very fond of Butler, but Frances she loved. I'm taking her—and Josephine, when she's better—under my own wing, you know. Of course the money comes to me—not that I want it now."

"You might be able to explain these people's psychology to us," Fen suggested.

"Not any longer," said Peace firmly. "I'm giving all that up and going into the Church."

They stared. "The Church!" they all exclaimed.

Peace seemed mildly hurt at their incredulity. "It seems the best way out of my doubts," he explained. "And I confess I've always thought the life attractive."

So there was no more to be said about that. But Fen was still worrying the question of psychology.

"James one can understand," he said. "He had a purely mercenary motive. Savernake, too—he was the superficially clever type to whom Fascism makes an immediate appeal. But Frances . . . she was in Germany, of course, but that doesn't mean anything. I suppose we shall never know now."

For the first time, Dallow spoke. "Isn't it possible, my *d*e-ear Professor, that there may have been something in the blood?"

"What do you mean?"

"She was of Tolnbridge blood on her father's side—a very old family in these parts. And there were real witches here—they were not all Elizabeth Pulteneys. I always think"—he glanced apologetically at Peace—"that psychology is wrong in imagining that when it has analysed evil it has somehow disposed of it."

"Then she was——"

"Witches ally themselves with the forces of the Devil wherever, and however, they appear. It isn't just a matter of participating in the rites of Walpurgis Night, nor of killing the neighbour who has slandered you. There is political evil as well."

"She made her sister a witch," said Geoffrey.

"It has always been done. The mother initiates her daughter; neighbours, sisters each other. . . ."

There was a long silence.

"One thing struck me," said Fen at last, turning to

Geoffrey. "Do you remember when she met us, just after seeing her own father killed?"

"Yes."

"Did anything particular strike you about her?"

"I thought she seemed happy."

"Yes. I think she was."

There was again silence. From the lawn below, where Garbin and Spitshuker were pacing together, fragments of argument floated up.

"It seems to me that when you insist on regarding the Old Testament simply as a historical record of the search of the Jewish people for God you are falling into the Marcionite heresy. Marcion . . ."

"You've made no attempt to answer my point about the literal interpretation of Genesis . . ."

"My dear Garbin . . ."

Towering beyond the garden stood the cathedral, restored again to quiet and worship, abandoned to the ghosts of Bishop John Thurston and Elizabeth Pulteney—*requiescant in pace!* The sky was clouding over, and a fresh wind presaged a gale later. But it was a clean, strong, cool wind.

Fen, who had finished packing, put on his raincoat and his extraordinary hat.

"Come on, Geoffrey," he said. "We've got to catch this train, and we must look in on Fielding on the way. How is he, by the way?" he enquired of the Inspector.

"Better," said the Inspector. "That C.I.D. chap Phipps has been talking to him, and I think promised to try and get him some routine office job connected with the counter-espionage. He's not well enough to bounce about with joy yet, but he would if he could."

"Some people," said Fen, "simply never learn from experience." He moved towards the door.

"I still think," said Geoffrey, following him, "that as detection this business simply won't do."

Fen turned in the doorway. "It wouldn't but for one thing."

"Well?"

"You remember Spitshuker told us about Butler picking a four-leaf clover at the gate from the clergy-house garden into the cathedral grounds? After Butler had decided to go up to the cathedral, Frances, according to her own account, went straight up to her room. Even if she had looked out she couldn't have seen at that distance what her father was doing. And we know that he wasn't in the habit of wearing four-leaf clovers in his buttonhole. So when she met us and told us he was wearing one, do you see, that rather gummed up the works. If she knew he was wearing it, she must have been at the cathedral. And if she was at the cathedral she must—mustn't she?—have seen him die."